"**N**ew York Dead has elements of *Psycho,
Silence of the Lambs,* and
Broadcast News. . . . Good, escapist fun."
Orlando Sentinel

"**W**oods is a world-class mystery writer.
And he's getting better and better. . . . I try
to put Woods's books down, and I can't.
The pace is terrific without being breathless.
His prose style is fluid, his dialogue
plentiful and excellent."
Houston Chronicle

"**M**ove over, Raymond Chandler. . . .
[Barrington] is an intriguing character in a
fast-moving, well-written mystery
that's just a little on the different side."
Washington Times

"**W**oods . . . is one of the best around
at tense, fast-paced plotting."
St. Petersburg Times

"**S**tuart Woods is a wonderful storyteller
who could teach Robert Ludlum
and Tom Clancy a thing or two."
The State (SC)

"**H**e tells a terrific yarn"
Boston Globe

Books by Stuart Woods

Chiefs
Run Before the Wind
Deep Lie
Under the Lake
White Cargo
Grass Roots
Palindrome
New York Dead
Santa Fe Rules
L.A. Times
Dead Eyes
Heat
Imperfect Strangers
Choke
Dirt
Dead in the Water
Swimming to Catalina
Orchid Beach
Worst Fears Realized
The Run

L.A. Dead
Cold Paradise
Orchid Blues
The Short Forever
Blood Orchid
Dirty Work
Capital Crimes
Reckless Abandon
The Prince of Beverly Hills
Two Dollar Bill
Iron Orchid
Dark Harbor
Short Straw
Fresh Disasters
Shoot Him if He Runs
Beverly Hills Dead
Santa Fe Dead
Hot Mahogany

STUART WOODS

NEW YORK DEAD

HARPER

An Imprint of HarperCollins*Publishers*

HARPER

An Imprint of HarperCollins*Publishers*
10 East 53rd Street
New York, New York 10022-5299

Copyright © 1991 by Stuart Woods
ISBN 978-0-06-171186-2

First Harper Premium paperback printing: April 2009
First Harper paperback special printing: October 1995
First HarperPaperbacks printing: September 1992
First HarperCollins hardcover printing: October 1991

HarperCollins® and Harper® are registered trademarks of Harper-Collins Publishers.

Printed in the United States of America

Visit Harper paperbacks on the World Wide Web at
www.harpercollins.com

10 9 8 7 6 5 4 3 2 1

This book is for
Nick Taylor and Barbara Nevins,
who are New York Alive

NEW YORK
DEAD

1

Elaine's, late. The place had exhausted its second wind, and half the customers had gone; otherwise she would not have given Stone Barrington quite so good a table—number 4, along the wall to your right as you enter. Stone knew Elaine, had known her for years, but he was not what you would call a regular—not what Elaine would call a regular, anyway.

He rested his left leg on a chair and unconsciously massaged the knee. Elaine got down from her stool at the cash register, walked over, and pulled up a chair.

"So?"

"Not bad," he said.

"How about the knee?" Anybody who knew him knew about the knee; it had received a .22-caliber bullet eleven weeks before.

"A lot better. I walked up here from Turtle Bay."

"When's the physical?"

"Next week. I'll tap-dance through it."

"So what if you fall on your ass, tap dancing?" Elaine knew how to get to the point.

"So, then I'm a retiree."

"Best thing could happen to you."

"I can think of better things."

"Come on, Stone, you're too good looking to be a cop. Too smart, too. You went to law school, didn't you?"

"I never took the bar."

"So take the bar. Make a buck."

"It's fifteen years since I graduated."

"So? Take one of those cram courses."

"Maybe. You're coming on kind of motherly, aren't you?"

"Somebody's gotta tell you this stuff."

"I appreciate the thought. Who's the guy at the bar?" To a cop's eye the man didn't fit in somehow. He probably wouldn't fit anywhere. Male Caucasian, five-six, a hundred and seventy, thinning brown hair, thick, black-rimmed glasses adhesive-taped in the middle.

"In the white coat? Doc."

"That his name or his game?"

"Both. He's at Lenox Hill, I think. He's in here a lot, late, trying to pick up girls."

"In a hospital jacket?"

"His technique is to diagnose them. Weird, isn't it?"

Doc reached over to the girl next to him and peeled back her eyelid. The girl recoiled.

Stone laughed out loud and finished the Wild

Turkey. "Bet it works. What girl could resist a *doctah?*"

"Just about all of them is my guess. I've never seen him leave with anybody."

Stone signaled a waiter for the check and put some cash on the table.

"Have one on me," Elaine said.

"Rain check. I've had one too many already." He stood up and pecked her on the cheek.

"Don't be such a stranger."

"If I don't pass the physical, I'll be in here all the time. You'll have to throw me out."

"My pleasure. Take care."

Stone glanced at Doc on the way out. He was taking the girl's pulse. She was looking at him as if he were nuts.

Stone was a little drunk—too drunk to drive, he reckoned, if he had owned a car. The night air was pleasant, still warm for September. He looked up Second Avenue to see a dozen cabs bearing down on him from uptown. Elaine's was the best cab spot in town; he could never figure out where they were all coming from. Harlem? Cabdrivers wouldn't take anybody to Harlem, not if they could help it. He turned away from them; he'd walk, give the knee another workout. The bourbon had loosened it up.

He crossed Eighty-eighth and started downtown, sticking to the west side of the street. He lengthened his stride, made a conscious effort not to limp. He remembered walking this beat, right out of the academy; that was when he had started drinking at Elaine's, when he was a rookie in the 19th Precinct, on his way home after walking his tour. He walked it now.

A cop doesn't walk down the street like anybody else, he reflected. Automatically, he checked every doorway as he swung down Second Avenue, ignoring the pain, leaning on the bourbon. He had to prevent himself from trying the locks. Across the street, half a dozen guys spilled out of a yuppie bar, two of them mouthing off at each other, the others watching. Ten years ago, he'd have broken it up. He would have now, but it didn't look like it would last long. The two guys turned away from each other, hurling insults. Neither was willing to throw the first punch.

At Eighty-sixth Street, two hookers were working the traffic. He'd have ignored them on his beat; he ignored them now. He remembered when Eighty-sixth was Germantown, when the smell of sauerbraten wafted from every third doorway. Somewhere along here there had been a place called the Gay Vienna that served kalbshaxe—a veal shank that looked like a gigantic drumstick. The place had had a zither player, the only one he'd ever heard. He'd liked it. He'd lived over on Eighty-third, between York and East End, had had a Hungarian landlady who made him goulash. She'd put weight on him, too much weight, and it had stuck. He'd lost it now, five weeks on hospital food. He was down to a hundred and eighty, and, at six-two, he looked slender. He vowed not to gain it back. He couldn't afford the alterations.

Stone rubbed his neck. An hour in one of Elaine's hard, armless chairs, leaning on the table, always made his neck and shoulders tight. About Seventieth Street, he started to limp a little, in spite of himself. In the mid-Sixties, he forgot all about the knee.

It was just luck. He was rolling his head around, trying to loosen the neck muscles, and he happened to be looking up when he saw her. She was free-falling, spread-eagled, like a sky diver. Only she didn't have a parachute.

Con Edison was digging a big hole twenty yards ahead, and they had a generator going, so he could barely hear the scream.

Time slowed down; he considered whether it was some sort of stunt and rejected the notion. He thought she would go into the Con Ed hole, but she didn't; instead, she met the earth, literally, on the big pile of dirt the workmen had thrown up. She didn't bounce. She stuck to the ground as if she had fallen into glue. Stone started to run.

A Con Ed man in a yellow hard hat jumped backward as if he'd been shotgunned. Stone could see the terrified expression on his face as he approached. The man recovered before Stone got there, reached down, and gingerly turned the woman onto her back. Her eyes were open.

Stone knew her. There was black dirt on her face, and her red hair was wild, but he knew her. Shit, the whole city knew her. More than half the population—all the men and some of the women—wanted to fuck her. He slowed just long enough to glance at her and shout at the Con Ed man. "Call an ambulance! Do what you can for her!" He glanced up at the building. Flush windows, none open; a terrace up top.

He sprinted past the scene, turned the corner of the white-brick, 1960s apartment building, and ran into the lobby. An elderly, uniformed doorman was sound asleep in a chair, tilted back against the wall.

"Hey!" Stone shouted, and the man was wide awake and on his feet. The move looked practiced. Stone shoved his badge in the old man's face. "Police! What apartment has a terrace on the Second Avenue side?"

"12-A, the penthouse," the doorman said. "Miss Nijinsky."

"You got a key?"

"Yeah."

"Let's go!"

The doorman retrieved a key from a drawer, and Stone hustled him toward the elevators. One stood open and waiting; the doorman pushed twelve.

"What's the matter?" the man asked.

"Miss Nijinsky just took a dive. She's lying in a pile of dirt on Second Avenue."

"Jesus God."

"She's being introduced to him right now."

It was a short building, and the elevator was slow. Stone watched the floor numbers light up and tried to control his breathing. When they hit eleven, he pulled out his gun. As the elevator slowed to a stop on twelve, he heard something, and he knew what it was. The fire door on twelve had been yanked open so hard it had struck the wall. This noise was followed by the sound of somebody taking the steel steps of the fire stairs in a hurry. The elevator door started to open, and Stone helped it.

"Stay here, and don't open the apartment door!" he said to the doorman.

The fire door was opposite the elevator; he yanked it open. From a floor below, the ring of shoe leather on steel drifted upward. Stone flung himself down the stairs.

The guy only had a floor's start on him; Stone had a chance. He started taking the steps two at a time. "Stop! Police!" he shouted. That was procedure, and, if anybody was listening, he wanted it heard. He shouted it again.

As he descended, Stone got into a rhythm— bump de bump, bump de bump. He concentrated on keeping his footing. He left the eighth floor behind, then the sixth.

From the sound of it, he was gaining. Aiming carefully, he started taking the steps three at a time. Whoever was below him was hitting every one. Now Stone was barely a flight of stairs behind him. At the third-floor level he caught sight of a shadow. The ringing of the steel steps built to a crescendo, echoing off the cinder-block walls of the staircase, sounding much like a modern composition a girl had once dragged him to hear.

The knee was hurting badly now, and Stone

tried to think ahead. If the man got out of the stairwell before he could be caught, then he'd have the advantage on level ground, because Stone wouldn't be able to run him down before the knee went. Stone made a decision; he'd go for a flight at a time.

On the next landing, he took a deep breath and leaped. He landed right, pushed off the wall, and prepared to jump again. One more leap down the stairs, and he'd have his quarry in sight. This time, as he jumped, something went wrong. His toe caught the stamped tread of the steel step—not much, just enough to turn him in midair—and he knew he would land wrong. When he did, his weight was on the bad knee, and he screamed. Completely out of control now, he struck the wall hard, bounced, and fell backward down the next flight of stairs.

As he came to rest hard against the wall, he struggled to get a look down the stairs, but he heard the ground-floor door open, and, a moment later, he heard it slam. He hunched up in the fetal position, holding the knee with both hands, waiting for the pain to subside just enough to allow him to get to his feet. Half a minute passed before he could let go of the knee, grab the railing, and hoist himself up. He recovered his pistol, and, barely letting his left foot touch the floor, lurched into the lobby. The guy was gone, and there was no hope of catching him now. Swearing, he hammered the elevator button with his fist.

He pressed his cheek against the cool stainless steel of the elevator door, whimpering with pain and anger and sucking in deep breaths.

The bust of the century, and he had blown it.

2

There were only two apartments on the twelfth floor, and the doorman was standing obediently in front of 12-A. The door was open.

"I told you not to open it," Stone said irritably.

"I didn't," the old man said indignantly. "It was wide open. I didn't go in there, either."

"Okay, okay. You go on back downstairs. There'll be a lot of cops here in a few minutes; you tell them where I am."

"Yessir," the doorman said and headed for the elevator.

"Wait a minute," Stone said, still catching his breath. "Did anybody come into the building the last half hour? Anybody at all?"

"Nope. I wake up when people come in. I always do," the old man said defensively.

Sure. "What time did Miss Nijinsky come home tonight?"

"About nine o'clock. She asked for her mail, but

there wasn't any. It had already been forwarded to the new address."

"She was moving?"

"Tomorrow."

"What sort of mood was she in?" Stone asked.

"Tired, I'd say. Maybe depressed. She was usually pretty cheerful, had a few words to say to me, but not tonight. She just asked for her mail, and, when I told her there wasn't any, she just sighed like this." He sighed heavily. "And she went straight into the elevator."

"Does she normally get many visitors in the building?"

"Hardly any. As a matter of fact, in the two years she's been here, I don't remember a single one, except deliverymen—you know, from the department stores and UPS and all."

"Thanks," Stone said. "You go on back to your post, and we'll probably have more to ask you later."

Stone stepped into the apartment. He reached high to avoid messing up any prints on the door and pushed it nearly shut. A single lamp on a mahogany drum table illuminated the living room. The place was not arranged for living. The cheap parquet floor was bare of carpets; there were no curtains or pictures; at least two dozen cardboard cartons were scattered or stacked around the room. A phone was on the table with the lamp. Stone picked it up with two fingers, dialed a number, waited for a beep, then, reading off the phone, punched in Nijinsky's number and hung up. He picked his way among the boxes and entered the kitchen. More packed boxes. He found the small bedroom; the bed was still made.

Some penthouse. It was a mean, cramped, three-and-a-half-room apartment, and she was probably paying twenty-five hundred a month. These buildings had been thrown up in a hurry during the sixties, to beat a zoning restriction that would require builders to offset apartment houses, using less of the land. If they got the buildings up in time, they could build right to the sidewalk. There were dozens of them up and down the East Side.

The phone rang. He got it before it rang a second time.

"Yes?"

"This is Bacchetti."

"Dino, it's Stone. Where are you?"

"A joint called Columbus, on the West Side. What's up?"

"Hot stuff." Stone gave him the address. "Ditch the girl and get over here fast. Apartment 12-A. I'll wait five minutes before I call the precinct."

"I'm already there." Bacchetti hung up.

Stone hung up and looked around. The sliding doors to the terrace were open, and he could hear the whoop-whoop of an ambulance growing nearer. There was an armchair next to the table with the lamp and the phone, and next to it a packed carton with a dozen sealed envelopes on top. Stone picked up a printed card from a stack next to the envelopes.

Effective immediately,
Sasha Nijinsky is at
1011 Fifth Ave.
New York 10021.
Burn this.

The lady was moving up in the world. But, then, everybody knew that. Stone put the card in his pocket. The ambulance pulled to a halt downstairs, and, immediately, a siren could be heard. Not big enough for a fire truck, Stone thought, more like an old-fashioned police siren, the kind they used before the electronic noisemaker was invented.

He walked out onto the terrace, which was long but narrow, and looked over the chest-high wall. Sasha Nijinsky had not fallen—she had either jumped or been muscled over. Down below, two vehicles with flashing lights had pulled up to the scene—an ambulance and a van with SCOOP VIDEO painted on the top. As he watched, another vehicle pulled up, and a man in a white coat got out.

Stone went back into the apartment, found a switch, and flooded the room with overhead light. He looked at his watch. Two more minutes before this got official. Two objects were on the drum table besides the lamp and the phone. He unzipped her purse and emptied it onto the table. The usual female rubbish—makeup of all sorts, keys, a small address book, safety pins, pencils, credit cards held together with a rubber band, and a thick wad of money, held with a large gold paper clip.

He counted it: twelve hundred and eleven dollars, including half a dozen hundreds. The lady didn't travel light. He looked closely at the gold paper clip. Cartier.

Stone turned to the other object: a red-leather book with the word DIARY stamped in gold. He went straight to the last page, today's date.

Hassle, hassle, hassle. The moving men are giving me a hard time. The paparazzi have been on my ass all day. The painters haven't finished in the new apartment. My limo caught on fire on East 52nd Street this afternoon, and I had to hoof it to the network through hordes of autograph-seekers. And the goddamned fucking contracts are still not ready. For this I have a business manager, a lawyer, and an agent? Also, I haven't got the change-of-address cards done, and the ace researchers don't have notes for me yet on the Bush interview, and What's-his-name just called and wants to come over here right now! I am coming apart at the seams, I swear I am. As soon as he leaves, I'm going to get into a hot tub with a gigantic brandy and open a vein. I swear to God it's just not worth it, any of it. On Monday, I have to smile into a camera and be serious, knowledgeable, and authoritative, when all I want to do with my life is to go skydiving without a parachute. Fuck the job, fuck the fame, fuck the money! Fuck everybody!!!

Skydiving without a parachute: his very thought, what, ten minutes ago? He gingerly picked up the phone again and dialed.

"Homicide," a bored voice said.

"It's Barrington. Who's the senior man?"

"Leary. How's the soft life, Barrington?"

"Let me speak to him."

"He's in the can. I just saw him go in there with a *Hustler*, so he'll be awhile."

"Tell him I've stumbled onto a possible homicide. Lady took a twelve-story dive. I'm in her apartment now." He gave the address. "An ambulance is already here, but we'll need a team to work the scene. Rumble whoever's on call. Bacchetti and I will take the case."

"But you're on limited duty."

"Not anymore. Tell Leary to get moving."

"I'll tell him when he comes out."

"I wouldn't wait." He hung up. He had not mentioned the victim's name; that would get them here in too much of a hurry. He heard the elevator doors open.

"Stone?" Bacchetti called from outside the door.

"It's open. Careful about prints."

Dino Bacchetti entered the room as he might a fashionable restaurant. He was dressed to kill, in a silk Italian suit with what Stone liked to think of as melting lapels. "So?" he asked, looking around, trying to sound bored.

"Sasha Nijinsky went thataway," Stone said, pointing to the terrace.

"No shit?" Dino said, no longer bored. "That explains the crowd on the sidewalk."

"Yeah. I was passing, on my way home."

Dino walked over and clapped his hands onto

Stone's cheeks. "I got the luckiest partner on the force," he said, beaming.

Stone ducked before Dino could kiss him. "Not so lucky. I chased the probable perp down the stairs and blew it on the last landing. He walked."

"A right-away bust would have been too good to be true," Dino said. "Now we get to track the fucker down. Much, much better." He rubbed his hands together. "Whatta we got here?"

"She was moving to a new apartment tomorrow," Stone said. He beckoned Dino to the table and opened the diary with the pen.

"Not in the best of moods, was she?" Dino said, reading. "Skydiving without a parachute. The papers are going to love that."

"Yeah, they're going to love the whole thing."

Dino looked up. "Maybe she jumped," he said. "Who's to say she was pushed?"

"Then who went pounding down the stairs at the moment I arrived on the scene?" Stone asked. "The moving men?"

"No sign of a struggle," Dino observed.

"In a room full of cardboard boxes, who can say?"

"No glasses out for a guest, if What's-his-name did show."

"The liquor's packed, like everything else. I've had a look around, I didn't see any. She didn't sound in any mood to offer him a drink, anyway." Stone sighed. "Come on, let's go over the place before the Keystone Kops get here."

"Yeah, Leary's got the watch," Dino said.

The two men combed the apartment from one

end to the other. Stone used a penlight to search the corners of the terrace.

"Nothing," Dino said, when they were through.

"Maybe everything," Stone said. "We've got the diary, her address book, and a stack of change-of-address cards, already addressed. Those are the important people, I reckon. I'll bet the perp is in that stack." He took out his notebook and began jotting down names and addresses. Apart from the department stores and credit card companies, there were fewer than a dozen. Had she had so few friends, or had she just not gotten through the list before she died? He looked over the names: alphabetical. She had made it through the W's.

They heard the elevator doors open, and two detectives walked in, followed by a one-man video crew. He was small, skinny, and he looked over-burdened by the camera, battery belt, sound pack, and glaring lights.

"You, out," Dino said. "This is a crime scene."

"Why do you think I'm here?" the cameraman said. He produced a press card. "Scoop Berman," he said. "Scoop Video."

"The man said this is a crime scene, Scoop," Stone said, propelling the little man toward the door.

"Hey, what crime?" Scoop said, digging in his heels.

"Possible homicide," Stone replied, still pushing.

"There's no homicide," Scoop said.

"Yeah? How do *you* know?"

"Because she ain't dead," Scoop said.

Stone stopped pushing. "What are you talking about? She fell twelve stories."

"Hang on a minute, guys," Scoop said. He rewound the tape in his camera and flipped down a tiny viewing screen. "Watch this," he said.

Stone and Dino elbowed the other two cops out of the way and focused on the screen. An image came up; the camera was running toward the Con Ed site downstairs. It pushed past an ambulance man and zoomed in on the form of Sasha Nijinsky. She was wearing a nightgown under a green silk robe.

"Easy, now, lady," someone was saying on the soundtrack. "Don't try to move; let us do the moving."

A white-clad back filled the screen, and the camera moved to one side, then zoomed in tight on her face. She blinked twice, and her lips moved.

"Okay, here we go," the voice said, and the ambulance men lifted her onto a stretcher. The camera followed as they loaded the stretcher into the back of the ambulance. One man got in with her and pulled the door shut. The ambulance drove away, its lights flashing and its whooper sounding.

"I had to make a choice then," Scoop said. "I called in the incident, and then I went for the apartment."

"It's impossible," Dino said.

"You saw her move, saw her blink," Scoop said.

"Holy shit," Dino said.

"Okay," Stone said to the two cops. "You work

the scene with the technical guys, and then knock on every door in the building. I want to know if anybody saw anybody come into the building after nine o'clock tonight." He grabbed Dino's elbow. "Let's get out of here."

3

Stone hung up the car phone. "The company dispatcher says the wagon is going to Lenox Hill Hospital, but the driver hasn't radioed in to confirm the delivery yet."

"Seventy-seventh and Park," Dino said, hanging a right.

Dino always drove as if he'd just stolen the car. Being Italian didn't hurt either.

The two had been partners for nearly four years when Stone had got his knee shot up. It hadn't even been their business, that call, but everybody responded to "officer needs assistance." The officer had needed assistance half a minute before Stone and Dino arrived on the scene; the officer was dead, and the man who had shot him was trying to start his patrol car. He'd fired one wild shot before Dino killed him, and it had found its way unerringly to Stone's knee. It had been nothing but a run-of-the-mill domestic disturbance, until the moment the officer had died and the bullet had changed Stone's life.

Dino had won an automatic commendation for killing a perp who had killed a cop. Stone had won four hours in surgery and an extremely boring amount of physical therapy. He rubbed the knee. It didn't feel so terrible now; maybe he hadn't screwed it up as badly as he had thought.

They screeched to a halt at the emergency entrance to Lenox Hill, and Stone limped into the building after Dino.

"You've got a woman named Nijinsky here," Dino said to the woman behind the desk, flashing his badge. "We need to see her now."

"I didn't get her name, but she's in room number one, first door on your right. Dr. Holmes is with her."

Dino led the way.

"I'd never have guessed her name was Nijinsky," the woman said after them.

They found the room and a resident taping a bandage to a woman's forehead. The woman was black.

"Dr. Holmes?" Stone said.

The young man turned.

"Yes?"

Stone limped into the room. "You've got another patient, a woman, here."

"Nope, this is it," Holmes said. "An uncommonly slow night."

"You're sure?" Stone asked, puzzled.

The doctor nodded at the black woman. "The only customer we've had for two hours," he replied. He watched Stone shift his weight and wince. "What's wrong with you?"

"I just banged my knee; no problem."

"Let's have a look."

"Yeah," said Dino, "let's have a look."

Stone pulled up his trouser leg.

Dino whistled. "Oh, that looks great, Stone."

"Tell me about it," the doctor said.

Stone gave him an abbreviated history.

The doctor went to a refrigerator, came back with a flat ice pack, and fastened it to Stone's knee with an Ace bandage. Then he retrieved a small box of pills from a shelf. "Keep the ice on until you can't stand it anymore, and take one of these pills now and every four hours after that. See your doctor in the morning."

"What are the pills?" Stone asked.

"A nonsteroid, antiinflammatory agent. If you haven't completely undone your surgery, the knee will feel better in the morning."

Stone thanked him, and they left.

"What now?" Dino asked as they turned onto Lexington Avenue.

Stone was about to answer when they saw the flashing lights. At Seventy-fifth and Lexington there was a god-awful mess, lit by half a dozen flashing lights. "Pull over, Dino," he said.

Dino pulled over. Stone got out and approached a uniformed officer. He pointed at a mass of twisted metal. "Was that smoking ruin once an ambulance?" he asked the cop.

"Yeah, and what used to be a fire truck hit it broadside." He pointed at the truck, which was only moderately bent.

"What about the occupants?"

"On their way to Bellevue," the cop said. "Seven from the fire truck, two or three from the ambulance."

"Anybody left alive?"

"I just got here; you'll have to check Bellevue."

Stone thanked him and got back into the car.

"Is that the same ambulance?" Dino asked.

"It's the same service." Stone stuck a flashing light on the dashboard. "Stand on it, Fittipaldi."

Fangio stood on it.

The emergency room at Bellevue was usually a zoo, but this was incredible. People were lying on carts everywhere, overflowing into the hallways, screaming, crying, while harried medical personnel moved among them, expediting the more serious cases.

"What the hell happened?" Dino asked a sweating nurse.

"Subway fire in the Twenty-third Street Station," she replied, "not to mention half a dozen firemen and a couple of ambulance drivers. We caught it all."

"There's nobody at the desk," Stone said. "How can we find out if somebody's been admitted?"

"Your guess is as good as mine," she said, wheeling a cart containing a screaming woman down the hallway. "Paperwork's out the window."

"Come on," Stone said, "let's start looking."

Fifteen minutes later, they hadn't found her. Dino was looking unwell.

"I gotta get outta here, Stone," he said, mopping his brow. "I'm not cut out for this blood-and-guts stuff."

"Wait a minute," Stone said, pointing across the room at a man on a stretcher. "A white coat."

They made their way across the room to the stretcher. The man's eyes were closed, but he was conscious; he was holding a bloody handful of gauze to an ear.

"Are you an ambulance driver?" Stone asked. "The one the fire truck hit?"

The man nodded, then grimaced at the pain the motion brought.

"What happened to your patient?" Stone asked.

"I don't know," the man whimpered. "My partner's dead; I don't know what happened to her."

Stone straightened up. "Then she's got to be here," he said.

"But she's not," Dino replied. "We've looked at every human being, alive or dead, in this place. She is definitely not here."

They looked again, anyway, even though Dino wasn't very happy about it. Dino was right. Sasha Nijinsky wasn't there.

"Downstairs," Stone said.

"Do we have to?"

"You sit this one out."

Stone walked down to the basement and checked with the Bellevue morgue. There had been two admissions that evening, both of them from the subway fire, both men. Stone looked at them to be sure.

He trudged back up the stairs and went to the main admissions desk. "Have you admitted an emergency patient, a woman, named Nijinsky?" he asked. "Probably a private room."

"We don't have a private room available tonight," the nurse said. "In fact, we don't have a bed. If she came into the emergency room, she's on a gurney in a hallway somewhere."

Stone walked the halls on the way back to the ER, where he found Dino in conversation with a pretty nurse. "Say good night, Dino," Stone said.

"Good night, Dino," Dino replied, doing a perfect Dick Martin.

The nurse laughed.

"She's not here," Stone said.

"So, now what?"

"The city morgue," Stone said.

Compared with Bellevue, the city morgue, just up the street, was an island of serenity.

"Female Caucasian, name of Nijinsky," Dino told the night man. "You got one of those?"

The man consulted a logbook. "Nope."

"You got a Caucasian Jane Doe?"

"I got three of them," the man replied. He pointed. "They're still on tables."

Stone walked into the large autopsy room, the sound of his heels echoing off the tile walls. "Let's look," he said.

The first was at least seventy and very dirty.

"Bag lady," the attendant said.

The second was no older than fifteen, wearing a black leather microskirt.

"Times Square hooker, picked up the wrong trick."

"Let's see the third," Stone said.

The third fit Sasha Nijinsky's general description, down to the hair color, but she had taken a shotgun in the chest.

"Domestic violence," the attendant said smugly.

Stone couldn't tell if the man was for it or against it. "It's not she," he said.

"Don't talk like that," Dino whispered. "It's not her."

"It is not she," Stone said again. He produced a card and wrote his home number on the back, then handed it to the attendant. "This is extremely important," he said. "If you get a Nijinsky in here, or a white Jane Doe in her thirties, call me. And please pass that on to whoever relieves you. If someone overlooks her, heads will ricochet off these walls for days to come."

"I got ya," the man said, and he stapled Stone's card to his logbook. "They won't miss it here."

In the car, Dino, who was usually the most cheerful of souls, sighed deeply. "I got a feeling," he said.

"Oh, God, don't get a feeling," Stone whimpered. "Don't get Italian on me."

"I got a very serious feeling that this one is going to be a fucking nightmare," Dino said.

"Thanks, Dino. I needed that."

"And, Stone," Dino added, "never say, 'It's not she' to some guy at the morgue. He'll think you're a jerk."

4

When Stone and Dino got to the precinct, the two detectives who had been at the Nijinsky apartment were sitting at their desks, cataloging evidence.

"So?" one of them asked. "Is she alive, or what?"

"Or what," Dino said.

"So she croaked, then, or what?"

"Or what."

Stone tugged at his partner's sleeve. "Let's see Leary."

Lieutenant Leary, the squad's commanding officer, was in his tiny, glassed-in cubicle, reading Sasha Nijinsky's diary. He looked up and waved the two detectives in. "Well, it took a fuckin' celebrity swan dive to get you back on the street, didn't it, Barrington?"

"I saw it happen," Stone said. "From the street." He took Leary through everything that had happened at the apartment.

"So, where's Nijinsky now?" he asked.

"It's like this, I think," Stone said. "The ambulance was taking her to Lenox Hill when it got broadsided by a fire truck. Another ambulance was called and took the driver and his partner to Bellevue. The driver's alive, but doesn't know what happened to Nijinsky. The partner's dead."

"So, to ask my question again, where's Nijinsky?"

"We don't know. She wasn't at Bellevue. We looked at everybody there."

"Not in the Bellevue emergency room," Leary said.

"No. Not anywhere at Bellevue. We checked it out thoroughly. Not at the city morgue either. They'll call me if she shows up."

Leary looked bemused. "What the fuck is goin' on here?"

"Probably homicide—attempted homicide, if she's still alive."

"Because of the guy you chased down the stairs?"

"Yes."

"Maybe he was the pizza deliveryman, got there in time to see her take the dive, then ran."

"Maybe. It feels like a homicide."

"And maybe a kidnapping, too. If the lady fell twelve stories and then her ambulance got whopped by a fire truck, she ain't walking around out there somewhere, right?"

Dino piped up. "If she's dead, is it a corpsenapping? And is that a crime?"

Leary tapped the diary with a stubby finger. "You read this?"

"Only the last page," Stone said.

"The last page was one of her better days. This was a very unhappy lady."

"She was about to become the only female news anchor on a major network. I would have thought she had it all."

"Anybody would think so. But she sounds scared to me. Maybe afraid she couldn't cut it."

"Maybe. It's a natural enough reaction."

"The diary makes her sound like a suicide."

"Maybe," Stone said. "I don't think so."

"Okay, here's what happened, maybe," Leary said. "You get this big pileup on Lex, and *two* ambulances respond. You know how competitive they are. One goes to Bellevue with the driver and the other guy, and the other ambulance goes to some other hospital."

"That's what I figured," Dino said.

"Run it down," Leary replied. He handed the diary to Stone. "Read that and tell me she didn't try to knock herself off."

Stone and Dino spent the rest of the night calling every hospital in Manhattan and reading Sasha Nijinsky's diary.

When the day shift came on, Lieutenant Leary called a meeting and brought the new group up to date.

"Okay, now you know everything we know," he said to the four assembled teams. "The press knows about the dive, because this guy Scoop What's-his-name?—"

"Berman," Stone said.

"—Berman shows up and gets his tape. They don't seem to know that the lady hasn't been seen since, and I want to keep it that way as long as possible. This is Barrington and Bacchetti's case, reporting directly to me. Barrington, Bacchetti, go sleep. I don't want you back here before noon. The rest of you, check on every private clinic, every doctor's office in the five boroughs, if you have to. Check Jersey and Westchester, too. On Long Island, just check the fancy private clinics. I want this woman found this morning, dead or alive. When you find her, Stone and Bacchetti get the interview, unless it's deathbed stuff. Nobody, but nobody says a word to the press except me, for the moment. I don't have to tell you what this celebrity shit is like. The mayor'll be on the phone as soon as he wakes up, and he'll want to know. I'll ask him to buy us a few hours to find the woman."

As the detectives shuffled out, Leary called Stone and Dino back. "Barrington, I'm assuming you're up to this. You're still on limited duty, officially."

"I'm up to it, Lieutenant."

"I mean it about the sleep," Leary said. "You grab four or five hours. This one ain't likely to be over today, and I want you in shape to fuckin' handle it."

"Yessir," they replied in unison.

Stone limped up the steps of the Turtle Bay brownstone, retrieved the *Times* from the stoop, and let himself in. He was met by the combined scent of decay and fresh wood shavings. No messages on the answering machine in the downstairs hallway. Too tired and sore to take the stairs, he took the elevator to the third floor. It creaked a lot, but it made it.

His bedroom looked ridiculous. An ordinary double bed stood against a wall, with only a television set, an exercise machine, an old chest of drawers, and a chair to help fill the enormous room. He switched on the television and started to undress.

"Television journalist Sasha Nijinsky last night fell from the terrace of her twelfth-floor East Side penthouse. An off-duty police detective who was at the scene gave chase to someone who had apparently been in Ms. Nijinsky's apartment, but was, himself, injured and lost the possible perpetrator. Astonishingly, Ms. Nijinsky may have survived the fall. She was taken to a Manhattan hospital, and we have had no further word on her condition. We'll keep you posted as news comes in."

"You're guessing about the Manhattan hospital, sport," Stone said to the newscaster. "That was my guess, too."

He stripped off his clothes and stretched out on the bed, switching the channel to *The Morning Show.*

"Sasha Nijinsky has done just about everything in broadcast journalism, and she's done it fast," a pleasant young man was saying. They cut to a montage of shots from Nijinsky's career, and he continued, voice-over.

"Daughter of the Russian novelist Georgi Ni-jinsky, who was expelled from the Soviet Union more than twenty-five years ago, Sasha was six years old when she came to this country with her parents. She already spoke fluent English." There were shots of a bearded man descending from an airplane, a surprised-looking little girl in his arms.

"Sasha distinguished herself as an actress at Yale, but not as a student. Then, on graduation, instead of pursuing a career in the theater, as expected, she took a job as a reporter on a New Haven station. Four years later, she came to New York and earned a reputation as an ace reporter on the Continental Network affiliate. She spent another three years here, on *The Morning Show,* where she honed her interviewing skills, then she was sent to Moscow as the network's corre-spondent in the Soviet Union for a year, before being expelled in the midst of spy charges that she has always maintained were fabricated.

"On returning to this country, she further en-hanced her growing reputation, covering both national political conventions before the last elec-tion. Then her Sunday morning interview show, *Newsmakers,* pitted her against the nation's top political figures. She proved to be as tough as ever in those interviews, and it was said in Washing-ton that nobody wanted to go on her show, but everyone was afraid not to.

"Earlier this month, the industry was not sur-prised when it was announced that Sasha Nijin-sky would join anchorman Barron Harkness as co-anchor on the network's evening news, which, although still the leading network newscast, had recently slipped in the ratings. Harkness, an old colleague of Sasha's on *The Morning Show*, could not be reached for comment, as he is not due back until today from assignment in the Middle East."

Stone switched off the set. Make a note to talk to Harkness, he told himself, then he put the case from his mind. He thought, as he always did when he wanted to clear his head, about the house and his plans for it. It was in terrible condition.

He turned his thoughts to plumbing fixtures. In minutes, he was asleep.

5

Stone arrived at the station house at one o'clock sharp. The squad room was abuzz with detectives on the phone. He raised his eyebrows at one, and the man gave a huge shrug. A moment later, he hung up.

"Gather round," Stone said to the group. "Any luck?" he asked when they had assembled.

"Zilch. She's nowhere," a detective said.

"How many more places to check?" Stone asked.

"Not many."

"Add all the funeral parlors in the city to your list," Stone said. "Start with the ones in Manhattan. What else we got?"

"We got a suspect," Detective Gonzales said. He referred to a sheet of paper. "One Marvin Herbert Van Fleet, male Caucasian, forty-one, of a SoHo address."

"What makes him a suspect?" Stone asked.

"He's written Sasha Nijinsky over a thousand

letters the past two years." Gonzales held up a stack of paper.

Stone took the letters and began to go through them. "I want you all to myself," he quoted. "Come and live with me. I've got a nice place. . . . You and my mother will get along great." He looked up. "This is pretty bland stuff. Not even anything obscene. He doesn't so much as want to sniff her underwear."

"Nijinsky wanted him arrested, but apparently he didn't do anything illegal. She finally got a civil court order, preventing him from contacting her."

"What else have we got on him?"

"Interesting background," Gonzales said. "He went to Cornell Medical School, graduated and all, but never completed his internship."

"Where?"

"At Physicians and Surgeons Hospital."

"Pretty ritzy. Why didn't he finish?"

"File says he was dropped from the program as 'unsuited for a medical career.' There have been some complaints about him posing as a doctor, but since he apparently never actually treated anybody, there was nothing we could do. He worked at the Museum of Natural History for a while."

"What's he do now?"

"He's an embalmer at Van Fleet Funeral Parlor."

Stone felt a little chill. "Pick him up for questioning."

"Here's a photograph."

Stone looked at the picture of Marvin Herbert Van Fleet. "Hang on, this guy's got an alibi."

"How do you know that? We haven't asked him yet."

"Because I saw him at the bar at Elaine's twenty minutes before Nijinsky fell."

There was a brief silence. "Twenty minutes is a long time," Gonzales said.

"You're right," Stone agreed. "I left and walked down Second Avenue. He could have taken a cab and gotten there before I did. Pick him up. No, give me that address. Dino and I will talk to him."

Dino arrived, waving a magazine. He tossed it onto Stone's desk. "I had to wrestle two women for this," he said. "It just hit the newsstands this morning, and this must be the last copy in the city."

Stone picked it up. The new issue of *Vanity Fair*, and Sasha Nijinsky was on the cover. SASHA! BY HIRAM BARKER, WITH PHOTOGRAPHS BY ANNIE LEIBO-VITZ, a headline read. Stone laughed. "Now, *that's* timing. You read it yet?"

"Not yet," Dino said. "Be my guest."

The tone of the piece reeled back and forth between sycophancy and bitchiness. Nijinsky's career was recapped briefly, but a lot of space was devoted to her social and sex lives. All the unflattering stuff came from unnamed sources, including a report of a secret affair between Nijinsky and her old colleague on *The Morning Show*, and new co-anchor on the evening news, Barron Harkness. "They were never seen together in public," the source said, "and a lot of the staff thought they were screwing in her dressing room. She would never go into his."

Stone finished the piece and added Hiram Barker to his list of interviewees. He picked up the phone, dialed the Continental Network, and asked for Barron Harkness.

"Mr. Harkness's office," an interesting female voice said.

"This is Detective Stone Barrington of the Homicide Division, New York City Police Department," he said. "I'd like to speak with Mr. Harkness."

"I'm afraid Mr. Harkness is on an airplane somewhere over the Atlantic," the woman said. "This is Cary Hilliard, his assistant. May I help you?"

Stone remembered the television report that the anchorman had been on assignment in the Middle East. "I want to speak to Mr. Harkness regarding the . . ." (What was it? Not a homicide—not yet, anyway.) ". . . about Sasha Nijinsky. Can you tell me what time his plane is due in?"

"He won't be in the office before about five thirty," the woman said. "And he'll be going on the air at seven o'clock, on the evening news."

Stone liked the woman's voice. "I'd like to know the airline and flight number, please. It's important."

The woman hesitated. "What was your name again, please?"

"Detective Stone Barrington. I'm in charge of the Nijinsky case."

"Of course. He's due in on an Alitalia flight from Rome at four twenty, but he'll be met and helicoptered in. You'd do better to see him here. I know he'll want to talk to you. He's very fond of Sasha."

"At what time?"

"It'll be hell from the moment he arrives until the newscast is over. Come at a quarter to seven, and ask for me. I'll take you up to the control room, and you can talk to Barron as soon as he's off the air."

"Six forty-five. I'll see you then."

"Oh, we're not in the Continental Network building. We're at the Broadcast Center, at Pier Nineteen, at the west end of Houston Street."

"I'll see you at six forty-five." Stone hung up. He really liked her voice. She was probably a dog, though. He'd made the voice mistake before.

Dino had turned on the television, and a doctor was being interviewed on CNN about Nijinsky.

"Doctor, is it possible that Sasha Nijinsky could have survived her fall from twelve stories?"

"Well," the doctor replied, "as we've just seen on the videotape, she obviously survived, at least for a few moments, but it is unlikely in the extreme that she could recover from the sort of injuries she must have sustained in the fall. I'd say it was virtually impossible that she lived more than a minute or two after striking the earth."

"That still don't make it a homicide," Dino said.

"It's a homicide," Stone said. "If she's dead."

"Whaddaya mean 'if she's dead'?" Dino asked.

"Didn't you hear the doctor, there? She's a fuckin' pancake."

"Look," Stone said, "do you know what terminal velocity is?"

"Nope," Dino replied. Nobody else did either.

"An object in a vacuum, when dropped from a height, will accelerate at the rate of thirty-two feet per second, and continue accelerating—in a vacuum. But in an atmosphere, like the earth's, there will come a point when air resistance becomes equal to acceleration, and, at that point, the object will fall at a steady rate."

"But it'll keep falling," Dino said, puzzled.

"Sure, but it'll stop accelerating." Stone had everyone's undivided attention now. "I read a piece in the *Times* a few weeks ago about cats, and how cats have been known to fall from a great height and survive. There was one documented case where a cat fell twenty-six stories, landed on concrete, and survived with only a couple of broken bones."

"How the fuck could it survive a fall like that?" a detective asked.

"Like this," Stone said. He held out his hand, palm down. "When a cat starts to fall, he immediately orients himself feet first—you know that cats will always land on their feet, right?"

"Right," the detective said.

"Not only does he get into a feet-first position, but he spread-eagles into what's called the flying-squirrel position, like this." He spread his fingers. "Flying squirrels don't fly, like birds, they glide, because they have a membrane connecting their front and back legs, and, when they spread out, they're sort of like a furry Frisbee."

"But a cat ain't a flying squirrel," another detective said.

"No," Stone agreed, "and he can't glide like one. But by presenting the greatest possible area to the air resistance, a cat slows down his rate of acceleration and, consequently, his terminal velocity."

"You mean he falls slow," Dino said.

"Compared to a human being, anyway. A cat's terminal velocity is about sixty miles an hour. But a human being's terminal velocity is a hundred and twenty miles an hour. That's why a cat could survive a fall from twenty-six stories, when no human could."

The group digested this for a moment.

"But Sasha Nijinsky ain't no cat," Dino said.

"No," Stone said, "she's not." He looked up to see that Lieutenant Leary had joined the group. "But," he continued, "she fell from twelve stories, not twenty-six. And not onto concrete, but into a large pile of freshly dug earth. And look at this." He opened the *Vanity Fair* to its center spread and showed a photograph to the assembled detectives.

The shot was of Sasha Nijinsky, and she seemed to be flying. The earth was thousands of feet below her, and she was wearing a jumpsuit and a helmet and had an unopened parachute strapped to her back. She was grinning at the camera, exposing rows of large, white teeth; her eyes were wide behind goggles.

"Sasha Nijinsky was a sky diver," Stone said. "An experienced one, too, with more than a hundred jumps. And that"—he thumped the photograph with his forefinger—"was the position she was in when I saw her falling. Also, she was wearing a full-length nightgown and a bathrobe when she fell, and she might have gotten some extra air resistance by the ballooning out of those garments. When she fell, she automatically assumed the position she'd been trained to assume when free-falling. And, by doing that, she slowed down her rate of acceleration and, most important, her terminal velocity."

No one spoke for a long time. Finally, Dino broke the rapt silence. "Horseshit," he said.

"Maybe not," Stone said.

"Let me tell you something, Stone—I read that lady's diary, and I say she was suffering from too much fucking, too much fuckin' ambition, and too much fuckin' fame, all of it too fuckin' soon." Dino closed the magazine and, with his finger, drew an X over her face. "That girl *jumped* off that terrace. She ain't no cat, and she ain't no flying squirrel."

"I think somebody helped her," Stone said. "And she may still be alive."

Dino shook his head slowly. "I'll tell you what she is. She's New York Dead."

6

The Van Fleet Funeral Parlor had a Gramercy Park address, but it was around the corner, off the square.

"Italians know all about death," Stone said to Dino. "What do you know about this place?"

Dino shrugged. "It's not Italian, so what could I know? The location tells us, don't it? Good address, not so good location. If you don't want to pay for a first-class funeral at Frank Campbell's, where the elite meet to grieve, then you go to, like, Van Fleet's. It's cheaper, but it's got all the fuckin' pretensions, you know?"

Dino parked in a loading zone and flipped down the sun visor to display the car's ID. They walked back half a block and entered the front door, following a well-dressed couple. They stopped in a vestibule while the couple signed a visitors' book, presided over by a man in a tailcoat.

"The Wilson party?" the man asked Dino, in unctuous tones.

"The NYPD party," Dino said, flashing his shield. "Who runs the place?"

The man flinched at the sight of the badge. "That would be Mrs. Van Fleet," he said. "Please stay here, and I'll get her. Please remember there are bereaved here."

"Yeah, yeah," Dino said.

"You don't like the fellow?" Stone said when the man had gone.

"I don't like the business," Dino said. "It's a creepy business, and people who do it are creepy."

"Somebody's got to do it," Stone said. "We'll do better if you don't give them a hard time."

Dino nodded. "You talk to the creeps, then."

As they waited, Stone looked around. In a large, somewhat overdecorated sitting room to their left, two dozen people talked quietly, while some gathered around an elderly woman who seemed to be receiving the condolences. He looked right and was surprised to see a bedroom. On the four-poster bed, under a lace coverlet, lay a pretty woman in her late thirties. Several people stood around the bed, and one knelt at some sort of altar set at the foot. It took Stone a moment to realize that the woman on the bed was the guest of honor. She appeared to be sleeping.

A door opened at the end of the hallway ahead of them, and a short, thin, severely dressed woman of about sixty approached them. She walked with her hands folded in front of her; it would have been an odd posture anywhere but here.

"Yes?" the woman said, her face expressionless.

"Good afternoon," Stone said. "I am Detective Barrington, and this is Detective Bacchetti, New York City Police. I believe you have an employee here named Marvin Herbert Van Fleet."

"He's not an employee," the woman said. "He's a partner in the firm, he's our chief . . . technical person, and he's my son."

Stone nodded. "May we see him, please?"

"Now?"

"Please."

"I'm afraid he's busy at the moment."

"We're busy, too," Dino said, apparently unable to contain himself.

Stone shot him a sharp glance. "I'm afraid we can't wait for a more convenient time," he said to the woman.

"One moment, please," Mrs. Van Fleet said, not happy. She walked down the hallway a few paces, picked up a phone, dialed two digits, and spoke quietly for a moment. She hung up and motioned to the detectives.

They followed her down the hallway. She turned right through a door and walked rapidly down another hall. The decor changed to utilitarian. A vaguely chemical scent hung in the air. She stopped before a large, metal swinging door and indicated with a nod that they were to enter. Then she brushed past them and left.

Stone pushed the door open and, followed by Dino, entered a large room with a tile floor. Before them were six autopsy tables, two of them occupied by bodies covered with sheets. At the far end of the room, the body of a middle-aged woman lay naked on another table. A man stood with his back to her, facing a counter built along the wall. Memories of dissecting frogs in high school biology swept over Stone; the smell of formaldehyde was distinct.

"Marvin Van Fleet?" Stone said.

A sharp, metallic sound was followed by a hollow rattling noise. The man turned around, and Stone saw a soft drink can on the tabletop.

"Herbert Van Fleet," the man said. "Please call me Doc. Everybody does."

The man was not handsome, Stone thought, but his voice was—a rich baritone, expressive, without any discernible accent. A good bedside voice. The detectives walked briskly to the end of the room, their heels echoing off the tile floor. They stopped at the head of the autopsy table. Stone introduced himself and Dino.

"I've been expecting you," Van Fleet said. He stepped over to the naked body on the table and picked up the forceps that rested beside the head.

"Oh? Why is that?" Stone replied.

"Well, of course I heard about Miss Nijinsky on television this morning. Given the nature of our relationship, I thought perhaps someone would come to see me." He produced a curved suturing needle and clamped it in the jaws of the forceps.

"Did you and Sasha Nijinsky have a relationship?" Stone asked.

Van Fleet looked thoughtful for a moment.

"Why, yes, we did. I was her correspondent, although she seemed to think of me as an antagonist, which I never intended myself to be. She was my . . ." He paused. "She was an object of interest to me, I suppose. I greatly admired her talents. Do you know how she's doing?" he asked, concernedly. "She's in the hospital, they said on television."

"We don't have any information on her condition," Stone said. God knew that was true.

Van Fleet nodded sadly. He bent over the corpse, peeled back the lips with rubber-gloved fingers, and inserted the needle in the inside of the upper lip, passing it through the inside of the lower lip, then pulled it tight.

Stone stopped asking questions and watched with a horrible fascination. So did Dino. Van Fleet continued to skillfully manipulate the forceps and the needle, until the web of thread reached across the width of the mouth. Then he pulled the thread tight, and the mouth closed, concealing the stitching on the inside of the lips. Van Fleet made a quick surgical knot, snipped off the thread, and tucked the end out of sight at the corner of the mouth.

"Shit," Dino said.

"Mr. Van Fleet, could you leave that until we're finished, please?" Stone said.

"Of course."

"Can you account for your whereabouts between two and three A.M. this morning?"

"*You* can account for my whereabouts at two," Van Fleet said, smiling. "I was where you were."

"I remember," Stone said. "At what time, exactly, did you leave Elaine's?"

"A few minutes after you did," Van Fleet said. "About two twenty, I'd say. Maybe the bartender would remember."

"Where did you go then?"

"I drove down Second Avenue, and in the sixties I saw a sort of commotion. It seemed that someone had been hurt. I have some medical skills, so I stopped to see if I could help. They were loading a stretcher into an ambulance. I didn't know it was Sasha until this morning, when I turned on *The Morning Show*."

"Who else was at the scene when you stopped?" Stone asked.

"Two ambulance men, two or three Con Ed men, and a man with a television camera."

"What did you do then?"

"I went home."

"What route did you take?"

"I continued down Second Avenue all the way to Houston, then turned right, then left on Garamond Street. That's where I live."

"Did you see anyone you knew?"

"At two thirty in the morning?"

"Anyone at all. Someone else in your building?"

"There is no one else in my building. I live over a former glove factory."

"We'd like to see your apartment. May we go there now?"

"Why?"

"It would help us in our investigation. If you

had nothing to do with what happened to Miss Nijinsky, then we'd like to be able to cross you off our list of suspects."

"I'm a suspect?" Van Fleet asked, surprised. "What do you suspect me of?"

"Well, we haven't established the cause of . . . what happened, yet."

"Was there a crime?"

"We haven't determined that yet."

"My impression from the news was that Sasha's fall was a suicide attempt."

"That's certainly a possibility. We treat any unknown cause of death as homicide, until we know otherwise."

"Then you suspect me of a homicide you're not sure was committed?"

"As I said, Mr. Van Fleet, everyone who had anything to do with her is a suspect, until we know for sure what happened. Do you object to our seeing where you live?"

Van Fleet shrugged. "Not really, but I think I should ask my lawyer how he feels about it."

"That's your right."

"Unless you have a search warrant."

"We can get one if we feel it's necessary."

"If a judge feels it's necessary, you mean."

"We can get a search warrant."

"I watch a lot of police shows on television, you see. I understand these things."

"You object to our seeing your apartment, then?"

"No, I don't, not really. However, I don't think you have a good enough reason to ask. If you do have a good enough reason, then you can get a search warrant, can't you?"

"It would certainly make us feel better about you if we had your cooperation, Mr. Van Fleet."

"Please don't misunderstand me, Detective Barrington, I'm most anxious to help. I greatly admire Sasha, and I would do anything I could to help you resolve what happened to her. But I don't really see how visiting my home would help you, and I think such a visit would be an unwarranted invasion of my privacy. Of course, a judge may feel differently, and, if so, I'll be happy to cooperate."

"I see," Stone said. He was getting nowhere.

"Is there anything else I can do to help you?"

"Not at the moment, Mr. Van Fleet. I expect we'll talk again."

Van Fleet nodded. "Any time. My pleasure. But there's something I think you should consider."

"What's that?"

"It's quite true that I have a history of what some people would call annoying Sasha Nijinsky. But I'm sure you can tell from the letters I wrote her that I had only admiration for her, that, certainly, I had no reason to cause her harm."

"We'll take that into consideration in our inquiry," Stone said.

"I hope you will, Detective Barrington, because, while I will help you in any way I feel I reasonably can, I do not intend to have my privacy unduly disturbed, nor do I wish to have my name splashed about in the tabloids, nor my professional reputation besmirched."

"Well, we'll leave you to your work, Mr. Van Fleet."

"Call, if you think of anything else."

"We will."

The front of the funeral parlor was deserted when they passed back through.

"He's dirty," Dino said, when they were on the street again.

"I don't know," Stone replied. "He said pretty much what I'd have said in the circumstances, if I were innocent."

"Maybe he's not dirty on Nijinsky, but he's dirty on something," Dino said emphatically. "He's a gold miner, for a start."

"A what?"

"A gold miner. You're so fucking naive, Stone, you really are. When we got there, he had just finished pulling that corpse's gold teeth. He put 'em in the Coke can. Didn't you hear it rattle? Why do you think he was sewing her mouth shut? Doesn't want anybody poking around in there, that's why."

"Jesus Christ, Dino, how do you think of this stuff?"

"I got a suspicious nature, didn't you know that?"

"I knew that."

"I think when this Nijinsky thing is over, we want to take a closer look at fuckin' Doc Van Fleet."

"Let's not wait until then," Stone said.

They reached the car, and Dino looked at his

watch. "You still want me to meet Barron Harkness's plane?"

"Yeah. I wanted us to see Hiram Barker this afternoon, but seeing if Harkness is on that airplane is more important."

"You go on and see Barker, and I'll meet the plane."

"It would be better if we both were there."

"Fuck procedure. We got a lot to do, right? I'll meet you at the TV studio at six forty-five, and we'll do Harkness together."

"Okay, you take the car, and I'll get a cab."

As Dino drove away and Stone looked for a cab, he drew deep breaths of fresh, polluted New York City air into his lungs. From now on he'd have different memories when he caught the scent of formaldehyde.

7

Stone went to the *Vanity Fair* offices in mid-town and, after a phone call was made, he was given Hiram Barker's address. As he entered the lobby of United Nations Plaza, he remembered a line about the apartment house from an old movie: "If there is a god," a character had said, "he probably lives in this building." After another phone call, the deskman sent him up to a high floor.

"I can just imagine why you're here," Barker said as he opened the door.

He was larger than Stone had expected, in both height and weight, a little over six feet tall and broad at the middle. The face was not heavy but handsome, the hair sleek and gray, slicked straight back.

"I'm Hi Barker," he said, extending a fleshy hand. He waved Stone into a spacious, beautifully furnished living room with a view looking south toward the United Nations.

Stone introduced himself. He heard the tinkling of silver in the background; he saw a woman enter the dining room and begin to set the table.

"Can I get you something to drink?" Barker asked solicitously.

Stone was thirsty. "Perhaps some water."

"Jeanine, get the gentleman some Perrier," Barker said to the woman.

She left and returned with a heavy crystal glass, decorated with a slice of lime.

"Sit you down," Barker said, waving at one end of a large sofa, while flopping down at the other end, "and tell me what I can do for you." He cocked his head expectantly.

"You can tell me where you were between two and three this morning," Stone said.

Barker clapped his hands together and threw his head back. "I've been waiting all my life for a cop to ask me that question!" he crowed.

Stone smiled. "I hope I won't have to wait that long for an answer."

"Dear me, no." Barker chuckled. "I got home about one thirty from a dinner at the de la Rentas', then went straight to bed. The night man downstairs can confirm that—ah, the time, not the bed part. Security is ironclad here, you know. We've got Arabs, Israelis, *and* Irish in the building, and nobody, but *nobody*, gets in or out without being seen."

Stone didn't doubt it.

"Am I a suspect then?"

"A suspect in what?" Stone asked.

"Oh, God, now I've done it! I'm not even supposed to know there's a crime!"

"Is there?"

"Well, didn't somebody help poor Sasha out into the night?"

"I'd very much like to know that," Stone said, "and I'd like to know why you think so."

"She wasn't the sort to take a flying leap," Barker said more seriously.

"That's why I've come to see you, Mr. Barker."

"Hi, please call me Hi. I'll be uncomfortable if you don't."

"Hi it is then."

"And why is it you've come to see me?"

"Because of your *Vanity Fair* piece. I've read it, and it seemed extremely well researched."

"That's a very astute observation," Barker said. "Most people would have thought it produced from gossip. No, I spent a good six months on that. I was researching it even before Tina at the magazine knew I wanted to do it."

"And you talked with Miss Nijinsky at some length?"

"I did, a good six hours over three meetings."

"Did you make any tape recordings?"

"I did, but when I finished the piece I returned the tapes to her, as agreed."

"You didn't, perhaps, make a copy?"

Barker's eyes turned momentarily hard. "No. That's not the way it's done."

"How well did you know her before you began research for the article?"

"We had a cordial acquaintance. We'd been to a few of the same dinner parties. That was before the piece. By the time I finished it, I think I knew her as well as anybody alive."

"You can do that in six hours of conversation?"

"If you've done six months of research beforehand, and if nobody else knows the person at all."

"She had no close friends?"

"None in the sense that any normal person would call close."

"Family?"

"She hardly ever saw them after she left home to go to college. I think she was close to her father as a young girl, but she didn't speak of him as a confidant, not in the least."

"Did she have any confidants?"

"Not one, as far as I could tell. I think by the time we had finished, she thought of me as one." Barker shook his head. "But no, as well as I got to know her, she never opened up to me. I took my cues as much from what she didn't say as what she said. There was a sort of invisible, one-way barrier between that young woman and the rest of the world; everything passed through it to her, but very little passed out."

"Do you think she was a possible suicide?"

"Not for a moment. Sasha was one tough cookie; she had goals, and she was achieving them. Christ, I mean, she was on the verge of the biggest career any woman ever had in television news. Bigger than Barbara Walters. That sort of person commits suicide only in trashy novels."

"All right," Stone said, "let's assume murder."

Barker grinned. "Let's."

"Who?"

Barker crossed his legs, clasped his hands behind his neck, and stared out at the sweep of the East River. "Two kinds of people might have murdered Sasha Nijinsky," he said. "First, people she hurt on the way up—you know, the secretary she tyrannized, the people she displaced when she got promotions—there was no shortage of those. But you'd have to be a raving lunatic to kill such a famous woman just for revenge. The chances are too good of getting caught and sent away."

"What's the other kind of person?" Stone asked.

Barker grinned again, still looking at the river. "Whoever had the most to lose from Sasha's future success," he said.

"That's an interesting notion," Stone said, and he meant it. "Who did you have in mind?"

"I'll tell you," Barker said, turning to face him, "but if you ever quote me, I'll call you a liar."

Stone nodded. "It'll be just between us."

"Well," Barker said, drawing it out. "There's only one person in the world I can think of who would suffer from Sasha Nijinsky's future success."

"Go on," Stone said.

"Her new co-anchor, who else? The estimable Mr. Barron Harkness, prizewinning television journalist, square-jawed, credible, *terribly vulnerable* Barron Harkness."

"I take it you don't like Mr. Harkness."

"Who does, dear boy? He lacks charm." Barker

said this as if it were the ultimate crime. "Sasha would have blown him out of the water in less than a year. His ratings had slipped badly, you know—after a winning streak last year, he has slipped to a point or two behind Brokaw, Jennings, and Rather, and he's still sinking. He's already worked at ABC and NBC, and neither would have him back; and I know for a fact that Larry Tisch despises him, so that shuts him out of CBS. Then here comes Sasha, hipping him over at the anchor desk, loaded for bear. A power struggle began the day the first rumor hit the street about Sasha's new job, and, if Harkness lost, where would he go? He'd be making solemn pronouncements on Public Radio, like Dan Schorr, and his ego would never accept that. No, sir, Barron Harkness is a man with a motive."

"I think I should tell you," Stone said, looking at his watch, "that Barron Harkness got off an airplane from Rome just about an hour ago."

Barker's face fell. "I'm extremely sorry to hear it," he said. "But," he said, brightening, "if I were you I'd make awfully sure he was really on that plane."

"Don't worry," Stone said, "that's been done. Tell me, would it violate some journalistic ethic if you gave me a list of the people you interviewed about Miss Nijinsky?"

Barker shook his head. "No. I'll do even better than that; I'll give you a paragraph on each of them and my view as to the value of each as a suspect."

"I'd be very grateful for that."

The writer turned sly. "It'll have to be a trade, though."

"What do you want?"

"When you find out what's happened to Sasha and who is responsible, I want a phone call before the press conference is held."

Stone thought for a moment. It wasn't a bad trade, and he needed that list. "All right, you're on."

"It'll take me a couple of hours."

"You have a fax machine?"

Barker looked hurt. "Of course."

Stone gave him a card. "Shoot it to me there when you're done." He got up.

Barker rose with him. "I'm having a few friends in for dinner this evening, as you can see," he said, waving a hand at the dining room. "Would you like to join us?"

"Thanks," Stone said, "but until I've solved the Nijinsky problem, there are no dinner parties in the picture."

"I understand," Barker said, seeing him out. "Perhaps another time?"

"Thank you," Stone said. While he waited for the elevator, he wondered why Hi Barker would ask a policeman to dinner. Well, he thought, as he stepped from the elevator into the lobby, if he solved this one, he would become a very famous policeman.

As it turned out, he didn't have to wait that long. A skinny young man with half a dozen cameras draped about him was arguing with the doorman when he turned and saw Stone. "Right here, Detective Barrington," he called, raising a camera.

The flash made Stone blink. As he made his way from the building, pursued by the snapping paparazzo, he felt a moment of sympathy for someone like Sasha Nijinsky, who spent her life dodging such trash.

8

Stone had almost an hour and a half to kill before his appointment with Barron Harkness at the network. Rush hour was running at full tilt, and all vacant cabs were off duty, so he set off walking crosstown. He reckoned his knee could use the exercise anyway. He was wrong. By the time he got to Fifth Avenue, he was limping. He thought of going home for an hour, but he was restless, and, even though he had another interview to conduct, he wanted a drink. He walked a couple of blocks north to the Seagram Building and entered a basement door.

The Four Seasons was a favorite of Stone's; he couldn't afford the dining rooms, but he could manage the prices at the bar. He climbed the stairs, chose a stool at a corner of the big, square bar, and nodded at the bartender. He came in often enough to know the man and to be known, but not by name.

"Evening, Detective," the bartender said, sliding a coaster in front of him. "What'll it be?"

"Wild Turkey on the rocks, and how'd you know that?"

The man reached under the bar and shoved a *New York Post* in front of Stone.

The photograph was an old one, taken at a press conference a couple of years before. They had cropped out Stone's face and blown it up. DE-TECTIVE SEES SASHA'S FALL, the headline said. Stone scanned the article; somebody at the precinct was talking to a reporter.

"So, what's the story?" the bartender asked, pouring bourbon over ice. He made it a double without being asked.

"What's your name?"

"Tom."

"When I find out, Tom, you'll be among the first to know. I'll be here celebrating."

The bartender nodded and moved down the bar to help a new customer, a small, very pretty blonde girl in a business suit.

The bar wasn't the only reason Stone liked the Four Seasons. He looked at the woman and felt suddenly, ravenously hungry for her. Since his hospital time and the course of libido-dampening painkillers, he had given little thought to women. Now a rush of hormones had him breathing rapidly. He fought an urge to get up, walk down the bar, and stick his tongue in her ear. COP IN SEX CHARGE AT FOUR SEASONS, tomorrow's *Post* would say.

The bartender put a copy of the paper in front of her. She glanced at it, looked up at Stone, sur-prised, and smiled.

Here was his opening. Stone picked up his drink and shifted off the stool. As he took a step, an acre of black raincoat blocked his view of the girl. A man built like a pro linebacker had stepped between them, leaned over some distance, and pecked the girl on the cheek. He settled on a barstool between her and Stone. The girl leaned back and cast a regretful grimace Stone's way.

Stone settled back onto his stool and pulled at the bourbon. His fantasy raged on, out of control. A five-minute walk to his house and they were in bed, doing unspeakable things to each other. He shook his head to clear it and opened the paper, looking for something to divert him. His view of the girl was now completely obliterated by the hulk in the black raincoat. Stone suppressed a whimper.

The *Post* was the first paper to get the Nijinsky story in time for a regular edition, and they had made the most of it. There was a retrospective of photographs of Sasha, from tothood to *The Morning Show*. There were shots of her as a schoolgirl, as a teenager in a beauty contest, performing as an actress at Yale, on camera as a cub reporter— even shots of her at the beach in a bikini, obviously taken without her knowledge.

Sasha looked damn good in a bikini, Stone thought. He wondered where that very fine body was resting at the moment.

He read the article slowly, trolling for some new fact about her that might help. When the bourbon was finished, he looked at his watch, left a ten-dollar bill on the bar, in spite of the bartender's wave-off, and walked down to the street. The worst of rush hour was past, but rain was threatening, and half a dozen people were looking for cabs at the corner. The light turned red, and an off-duty cab stopped. Stone flipped open his wallet and held his badge up to the window. The driver sighed and pushed the button that unlocked the doors.

"Houston Street and the river," Stone said, and leaned his head back against the seat. Heavy raindrops began pounding against the windows. If he had been off women for a while, Stone reflected, he had been off booze, too, and the double shot of 101-proof bourbon had made itself felt. He dozed.

9

Stone was jerked awake by the short stop of the cab. He fumbled for some money, gave the cabbie five dollars, and struggled out of the cab. It was pouring rain now, and he got across the street as quickly as he could with his sore knee. A uniformed security guard sat at a desk, and Stone gave him Cary Hilliard's name. Before the man could dial the number, an elevator door opened, and a young woman walked out.

"Detective Barrington?" she asked, offering a hand.

"That's right," Stone replied, thinking how long and cool her fingers were. All of her, in fact, was long and cool. She was nearly six feet tall, he reckoned, slim but not thin, dressed in a black cashmere sweater that did not conceal full breasts and a houndstooth skirt that ended below the knee.

"I'm Cary Hilliard," she said. "Come on, let's go up to the studio. Barron will be on the air in a few minutes, and we can watch from the control room." They turned toward the elevator. "By the way, a Detective Bacchetti called and left a message for you. He said, and I quote, 'Your man was where he was supposed to be' and 'Tell Detective Barrington that I've been detained, and I'll see him tomorrow.'"

"Thank you." Detained, my ass, Stone thought. Detained by some stewardess, maybe.

She led him upstairs and through a heavy door. A dozen people worked in a room that held at least twenty-five television monitors and thousands of knobs and switches. "We can sit here," she said, showing him to a comfortable chair on a tier above the control console.

The whole of the top row of monitors displayed the face, in close-up, of Barron Harkness, "the idol of the airlanes," someone had called him, stealing Jan Garber's sobriquet. Tissue paper was tucked into his collar, and a woman's hand entered the frame, patting his nose with a sponge. "You've got a good tan, Barron," a voice said. "We won't need much of this."

Harkness nodded, as if saving his voice.

"One minute," somebody at the console said.

"I've got a thirty-second statement before the music," Harkness said into the camera.

"Barron," a man at the console said, "it's too late to fit it in; we're long as it is."

"Cut the kid with the transplant before the last commercial," Harkness said.

"Barron . . . ," the man nearly wailed.

"Do it."

Someone counted down from ten, and stirring music filled the control room. Barron Harkness arranged his face into a serious frown and looked up from his desk into the camera. "Good evening," he said, and his voice let the viewer know that something important was to follow. "Last night, a good friend of this newcast and of many of us personally was gravely injured in a terrible accident. Sasha Nijinsky was to have joined me at this desk tonight, and she is badly missed. All of us here pray for her recovery. All of us wish her well. All of us look forward to her taking her place beside me. We know you do, too."

Music swelled, and an announcer's voice heralded the evening news. Stone watched as Harkness skillfully led half a dozen correspondents through the newscast, reading effortlessly from the TelePrompTer and asking an occasional informed question of someone in Tehran, Berlin, or London, while the control room crew scrambled to squeeze his opening statement into their allotted time.

During a commerical break, Cary turned to Stone. "What do you think?" she asked.

"Very impressive," he said, looking directly at her.

She laughed. "I meant about the newscast."

"Not nearly as impressive."

"Well, Barron's a little self-important," she said, "but nobody does this better."

"Read the news?"

She laughed again. "Oh, come on, now, he's

reported from all over the world; he doesn't just read."

"I'll take your word for it."

The newscast ended, and she led Stone out another door and down a spiral staircase to the newsroom set. A dozen people were working at computer terminals.

"They're already getting the eleven o'clock news together," Cary said.

Barron Harkness was having the last of his makeup removed. He stood up and shook Stone's hand firmly. "Detective," he said.

To Stone's surprise, Harkness was at least six four, two twenty, and flat bellied. He looked shorter and fleshier on camera.

"Come on, let's go up to my office," Harkness said.

They climbed another spiral staircase, entered a hallway, and turned into Harkness's office, a large, comfortably furnished room with a big picture window looking down into the newsroom. Harkness waved Stone to a leather sofa. "Coffee? I'm having some."

"Thank you, yes," Stone said. He could use it; he fought off the lassitude caused by the bourbon and the newscast.

Cary Hilliard disappeared without being told, then came back with a Thermos and two cups. Both men watched her pour, then she took a seat in a chair to one side of Harkness's desk and opened a steno pad. "You don't mind if I take notes?" she asked Stone.

"Not at all," he replied. "Forgive me if I don't take any; I remember better if I do it later." He turned to Harkness. "Mr. Harkness—"

"Please call me Barron; I'd be more comfortable. And your first name?"

"Stone."

"A hard name," he said, smiling slightly.

"I'll try not to be too hard on you."

"Where is Sasha Nijinsky? What hospital?"

"I'm afraid I don't have any information on that."

Harkness's eyebrows went up. "I understood you were in charge of this investigation."

"That's nominally so, but I'm not the only investigator on the case, and I don't have all the information." That wasn't strictly true; he did have all the information there was; there just wasn't much.

"I trust *somebody* knows what hospital she's in. Certainly nobody at the network does."

"I expect somebody knows where she is," Stone said. "I understand you were traveling last night?"

"Yes, from Rome. I expect you've already checked that out."

"What time did you arrive at Kennedy?"

"Four thirty or five."

Stone nodded. "Mr. Harkness, did Sasha Nijinsky have any enemies?"

Unexpectedly, Harkness broke into laughter. "Are you kidding? Sasha climbed over half the people at the network to get where she is, and the other half are scared shitless of her."

"I see. Did any of them hate her enough to try to kill her?"

"Probably. In my experience, lots of people kill who have less cause than Sasha's victims."

That was Stone's experience too, but he didn't say so. "Who among her enemies do you think I should talk to?"

"Christ, where to begin!" Harkness said. "Oh, look, I'm overstating the case. I don't think anybody around here would try to kill Sasha. Do you think somebody kicked her off that terrace?"

"We have to investigate all the possibilities," Stone said.

"Well, I can't imagine that, not really. Maybe she caught a burglar in the act? Something like that?"

"It's possible," Stone said. It was, too, given that the doorman spent his evenings sound asleep. "We're looking at known operators in her neighborhood."

"On the other hand," Harkness said, "Sasha was one tough lady; I don't think a burglar could get the best of her. I'll tell you a story, in confidence. After the last elections, Sasha and I left this building very late, and, before we could get to the car that was waiting for us, a good-sized black guy stepped out of the shadows. He had a knife, and he said whatever the ghetto version of 'your money or your life' is these days. Before I even had time to think, Sasha stuck out her left arm, straight, and drove her fist into the guy's throat. He made this gurgling noise, dropped the knife, and hit the pavement like a sack of potatoes. Sasha stepped over, kicked the knife into the river, and said, 'Let's go.' We got into the car and left. Now *that* is what Sasha can be like. She'd been studying one of those martial arts things, and, when most people would have turned to jelly in the circumstances, she used what she knew. Me, I'd have given the guy anything he wanted." Harkness put his feet on his desk. "Now, do you think a burglar—or anybody else, for that matter—could heave somebody like that over a balcony railing?"

"You could be right," Stone said. You could be the guy who heaved her over the edge too, he thought. You're big enough and in good enough shape to handle a woman—even one who had martial arts training. "That brings us to another possibility. Did Sasha strike you as the sort of person who might take her own life?"

Harkness looked down at the carpet for a moment, drumming his fingers on the desk noisily. "In a word, yes," he said. "I think there was something of the manic-depressive in Sasha. She was high at a lot of times, but she was down at times, too. She could turn it off, if she was working; she could look into that camera and smile and bring it off. But there must have been times, when she was all alone, when it got to her."

"Did you ever see it get to her?"

"Once or twice, when we were doing *The Morning Show* together. I remember going into her dressing room once, five minutes before airtime, and she was in tears over something. But when we went on the air, she was as cheerful as a chipmunk."

"Do you know if she ever saw a pyschiatrist?"

"Nope, but I'd bet that, if she did, she didn't tell him much. Sasha plays her cards very close to that beautiful chest."

Stone nodded, then stood up. "Well, thank you, Mr.—ah, Barron. If anything else comes up, I hope I can call you."

"Absolutely," Harkness said, rising and extending his hand. "Just call Cary; she always knows where to find me."

"Come on, I'll walk you down," Cary said, leading the way. Passing through the outer office, she tossed her steno pad on a desk and grabbed a raincoat from a rack. On the elevator, she turned to Stone. "Well, now you've had the Harkness treatment," she said. "What did you think?"

Stone shrugged. "Forthright, frank, helpful."

She smiled. "You got Barron's message."

The elevator reached the lobby, and, when the doors opened, they could see the rain beating against the windows.

"Can I give you a lift?" she asked. "I've got a car waiting, and you'll never get a cab down here at this time of the evening."

"Sure, I'd appreciate that." He took a deep breath. "If you're all through with work, how about some dinner?"

"You're off duty now?"

"The moment you say yes."

She looked at him frankly. "I'd like that."

They ran across the pavement to the waiting Lincoln Town Car, one of hundreds that answer the calls of people with charge accounts.

"Where to?" Cary said, as they settled into the back seat.

"How about Elaine's?" Stone said.

"Can you get a table without a reservation?"

"Let's find out."

"Eighty-eighth and Second Avenue," she said to the driver.

Stone turned to her. "I got the impression from what you said in the elevator that I shouldn't necessarily believe everything Barron Harkness tells me."

"Why, Detective," Cary said, her eyes wide and innocent. "I never said that." She scrunched down in the seat and laid her head back. "And, anyway, you're off duty, remember?"

10

Elaine accepted a peck on the cheek, shook Cary's hand, and gave them Woody Allen's regular table. Stone heaved a secret sigh of relief. This was no night for Siberia.

"I'm impressed," Cary said when they had ordered a drink. "Whenever I've been in here before, we always got sent to Siberia."

"You've clearly been coming here with the wrong men," Stone replied, raising his glass to her.

"You could be right," she said, looking at him appraisingly. "You're bad casting for a cop, you know."

"Am I?"

"Don't be coy. It's not the first time you've been told that."

Pepe, the headwaiter, appeared with menus. Stone waved them away and asked for the specials.

"No, it's not the first time I've been told that," Stone said, when they had chosen their food.

"I'm told that every time a cop I don't know looks at me."

"All right," she said, leaning forward, "I want the whole biography, and don't leave anything out, especially the part about why you're a cop and not a stockbroker, or something."

Stone sighed. "It goes back a generation. My family, on my father's side, was from western Massachusetts, real Yankees, mill owners."

"Barrington, as if Great Barrington, Massachusetts?"

"I don't know; I didn't have a lot of contact with the Massachusetts Barringtons. My father was at Harvard—rather unhappily, I might add—when the stock market crash of 'twenty-nine came. His father and grandfather were hit hard, and Dad had to drop out of school. This troubled him not in the least, because it freed him to do what he really wanted to do."

"Which was?"

"He wanted to be a carpenter."

"A *carpenter?* You mean with saws and hammers?"

"Exactly. He took it up when he was a schoolboy at Exeter, and he showed great talent. My grandfather was horrified, of course. Carpentry wasn't the sort of thing a Barrington did. But when he could no longer afford to keep his son in Harvard, well . . ."

"What does this have to do with your being a cop?"

"I'm coming to that, eventually. Dad got to be

something of a radical, politically, as a result of the depression. He gravitated to Greenwich Village, where he fell in with a crowd of leftists, and he earned a living knocking on people's doors and asking if they wanted anything fixed. He lived in the garage of a town house on West Twelfth Street and didn't own anything much but his tools.

"He met my mother in the late thirties. She was a painter and a pianist and from a background much like Dad's—well-off Connecticut people, the Stones—who'd been wiped out in the crash. She was younger than Dad and very taken with the contrast between his upper-class education and his working-class job."

Cary wrinkled her brow. "Not Matilda Stone."

"Yes."

"Her work brings good prices these days at the auctions. I hope you have a lot of it."

"Only three pictures; her favorites, though."

"Go on with the autobiography."

"They lived together through the war years— the army wouldn't take Dad because he was branded as a Communist, even though he never joined the party. They had a tough time. Then, after the war, Dad rented a property on Hudson Street, where he finally was able to have a proper workshop. Some of Mother's friends, who had done well as artists, began to hire him for cabinetwork in their homes, and, by the time I was born, in 'fifty-two, he was doing pretty well. Mother's work was selling, too, though she never got anything like the prices it's bringing no, and, by the time I was old enough to notice, they were living stable, middle-class lives.

"When I was in my teens, Dad had quite a reputation as an artist-craftsman; he was building libraries in Fifth Avenue apartments and even designing and making one-of-a-kind pieces of furniture. The Barringtons and the Stones were very far away, and I didn't hear much about my forebears. Somehow, though, my parents' backgrounds filtered down into my life. There were always books and pictures and music in the house, and I suppose I had a sort of Yankee upbringing, once removed."

"Did you go to Harvard, like your father?"

"No; that would have infuriated him. I went to NYU and walked to class every day. By about my junior year, I had decided to go to law school. I didn't have any real clear idea about what lawyers actually did—neither did a lot of my classmates in law school for that matter—but, somehow, it sounded good. I did all right, I guess, had a decent academic record, and, in my senior year, the New York City Police Department had a program to familiarize law students with police work. I worked part-time in a station house, I rode around in a blue-and-white, and I just loved it. The cops treated me like the whitebread college kid I was, but it didn't matter, the bug had bit. I took the police exam, and, almost immediately after I got my law degree, I enrolled in the Police Academy. In a way, I think I was imitating my father's choice of a working-class life."

"You never took the bar?"

"I couldn't be bothered with that. I was hot to be a cop."

"Are you still?"

"Yes, sort of. I love investigative work, and I'm good at it. I had a couple of good collars that got me a detective's shield; I had a good rabbi—a senior cop who helped me with promotion; he's dead now, though, and I seem to have slowed down a bit."

"But you're different from other cops."

Stone sighed again. "Yes, I guess I am. I've been an outsider since the day I started at the academy."

"So you're not going to be the next chief of police?"

Stone laughed. "Hardly. You could get good odds at the 19th Precinct that I'll never make detective first grade."

"What are you now?"

"Detective second."

"So, you're thirty-eight years old, and . . ."

"Essentially without prospects," Stone said, shrugging. "I can look forward to a pension in six years; a better one, if I can last thirty."

"Why are you limping?"

Stone told her about the knee, keeping it as undramatic as possible. She listened and didn't say anything. "Now it's your turn," he said, "and don't leave out anything."

"My bio is much simpler," she said. "Born and grew up in Atlanta; the old man was a lawyer, now a judge; two years at Bennington, which my father thought was far too radical—I was wearing only black clothes and not washing my hair enough—so I finished at the University of Georgia, in journalism. Summer between my junior and senior years, I got on the interns' program at the network, and, when I graduated, they offered me a job as a production assistant. I'm thirty-two years old, and I'm still a production assistant."

"But at a higher level, surely? After all, you're assisting Barron Harkness."

She laughed. "It's a nice place to work, if your father can afford to send you there. The perks aren't bad." She looked at him sideways. "You skipped something."

"What?"

"Married?"

"Nope."

"Never? Why not?"

"Just lucky, I guess."

"Cynic."

"Probably."

"No girl?"

"Not at the moment. I was seeing somebody for a couple of years. When I was in the hospital, she accepted a transfer to LA."

"Sweet."

Stone shrugged. "I didn't come through with the commitment she wanted; she took a hike." He imitated her sidelong glance. "What about you?"

She sighed. "The usual assortment of yuppies during my twenties. I'm just out of a relationship with a married man."

"Those don't work, I'm told."

"This one sure didn't. He kept me on the hook for four years, and then he just couldn't bring himself to leave his wife."

"That's the drill. Still hurting?"

"Now and then, if I don't watch myself. I think I'm relieved, more than anything else."

"Was it Harkness?"

"No; he wasn't in the TV business. Advertising."

"For what it's worth, I think the guy's nuts."

She smiled, a wide mouth full of straight, white teeth. She started to speak, but didn't. Instead, she concentrated on her pasta.

Stone watched her, and he felt the possibilities in his gut.

When they left Elaine's, the rain had stopped, and the air was cool. The car still waited for them.

"Can I drop you?" she asked. "It's one of the perks of the job; I think I probably spend more of the network's money on cars than they pay me."

"Sure, thanks. It's early; I'll give you a night-cap at my house."

"Sold."

They got into the car, and Stone gave the driver his address.

She looked at him, eyebrows arched. "That's a pretty expensive neighborhood. You on the take?"

Stone laughed. "Nope. I'll explain later."

They drove straight down Second Avenue, and at Sixty-ninth Street they ran into a wall of flashing lights. A uniformed cop was waving traffic through a single open lane.

"Pull over here," Stone said to the driver. He

opened the car door and turned to Cary. "Give me a couple of minutes, will you?" He flashed his badge at a uniform and crossed the yellow tape. A Checker cab was stopped at the intersection, and a small group had gathered around the driver's open door. Stone saw Headly, from the detective squad.

Headly nodded. "Cabdriver caught one in the head," he said to Stone. "Looks like he was stopped for the light, somebody pulled up next to him, and just popped him one."

Stone glanced into the cab at the dead driver, sprawled across the front seat. There was a lot of blood. "You got it covered?" he said to Headly.

"Yeah," the detective replied.

Suddenly the cab was bathed in bright light. Stone turned, shielding his eyes.

"Howdy, Stone," Scoop Berman said, still operating his camera. "You on this one?"

"It's Headly's," Stone said. "You can give him the hard time." He stepped out of Scoop's lights and bumped into Cary Hilliard, who was staring at the dead driver. He took her elbow. "You don't want to see that," he said, turning her toward their car. "How'd you get past the tape?"

"Press card," she said, showing a blue, plastic shield on a string around her neck. She took it off and stuffed it into her handbag.

In the car they were both quiet for a block or two.

"You see a lot of that stuff?" she asked finally.

"Enough. More than I'd like to see. Did it upset you?"

She shook her head. "I didn't get a good enough look, thank God. I faint at the sight of blood."

They turned into Turtle Bay, and the car stopped.

"Wait for me," Cary said to the driver.

They climbed the steps, and Stone opened the front door of the house.

"You've got the duplex?" Cary asked, surprised.

"I've got the house," Stone replied. He flipped on the hall light.

"You *are* on the take," she said, laughing. "No honest cop could ever afford a house in Turtle Bay."

"Would you believe I inherited it?"

"No, I wouldn't."

"I did. My Great-Aunt Elizabeth, my grandfather's sister, married well. She always had a soft spot for my father, and she willed it to him. She outlived him, though, only died early this year at the age of ninety-eight, and so her estate came to me."

Stone led her into the library.

"It's a mess," she said, looking around at the empty shelves, stripped of their varnish, the books stacked on the floor, the rug rolled up, the furniture stacked in a corner, everything under sheets of plastic.

"It is now," Stone said, "but I'm working on it. My father designed and built this room; it was his first important commission, right after World War II. Everything is solid walnut. You could still buy it in those days; now all you can get is veneer, and that's out of sight."

"It's going to be magnificent," she said.

He led her through the other rooms, pointing out a couple of pieces that his father had built. "Most of the upholstered furniture is out being re-covered. My plan is to do the place up right, then sell it and retire on the proceeds, one of these days."

"Why not just sell it now?" she asked.

"I had a real estate lady look at it. She says I can triple the price if I put it in good shape—new heating, plumbing, kitchen—the works."

"How can you afford to do that?"

"There was a little money in Aunt Elizabeth's estate. I'm putting it all into the house and doing most of the work myself, with a couple of helpers and the occasional plumber and electrician."

"Where are your mother's pictures?"

"In my bedroom."

"May I see them?"

Stone took her up in the old elevator. "I keep meaning to get this thing looked at," he said over the creaking of the machinery, "but I'm afraid they'll tell me it needs replacing."

She stood in the bedroom and looked around. "This is going to be wonderful," she said. "I hope to God you've got decent taste."

"I'm not all that sure that I do," he lied. "I could use some advice."

"You may get more of that than you want; doing interiors is almost my favorite thing." She walked across the room and stood before the three Matilda Stones. There were two views of West Ninth and West Tenth streets and an elevated view of Washington Square. "These are superb," she said. "You could get half a million for the three, I'll bet, but don't you dare."

"Don't worry. They're a permanent fixture."

"They belong in a house like this," she said, "and so do you. Can't you think of some way to hang on to it? Go on the take, or something?"

"I have this fantasy," he said. "I'm living in this house; it's in perfect condition; there are servants in the servants' quarters, a cook in the kitchen, and money in the bank. I don't dare let myself dwell on it; it's never going to happen, I know that." He turned from the pictures and looked at her. "You said interior decorating was almost your favorite thing. What's your favorite?"

She stepped out of her heels and turned to face him. "I'm five-eleven in my stocking feet; does that turn you off?"

Stone looked her up and down—the luxuriant, dark hair; the chiseled face; the full breasts under the black cashmere; the long legs finishing in slender feet. He hooked an arm around her narrow waist and pulled her to him.

She smiled and rubbed her belly against his. "Apparently not," she said, then kissed him.

Stone slid down a long, velvet tunnel of desire, made no attempt to slow his fall. Their clothes vanished, and they found the bed. Stone made to move on top of her, then cried out when his swollen knee took his weight.

She pushed him onto his back, kissed the knee, kissed his lips and his nipples, kissed his navel and his penis, took him in her mouth, nearly swallowed him, brought him fully erect, then slid him inside her.

Stone looked up at the long body, the firm breasts, freed from the cashmere, the lips parted in ecstasy, the glazed eyes. She sucked him inside her again and again. When he thought he would come, she stopped and sat still, kissing his ears and his eyes, then she began again. Half an hour seemed to stretch into weeks, until, bathed in sweat, his face buried between her breasts, he came with her, and their cries echoed around the underfurnished room.

They lay in each other's arms, spent, breathing hard, caressing.

"You never told me what your favorite thing was," Stone said.

"That was it," Cary replied, kissing him.

Stone woke to broad daylight, and she was gone. A card was propped on the mantelpiece. There were phone numbers for home and work and an address: 1011 Fifth Avenue.

11

Stone arrived in the detectives' squad room of the 19th Precinct feeling rested, refreshed, fulfilled, and in an extremely good mood. The good mood was tempered somewhat by the rows of empty desks in the room. Twenty-four hours earlier, they had been filled with detectives doing his bidding, chasing down every lead on the Sasha Nijinsky disappearance, leaving only to interview her co-workers and acquaintances, again at his bidding. He had the sickening feeling that his time at the head of the investigation had come to an end.

Dino was in Lieutenant Leary's glassed-in office at the end of the large room. Stone rapped on the glass and joined them. "Where is everybody?" he asked Dino as he pulled up a chair.

"On the cabdriver thing," Dino said.

Stone turned to Leary. "Lieutenant, you're not going to pull my guys off this investigation and put them on a cabdriver murder, are you?"

"Yeah," Leary said, "but it's *three* murders."

"The cabdriver and who else?" Stone asked.

"The cabdriver and two other cabdrivers," Leary said. "Don't you watch TV or nothing?"

"I got a late start this morning," Stone said. "You mean three cabdrivers on the same day?"

"On the same night, all within an hour of each other," Leary said. "We got a fucking wildcat cabdrivers' strike going, you know that? Park Avenue is a parking lot. There's two thousand cabs just sitting there. You didn't notice?"

"Park Avenue isn't on my way to work," Stone said.

"You're lucky you and Bacchetti are still on Nijinsky," Leary said. "The mayor wasn't interested personally, you wouldn't be. What've you got on the lady?"

"Zip," Dino said.

"Some ideas," Stone said, shooting Dino a glance.

"What ideas?" Leary asked.

"We want a search warrant on Van Fleet," Stone said.

"Dino's been telling me about him," Leary replied. "I like him for this. You got enough for the warrant?"

"The letters ought to do it. We can demonstrate his undue interest in Nijinsky."

"See Judge O'Neal," Leary said. "She's got a hair up her ass about anything to do with any crime against women. She'll buy the letters."

"Right."

"What else you got?"

"Zip," Dino replied.

Stone shrugged. "It's not as though the effort hasn't been made. Every single co-worker has been interviewed; every hospital, clinic, and funeral parlor in the city, Long Island, and New Jersey has been contacted. I want to go through all her stuff today, just as soon as we've searched Van Fleet's place."

"I buy the effort," Leary said. "It's a bitch, ain't it?"

"It is," Dino agreed. "I never knew of nobody going up the pipe like this broad. It's spooky."

"I'll call the chief this morning; he'll talk to the mayor. I'll tell 'em we need more time."

"We do," Stone said.

"Go to it." Leary put his feet on his desk and picked up the telephone.

Stone followed Dino out of Leary's office. "You call Judge O'Neal's secretary for an appointment. I've got a call to make." He sat down at his desk, dug out Cary's card, and called her direct line. He got her on the first ring.

"Cary Hilliard."

"Morning."

"Well, good morning to you!" She was laughing.

"How are you?"

Her voice moved nearer the phone, and she whispered. "I'm sore as hell, and I feel great!"

"Same here"—Stone laughed—"but I'm not sure great describes it; it's somewhere above that."

"I'm free this evening," she said.

"No you're not; you've got a dinner date."

"I'll be done here by seven forty-five. Have you been to the Tribeca Grill?"

"Is that De Niro's new place?"

"That's it. Shall I book us a table?"

"Come to my house first, for a drink."

"You're on. I'll book for nine o'clock. See you at eight."

"You betcha."

When Stone hung up, Dino was looking at him.

"You got laid, didn't you?"

"What are you talking about?" Stone dissembled.

"I can tell." Dino batted his eyes rapidly. "You're just *glowing* all over."

"Jesus Christ! Do I have to take this shit from my own partner?"

"You betcha," Dino said, imitating Stone.

"What about Judge O'Neal?"

"Half an hour."

"What are we going to do for some help with the search?" Stone asked. "Nobody here."

"Well, shit," Dino replied, "if you and me between us can't find a corpse in a funeral parlor, we ought to turn in our papers."

Stone led the way out. "She's still alive, Dino. I can feel it."

"When I can feel *her*, I'll believe it," Dino called after him, hustling to keep up.

Judge O'Neal was youngish, blonde, and extremely good-looking. She sat in her high-backed, leather chair, her robes thrown open and her legs crossed, and contemplated Stone.

Stone contemplated right back. The woman had been wearing an engagement ring during the year since he had first come across her, or he would have asked her out.

"The letters are enough for me," O'Neal said, "even if he doesn't talk dirty. A thousand letters is weird enough for a warrant. Nobody's going to overrule."

"I shouldn't think so," Stone said. "By the way, we've included his place of work in the warrant."

"Off the record, Detective, for my own curiosity, what do you think happened to this woman?"

"Off the record, Judge, I am completely baffled, but I think she may still be alive."

O'Neal's eyebrows went up. "Get serious."

Stone explained his terminal velocity theory.

O'Neal shook her head vigorously, and the blonde hair swirled around her shoulders. *"That,"* she said, "is the wildest theory I ever heard."

"It may not be plausible, but it's possible."

Judge O'Neal uncrossed her legs and leaned on her desk, resting her chin in her hand. "I've got a hundred bucks says she's stone dead—you should excuse the expression."

Stone laughed. "I'll take your bet, but the loser buys dinner."

O'Neal pursed her red lips for a moment, then smiled. "You're on," she said, signing the warrant.

In the car, Dino looked sideways at Stone while dodging a bicycle messenger. "Jesus, Stone, why didn't you just fuck her right there on the desk? I'd have been happy to watch."

"Come on, Dino."

"She's got the hots for you, I'm telling you."

"She's wearing an engagement ring."

"So what the fuck? She was wearing a wedding ring, that's maybe cause for pause, maybe. A diamond ring is an open door. Anyway, you got a dinner date, just as soon as we find Sasha, dead or alive."

Stone glanced at his watch. "Van Fleet should be at the funeral parlor by now. We'll serve him there, then do the apartment."

12

Herbert Van Fleet's mother didn't like it. Stone and Dino waited quietly while Mrs. Van Fleet called her lawyer.

She returned grim faced. "All right, how do you want to go about this?"

"We'd like to see every room in the building," Stone said.

"What are you looking for?" she demanded.

"Anything that might help us in our investigation," Dino said, none too politely.

Seething, the woman took them through the building. Stone saw nothing out of the ordinary—at least, out of the ordinary for a funeral parlor. They finished up in the embalming room, where Herbert Van Fleet was working on a corpse. A tube ran from the man's stomach to a pump, and the machine whirred quietly. Stone looked away.

Van Fleet looked up without surprise. "Well, well, look who's back. I'm not answering any further questions, gentlemen, except in the presence of my lawyer."

Stone handed him the warrant, and, while Van Fleet read it carefully, he went to a row of large drawers.

"I'll do this," Stone said to Dino. "I wouldn't want you to faint on me."

Two elderly men were the only occupants of the refrigerated storage drawers. Stone and Dino had a look in an adjacent storage room, then returned.

"All right," Van Fleet said, "when do you want to go to my apartment?"

"Immediately," Stone replied.

Van Fleet turned to his mother. "But what about Mr. Edmonson?" he asked plaintively, gesturing toward the corpse on the table.

"Just pop him in the fridge," Dino said. "He'll keep."

"You'd better go with them," Mrs. Van Fleet said to her son. "They'll wreck your place if you're not there."

Van Fleet nodded, went to a sink, washed his hands, removed his rubber apron, revealing that he was dressed in a three-piece suit, and said to the officers, "I'm ready."

Van Fleet didn't speak on the way downtown. His building was in SoHo, near the river, and the street seemed to have been missed in the gentrification of the area. A sign on the dusty windows of the empty ground floor read WEIN-STEIN'S FINE GLOVES. Van Fleet unlocked a steel door and led them into a vestibule and onto a freight elevator.

"Who else lives in the building?" Stone asked.

"Nobody," Van Fleet replied genially. "My mother and I bought it as an investment last year. I had planned to renovate the rest of the building and rent lofts, but I ran out of money. Maybe next year."

"Did the glove factory occupy the whole place?"

"No, there was a kosher meat-processing plant and a piecework sewing business, and offices on the top floor, where I live."

The elevator stopped. Van Fleet pushed back the gate and unlocked another large steel door.

"It's sort of like a fortress, isn't it?" Dino said.

"I shouldn't have to tell *you* what a problem burglary is in this city," Van Fleet said. Inside the door, he tapped a code into a keypad. "I've got a very decent alarm system, too."

Stone watched him.

Van Fleet led them into a large, open space. A kitchen had been built in a corner at the far end and a bedroom in the other corner. These rooms were separated from the rest of the loft by a framework of lumber that had not yet had plasterboard applied to it. "I'm doing most of the work on the place myself," Van Fleet said.

Light flooded the loft from three sides; the other abutted another building.

"Nice place, Herb," Dino said admiringly.

"You may call me Mr. Van Fleet," Van Fleet said, almost sweetly. He turned to Stone. "*You* may call me Herbert, if you wish."

"Thank you, Herbert," Stone said. "I feel for you,

doing your own remodeling. I'm doing the same, myself." He said this while walking the length of the highly polished oak floor, the expanse of which was broken only by an occasional Oriental rug. A sofa, two chairs, a lamp, and a television set had been placed on one rug, an island of a living room surrounded by hardwood. The two detectives went methodically through the place, but there was hardly anywhere to hide anything. Van Fleet's desk rested against one wall. Stone opened the drawers and found nothing he wouldn't have seen in his own desk drawers: bills, stationery, office supplies.

"Let's see the rest of the building," Stone said to Van Fleet. His warrant did not cover the whole building, but he hoped the man wouldn't notice.

Van Fleet didn't. He went to a kitchen drawer and retrieved a large key ring, which jangled as he led them to the elevator. They walked through the building a floor at a time. Van Fleet may not have had the money to complete his development project, but he had cleaned out the building; it was as empty as any place Stone had ever seen.

"Anything else?" Stone said to Dino.

Dino shook his head.

"Can we offer you a lift uptown, Herbert?"

"Thank you, no," Van Fleet replied. "As long as I'm here, I'll have my lunch and get a cab later. Sorry I couldn't be more helpful," he said sweetly.

"You've been very helpful, Herbert," Stone said, "and we appreciate your cooperation."

"Have you found out anything else about Sasha?" Van Fleet asked.

"I'm afraid we can't discuss an investigation in progress," Stone said.

"The papers said you're making no progress at all," Van Fleet said, walking them to the front door.

"Don't believe everything you read in the papers," Dino said, as Van Fleet closed the door behind them.

Back in the car, Stone sighed. "Clean as a hound's tooth," he said.

"Yeah," Dino agreed, disconsolately.

"Let's go up to Sasha's and go through those boxes."

"Okay."

There was a different doorman on duty when the detectives arrived at the building. Stone flashed his badge and asked for his key to the Nijinsky apartment. The man handed it over silently.

The moment they stepped off the elevator, it was obvious that something was wrong. The police notice fixed to the apartment door had been removed.

"The seal's broken," Dino said. "What the fuck?"

Stone led the way into the apartment. It was completely empty. The two men stood there looking helplessly about them, as if waiting for inspiration. Stone bent over and picked up a card from the floor.

Effective immediately,

Sasha Nijinsky is at

1011 Fifth Ave.

New York 10021.

Burn this.

"The movers," Stone said.

"What?"

"The movers. She was moving the next morning."

"What's the new address?"

"Ten-eleven Fifth." Stone didn't mention that he knew someone else at that address.

"Let's go see the doorman."

Downstairs, Stone braced the doorman. "There was a police seal on the door of the Nijinsky apartment," he said. "Who broke it?"

"Jesus, Officer," the man pled, "I don't know nothing. The moving people showed up and took her stuff; that's all I know."

They drove uptown in silence. The building was across the street from the Metropolitan Museum of Art. The doorman greeted them.

"Can I help you, gentlemen?" he said, blocking the entrance.

Stone showed his ID. "Miss Nijinsky's apartment."

"Yes? What about it?"

"We'd like to see it. This is part of a police investigation. Did some moving people bring some furniture and boxes here yesterday?"

"Yes, but I'm afraid I can't let you into the apartment without permission, unless you've got a search warrant, of course."

Dino sighed loudly. "I guess you know the lady's in no condition to give permission."

The doorman shrugged. "My hands are tied," he said, "unless you get permission from the cooperative's board of directors. If one of them says it's okay, I'll let you in."

"Who's the chairman of the cooperative's board?" Stone asked.

The doorman went to a tin box on his desk and produced an index card. He handed it to Stone.

The name on the card was Barron Harkness.

Stone registered this for a moment, then showed the card to Dino. "May I use your telephone?" he asked the doorman.

"Sure," the man said, placing a phone on the desk.

"An interesting connection, wouldn't you say?" he asked Dino. He checked his notebook and dialed the number of the network.

13

A woman answered Harkness's phone, a voice Stone didn't recognize.

"Barron Harkness, please. My name is Barrington; he knows me."

"I'm sorry, Mr. Barrington, Mr. Harkness is in a meeting. May I have him return the call?"

"Let me speak with Cary Hilliard, please."

"Ms. Hilliard is in the same meeting."

Stone tried not to sound annoyed. "Please take a note to Mr. Harkness. Tell him Detective Stone Barrington would like to speak with him at once, and that it's important."

"I'm sorry, but—"

"Please do it now. This is police business."

The woman hesitated. "All right," she said finally. "What is your number?"

"I'll hold."

An irritating minute passed, then: "Barron Harkness."

"Mr. Harkness, this is Stone Barrington. I'm at your apartment building, and I want your permission to enter Sasha Nijinsky's apartment. The doorman insists on speaking with you before allowing entry."

"But why?" Harkness asked. "Sasha never moved into the apartment; there's nothing there. Legally, she didn't even own the apartment; she was supposed to have closed on it the morning after she . . ."

"It appears that a moving company followed instructions she gave before her disappearance and moved her belongings into the apartment. The doorman let them in."

Harkness hesitated, then spoke. "I'll be right over there," he said, and hung up before Stone could speak further.

Stone replaced the receiver and turned to Dino. "Harkness is coming over here."

"Why?" Dino asked.

"Who knows? Maybe he's being protective of his building's reputation."

The doorman spoke up. "That sounds like Mr. Harkness," he said. "He and the board are very picky about what goes on here. That's why I wouldn't let you in. It woudda been my job, y'know."

Stone nodded, then joined Dino on a sofa in the lobby to wait for Harkness.

They didn't have to wait long. A black Lincoln Town Car pulled up at the curb, and Harkness strode into the building. He shook hands with Stone and was introduced to Dino. "All right," he said, "let's get this over with. I've got to get back to the office."

"We don't really need you for this," Stone said, "if you'd like to go back now."

Harkness fished a letter from an inside pocket and handed it to Stone. It was from a midtown law firm.

"You're her executor?" Stone asked. "But we don't even know that she's dead."

"I got the letter this morning; it was the first I'd heard of it." He shrugged. "I guess I'm representing Sasha in this," he said, "so, unless you want to get a search warrant, I'm going to have to go into that apartment with you."

"All right," Stone said.

"Eddie," Harkness said to the doorman, "I'll use my passkey. We won't need you."

On the elevator, Stone turned to Harkness. "You say you didn't know that Ms. Nijinsky had appointed you executor of her will?"

"Didn't have a clue," Harkness replied. "I was astonished, to tell you the truth."

"Mr. Harkness, did you and Sasha Nijinsky ever have a romantic relationship?"

Harkness looked him in the eye. "Stone, I haven't the slightest intention of answering that."

The elevator door opened, and they stepped into a vestibule; only two apartments opened onto it, 10-J and 10-K. Harkness opened the door to 10-J and led the way in. There was an entrance hall, then a large living room. Furniture had been dumped here and there, as if the moving men had no instructions, and the boxes Stone had seen at Sasha's old apartment were piled in the middle of the floor. Every one of them had been opened, and the woman's belongings were strewn across the floor.

"Now that's interesting," Dino said.

Stone picked up a yellow movers' receipt from the floor and handed it to Dino. "See if there's a working phone; if not, go down and use the doorman's. Get hold of the movers' supervisor and ask him what the hell went on here."

Dino took the receipt and went in search of a phone. "The one in the kitchen is working," he called out.

"Do you have any idea who might have opened these boxes?" Stone asked Harkness.

"Not a clue," Harkness replied. "As I said earlier, she didn't even own the apartment yet. It would have been like Sasha, though, to have her stuff moved at the moment she would have been closing the sale. She wasn't a woman who liked to be kept waiting."

"I want to go through her belongings," Stone said, "and I may want to remove some things for evidence. Have I your permission to do that?"

Harkness hesitated. "I think maybe I should talk to a lawyer, first. I want to do the right thing, here."

"Look, Barron," Stone said, "Sasha trusted you enough to put you in charge of her estate. There may be something here that will help us find out what happened to her, and we're going to need your cooperation."

Dino returned from the kitchen. "The supervisor at the movers' says his guys didn't open any boxes. I called the doorman on the house phone, and he confirms that they were sealed when he signed the receipt and let the movers out."

"So," said Stone, turning to Harkness, "somebody has been in here since the movers left."

"Don't look at me," Harkness said.

"You've got a passkey, right?"

"I'm chairman of the cooperative board. Look, I thought the apartment was empty. Why would I want to come in here?"

"Who else besides the doorman has a key to this apartment?"

"The owners would, the people who were selling to Sasha. They live in Connecticut; I'll get the phone number for you."

"Who lives in the other apartment across the vestibule, number 10-K?"

"My assistant, Cary Hilliard. You met her the other night."

Stone nodded. "And would she have a key?"

"No."

"Did she know that Sasha was moving in here?"

"No. Sasha wanted her change of address kept quiet until she had moved. She liked to control what people knew about her."

"Where do you normally keep your passkey?"

Harkness held up a gold key ring. "Here, with my other keys. They're always in my pocket. Always. I lost some keys once, and it was such a pain in the ass that I've had a thing about it ever since."

"Who else knew that Sasha was buying the apartment?"

"The owners; the board of directors, four other people besides me—they had to approve the buyer—the doorman, and, of course, anybody Sasha might have felt like telling."

Stone remembered Sasha's change-of-address cards, unmailed. "I want to go through this stuff. Are you going to cooperate, or am I going to have to go to the trouble of getting a search warrant?"

"All right"—Harkness sighed—"do what you have to do, but I'm going to be here while you're doing it." He walked across the room and settled his large frame in a chair. "Have at it," he said.

Nearly two hours later, Stone wrote a receipt and handed it to Harkness. "I want her checkbook and her other financial records—these two boxes here."

"When do I get them back?"

"When I've had a chance to go over them thoroughly, or when Sasha turns up alive, whichever comes first."

Harkness stared at the two boxes.

"Is there something you want to tell me?" Stone asked.

"No," Harkness replied. "If it will help to find out what happened to Sasha, you're welcome to the records."

They parted at the front door of the building, and the detectives lifted the two boxes into the trunk of their car. As they got in, Dino spoke up. "If Harkness keeps his keys in his pocket all the time, then his wife might have gotten to them when he was asleep. If he was fucking Sasha, the lady might have taken an interest in her moving into the building."

"I didn't think of that," Stone said. "I don't even know if Harkness has a wife."

"He's a big guy, isn't he? Wouldn't have much trouble tossing a lady off a balcony, he felt like it."

"I thought of that," Stone said.

14

"If you're going to start out the evening kissing like that, then we're never going to make it to dinner," Stone said, feeling her breasts against him. The front door was still open, and he kicked it shut.

"Couldn't help myself." She grinned. "Say, all the way over here, I've been wondering where in this house you're going to offer me a drink. I mean, the place is a wreck."

"Follow me," he said, and he led her to the kitchen.

She stood and looked around the room. "It's beautiful," she said. "You didn't do this yourself."

"I did, with a little help. I didn't build it, I just restored it, refinishing all the original cabinetwork and fitting in the new appliances. It's the only room in the house that's done, except for the floors."

"It's like a turn-of-the-century dream," she said, opening a cabinet. "And you've got your aunt's china, too."

"Hers and my mother's. I could feed an army, if I had a working dining room."

"We've got to find a way for you to keep this house, Stone. You deserve to live in it, really you do. I hate to think of your turning it over to some stranger, just for the money."

"I hate the idea, too, but that's the way it has to be. What would you like to drink?"

"Scotch."

They sat at the kitchen table.

"So how's the Sasha investigation going?"

"Stranger and stranger. Did you know she was going to be your next-door neighbor?"

Cary's jaw dropped. "In 10-J? You're kidding!"

"Barron didn't tell you?"

"Jesus, no." She looked thoughtful. "I wonder why not. I know most of what goes on with him, and if he got her into the building, why wouldn't he tell me that?"

"Did he get you into the building?"

"Yeah. Daddy paid, of course. Dammit, I'll bet Sasha paid less. The co-op market is soft right now, and I've been there two years; I bought in at the top."

"Did you know the people who lived there before?"

"The Warrens? Sure. I mean, they had me in for a drink when I moved in, and I had them in for a drink in return, and after that I just saw them in the elevator. The place was just a pied-à-terre for them; they live in Westport. He was in a Wall Street law firm, and he just retired."

"Did you have a key to 10-J?"

"No."

Stone told her about the day's events.

"Spooky!" she said. "And you wondered if *I* went through her stuff?"

"Had to ask."

"Did you talk to the Warrens?"

"I tried. The maid said they're in London. That lets them out, I guess."

"The painters have been in and out of there, but I guess they finished up before Sasha's stuff arrived. Anyway, the doorman would have let them in and locked up after them."

"Well, enough shoptalk. How was your day?"

It was nine before they reached the Tribeca Grill, riding in the inevitable black Lincoln. The headwaiter knew Cary and gave them a good table.

"Neat place," Stone said. "I've read about it. Is De Niro in here much?"

"From time to time. Sometimes I think a third of the people in here came just to catch a glimpse of him."

"Like those two couples," Stone said, nodding at a table in a less desirable part of the restaurant. They watched as one of the men, dressed in a silk suit and a pearl gray tie, offered the headwaiter money and had it refused.

"Tourists," Cary said.

"Not your ordinary tourists," Stone replied. "They're wise guys."

"Mafia? You know them?"

"I know the look. The suits, the women's clothes. Just about everybody else in here is casual, but they're dressed to kill. Here's how it goes: the wise guys like places they're known, where they're known to be connected; they're treated like princes—the best tables, the best wines on the house. Tonight, though, the ladies wanted to break out, wanted to come to De Niro's restaurant and see him up close. The guys went for it, because De Niro is Italian, he's their hero, and they're already regretting it. They got the worst table in the house, and the headwaiter won't be bought. They'll sulk all through dinner, and it'll be the last time for a while the ladies will get to go to a new restaurant."

Cary laughed. A wonderful sound, Stone thought. "Do you deal much with Mafia guys?"

"Not unless there's a homicide. My partner, Dino, grew up with them, though. Dino says that everybody he was in school with is either dead, in prison, or has his phones tapped by the FBI."

"I'd like to meet Dino."

"He'll charm you right out of your pants," Stone said.

She leaned close. "Only you can do that."

"I'm glad to hear it."

They dined well, and Cary pointed out the regulars to him, told him who the producers and directors were. When coffee came, she was quiet for a while.

"That's really strange, Barron not telling me that Sasha and I were going to be next-door neighbors," she said finally.

"It really seems to bother you," Stone said.

"It does. During the time I've been with Barron, he's come to trust me on just about everything, I think, and then, when there's something you'd think he would just naturally tell me about, he clams up. If Sasha's stuff hadn't got moved in there, I'd never have known about her buying the place."

"Is Barron married?"

"Sure. He and Charlotte celebrated their twentieth anniversary last year. Now, *that* could have something to do with it. Maybe he didn't want Dolly to know—but hell, that doesn't make any sense either. How could he move her into the building and expect to keep it from Dolly? And why would he think I would tell her, anyway? I've never told her about anything else he's done. I hardly know her."

"What's Charlotte like?"

"Straight arrow; utterly conventional. They were college sweethearts, and she worships the ground he slithers on."

"Now, *that* is the first hard word I've heard you say about him. He slithers, does he?"

"Oh, I guess I'm just mad because he didn't tell me about Sasha's moving into the building."

"Was Barron fucking Sasha?"

She turned and looked at him. "Are you on the job, Stone, or is this a personal conversation?"

He didn't blink. "Every cop is always on the job. There are times when I can't separate my work from my personal life. This is one of them."

She didn't blink either. "If you want to interrogate me about my boss, see me at my office. And I might lie to you."

"You should never lie to a policeman," he said.

"I will if I feel like it," she replied evenly.

The evening suddenly turned cool.

Later, when her black car stopped in front of the Turtle Bay house, she declined to come in with him.

Before he got out, he turned to face her. "I'm sorry. I apologize. I stepped over the line, and I'll try not to do it again."

She nodded, but didn't say anything.

He kissed her on the cheek, got out of the car, and closed the door.

She rolled down the window. "Stone," she called after him.

He turned and walked back to the car, leaned down close to her.

"Barron was fucking Sasha," she said. "Secretly, regularly, and for a long time. And I think I'm falling in love with you." She rapped on the back of the front seat and the car drove away, leaving Stone standing in the street.

15

When Stone arrived at the precinct, a well-dressed, obviously irritated man was sitting next to Dino's desk. Dino, unaccountably in the station house early, was interviewing him.

"Look, I've already explained," he said, looking uncomfortably around him. A very dirty, handcuffed black man was sitting at the next desk, admiring the man's clothes.

"Mr. Duncan, this is my partner, Stone Barrington. Stone, this is Mr. Evan Duncan, who has something interesting to tell us."

"How do you do, Mr. Duncan," Stone said, extending his hand. He stepped between Duncan and the black man.

"Would you please tell Detective Barrington what you saw, Mr. Duncan?" Dino asked politely.

Shielded from the black man and seeming to take confidence from the presence of Stone, who probably looked like most of the people he knew, Duncan nodded. "I'm an investment banker," he said. "My office is in Rockefeller Plaza." Having established that he was a person worthy of belief, he went on. "Last evening, about six thirty, a friend and I were leaving the Harvard Club, on West Forty-fourth Street. We had ordered a car from the club's service, and a black car pulled up and let a man out. I looked at the number on the window and thought it was car number twelve, which was the number on the slip the steward had given me, so I opened the door and started to get into the car." He paused, as if uncertain as to whether he should continue.

"Go on, Mr. Duncan," Stone said, nodding reassuringly.

"Well, there was a woman in the backseat. She turned to me, surprised that someone was getting into her car. I apologized and began backing out, and she said, 'Don't worry about it, all these cars look alike.' I closed the door and checked the number again, and it was number twenty-one, not twelve." He stopped and looked to Stone as if for approval.

Stone wondered if he had missed something. "Mr. Duncan . . ."

"You didn't tell him, Mr. Duncan," Dino said to the man.

"Oh, I'm sorry, I quite missed the main point, didn't I?" Duncan chuckled.

"Yes," Dino said.

"What *is* the main point?" Stone asked, baffled.

"Oh, well, the woman was Sasha Nijinsky," Duncan replied, as if Stone should have known it all along.

The hairs stood up on the back of Stone's neck. Here was an obviously solid citizen with a close-up sighting. "Why did you think it was Sasha Nijinsky?" Stone asked, hoping against hope that the man was not simply some upper-class fruit-cake.

"Well, I've seen her on television several hundred times."

"Sometimes people on television look different in person," Stone said.

"And I sat across the table from her at a dinner party less than two weeks ago," Duncan said firmly.

Stone looked at Dino. Dino made a how-about-that face.

"Did she recognize you?" Stone asked.

"I don't think so, and I was in and out of the car so fast that I never really engaged her in conversation. But it was Sasha Nijinsky, I'm absolutely certain of it. I wouldn't really have come in here about this, but my wife said it could be important, since Sasha is missing."

"Missing?" Stone asked. Nobody knew she was missing. The press still thought she was in some hospital or other.

Dino held up a fresh copy of the *Daily News*. SASHA VANISHES, a headline screamed.

Stone picked up the paper and opened it. "A source in the New York City Police Department confirmed last night that, since her fall from the terrace of her East Side penthouse apartment, Sasha Nijinsky has been missing, and no one knows if she is alive or dead." He didn't read the rest. Somebody, probably somebody in this room, was talking to a reporter.

"You did the right thing, Mr. Duncan," Stone said. "Now the car number was twenty-one, the time was about six thirty, you said?"

"That's right, just about exactly six thirty. That was the time I had ordered the car for."

"And the name of the car service?"

"Minute Man. I use them all the time."

Stone held out his hand. "Thank you very much for this information, Mr. Duncan," he said. "You may be sure that we'll check this out thoroughly."

Dismissed, Duncan retrieved his trench coat from Dino's desk and made his way out of the room, giving the leering black man a wide berth.

"Cat's out of the bag, huh?" Stone said to Dino.

"I think a more appropriate description of the situation is that the shit has hit the fan," Dino said. "Leary wants to see us."

"At least we've got some sort of lead," Stone said. "Let's call Minute Man first."

After a long wait for the information, Stone was told that a Minute Man car had picked up a Ms. Balfour at the Algonquin Hotel at six thirty and had delivered her to an East Sixty-third Street address. Stone scribbled it down. "The Algonquin is right down the block from the Harvard Club; the car must have been stopped in traffic when Duncan mistook it for his."

"Sounds good to me," Dino said.

Armed with their new information, the two

detectives faced Leary, who was an unhappy man. "I hope to God this is no fuckin' wild-goose chase," he said, when he had heard their story. "The chief of detectives has already been on the phone this morning, and I'm expecting a call from the mayor any minute."

As if on cue, the phone rang. Leary put his hand on it. "Get out of here and run down that lead," he said. "I'll buy you as much time as I can."

Stone and Dino sat in their car outside the address, an elegant town house on East Sixty-third Street.

"I'm scared," Dino said.

"I know how you feel," Stone replied.

"You know how much we need this to *be* something, don't you? I'd like to get a shot at the balls of the guy who leaked to the papers. I'd cut 'em off and make him eat 'em."

"I'd hold him down while you did it," Stone said. "All right, let's go."

They trudged up the front steps and rang the bell, then watched through iron grillwork as a uniformed maid approached the door.

"Yes?" she said, opening the door slightly.

Stone showed his badge. "My name is Detective Barrington. Is there a Ms. Balfour at this address?"

"Just a minute," the maid said, closing the door and shutting them out. She went to a telephone in the entrance hall, spoke a few words into it, then returned and opened the front door wide. "Please come in," she said. "Mrs. Balfour will be right down."

As they entered, Stone saw half a dozen pieces of matched luggage piled to one side of the front door. The detectives were shown to a small sitting room, and, as they sat down, the maid opened the door to another man, who began removing the baggage.

A moment later, there was the click of high heels on the marble floor of the entrance hall, and Sasha Nijinsky walked into the sitting room.

As the detectives got to their feet, Stone was swept with an overwhelming sense of relief that made him light-headed.

"I'm Ellen Balfour," Sasha Nijinsky said. "How may I help you?"

Something is wrong here, Stone thought. Relief began to be replaced by panic.

"Well?" the woman said into the stunned silence.

"Aren't you . . ." Stone couldn't get the words out.

"Oh, I see," the woman said, nodding her beautiful head gravely. "It's the third time this week I've been mistaken for her."

"Oh, shit," Dino said, involuntarily, then recovered himself.

The woman turned and looked at him.

"Excuse me, please," Dino pled.

"I wonder, Mrs. Balfour, if you have some personal identification?" Stone said, hoping against hope that this woman was Nijinsky and hiding it. "Something with a photograph?"

The woman opened her handbag and produced a New York driver's license with a very nice picture.

"I can only apologize for the intrusion," Stone said, returning the license to her. "A gentleman turned up at the precinct this morning and reported having seen Sasha Nijinsky."

"I'll bet it was the man from the Harvard Club last night," she said.

"It was."

"He looked as if he'd seen a ghost."

"He was very certain. He'd met Miss Nijinsky only a couple of weeks ago."

"I've been putting up with this for years," Mrs. Balfour said, "and I've resisted changing my hair, but now I'm just going to have to go for a new look, I guess. And after the newspaper stories this morning, I'm getting out of town."

"I don't blame you," Stone said.

"If you get any reports of sightings in the Hamptons, please ignore them," Ellen Balfour said. "My husband doesn't think this is funny anymore."

Back in the car, neither detective spoke until they were nearly back to the precinct.

"I guess we'd better get into Sasha's financial records," Stone said finally.

"Yeah," Dino replied disconsolately. Dino's idea of a financial record was the color of the sock he kept his money in. "Tell you what, I'll go through the interview reports again on the people you and I didn't talk to personally; you do the financial records, okay?"

"Okay," Stone said.

16

Stone was impressed with Sasha's records. She kept the kind of system that he kept meaning to set up for himself.

Her checkbook was the large, desk model, and every stub was fully annotated; she kept a ledger of the bills she received and paid; there was no preparer's signature on her tax returns, so she must have done them herself. It seemed that Sasha Nijinsky had never been late on a payment for anything, and, periodically, there was a large check written—usually between twenty-five and a hundred thousand dollars—to a brokerage account. The lady had been making a lot of money for years, and she knew how to save it.

Stone was surprised, then, when her most recent brokerage statement showed the value of her holdings was only thirty-seven thousand dollars and change. He began backtracking through the brokerage statements, which were bundled by year and secured with strong rubber bands. They made good reading. Figuring roughly, Stone estimated that Sasha had saved just under eight hundred thousand dollars during the past five years and that, through shrewd trading, this had grown to just over two million during that time. Then, eight months back, an even two million had been withdrawn, paid by the broker with a cashier's check made out to Cash.

Having an easily negotiable instrument of that size in her possession seemed at odds with Sasha's character as revealed in her records, Stone thought; the consequences of losing it would have been catastrophic for her, and he could find no record of the sum having been placed in any other of her accounts. Two million dollars was just gone. Furthermore, at the time she had disappeared, Sasha had been about to close a substantial real estate transaction which, according to her records, she had no ready funds to cover. And there was no record of a mortgage application or commitment letter. Strange.

"Dino, you keep at the interview reports," Stone said. "I think I'm going to pay Sasha's lawyer a visit."

"You find something?"

"No, I'm missing something. Or rather, Sasha is."

It was five o'clock when Stone presented himself at the midtown law offices of Woodman & Weld, and the receptionist fled her desk, clutching her coat, as soon as she had announced him.

"I'm Frank Woodman," a tall, athletic man in

his fifties said, extending his hand. "Come on back to the conference room; there's a meeting still going on in my office."

"I'm sorry if I've come at a bad time," Stone said, following Woodman down a plushly carpeted hallway.

"Not at all," Woodman said over his shoulder. "I'm happy to do anything I can to help Sasha." He led the way into an elegant conference room, which was furnished in English antiques, and sat down at the head of the table.

Stone took a chair. "Mr. Woodman, to get right to the point, two million dollars seems to be missing from Sasha's brokerage account."

Woodman nodded. "I know about that," he said, "but only because Sasha mentioned it in passing. I should tell you that, even as her sole attorney, I know less about Sasha's affairs than most lawyers in my position would know. She was . . . well, secretive, I guess I'd have to say."

"You say you know where the money is?"

"I said I knew *about* it," Woodman replied. "Sasha told me a few months ago that she had cashed in her chips after having done well in the market for several years. She showed me a cashier's check made out to Cash for two million."

"I thought you said she was secretive."

"She was, but we were having a drink in the Oak Bar of the Plaza one evening, and I guess she'd had a couple, and she showed me the check."

"Did she say what she was going to do with it?"

"Only that she was Federal Expressing it to a bank in the Cayman Islands the following morning. She said she was making an investment with a friend."

"She didn't say who the friend was?"

"No."

"Have you any idea who it might have been?"

"None."

"Is there some way I might trace the money?"

"I shouldn't think so. Cayman Islands banks are a lot like their Swiss counterparts, in that their transactions are held secret. It's said there's a lot of drug money down there. Even if I knew the name of the bank, and I do not, they wouldn't give you the time of day. They won't even give the IRS the time of day."

"It appears from her records that she had paid the taxes on her profits in the marker," Stone said.

"I've no doubt of that," Woodman replied. "Sasha was punctilious in her financial dealings. But when people put large sums of money into Swiss or Cayman banks, they're often trying to avoid paying taxes on the income from that investment. That she may very well have been trying to do, although I would have advised her against it, if she had asked me."

"Do you know how Sasha had planned to pay for her new apartment?"

"What new apartment?" Woodman asked, surprised.

"You didn't know that she was moving?"

"She never mentioned it to me," Woodman said. "Oh, a couple of years back she called me about the availability of mortgages on co-ops in the city, and I told her I would be happy to help her with an application, but, as far as I know, she never applied for a mortgage. Certainly, she had the income to raise one, if she had wished."

"Was Sasha the kind of client who might have been lured into a fast-buck investment by a friend?" Stone asked.

Woodman thought about that. "Yes," he said. "Sasha loved money, loved making it. But she would only have taken that sort of plunge if she had checked it out carefully, and if she trusted the friend implicitly." Woodman's eyebrows went up. "I find myself speaking of her in the past tense," he said. "Of course, I did read the papers this morning."

"Is that why you let Barron Harkness know that Sasha had appointed him executor of her estate?"

"I did that before I saw today's papers. When I heard about her fall and when I was unable to locate her, I wrote to Harkness simply as a precautionary step. It seemed the prudent thing to do."

Stone stood up. "Thank you for your time, Mr. Woodman," he said. "If you think of anything else that might help me, I'd appreciate a call, day or night." He gave Woodman a card.

"Of course," the lawyer said. "Do you think you can find your way back to reception? I'd like to rejoin my meeting."

"Sure, thanks," Stone replied. The two men shook hands, and Stone turned back toward the front of the office.

Halfway there, someone called his name. Stone stopped and backtracked a few steps to an open office door. A grinning man was rising from a desk.

Stone struggled for a name. "Bill Eggers?" he managed finally.

Eggers stuck out a hand. "Haven't seen you since graduation day," he said, "although I've seen your picture in the paper from time to time."

"So what have you been doing with yourself for all these years?" Stone asked. He remembered Eggers as a companionable fellow; they'd had a few beers after class more than once.

Eggers spread his hands. "This," he said. "I joined a downtown firm after law school, but I've been here for the past eight years."

"What sort of law are you practicing?"

"Oh, I'm the general dogsbody around here," Eggers said. "I do whatever needs doing—some personal injury, a little domestic work, the odd criminal case, when one of the firm's clients crosses the line."

"Sounds interesting." Stone looked around the plush office. Looked as though Eggers had done well at it too.

"More interesting than you would believe." Eggers laughed. "You seeing Woodman about Sasha?"

"Yeah."

"I wondered when you'd get around to him."

"It took me a few days; I've been pretty busy."

"Funny you turning up here; I've been thinking about you lately."

"Kind thoughts, I hope."

"The kindest, I assure you." Eggers looked at his watch. "I've got a client coming in any second, but I'd like to buy you a drink sometime, chew over some things."

"Sure," Stone said, fishing out a card. "Give me a week or two, though. The Sasha thing is taking a lot of time."

"Of course," Eggers said, extending his hand again. "We'll make it dinner, when you've got the time."

On his way home, Stone reflected on Bill Eggers's prosperous appearance, the handsome office, the prestigious law firm. Was it possible that Woodman & Weld might need someone with his background?

When he got home, there was a notice from the NYPD: his return-to-duty physical had been scheduled. Stone flexed the knee. Not bad; he'd begun to forget about it. He tried a couple of half knee bends. It was sore, but he could ace the physical.

17

"Can I buy you breakfast?" her low, pleasing voice said on the phone. "It's the first real day of autumn outside, and we'll have a walk in the park, too."

"Oh, yes." Stone exhaled. He was pitifully glad to hear from Cary. Their last, uncomfortable evening had been eating at him, and, in spite of her parting words, he had been unsure of his reception, should he call her.

"There's a little French place called La Goulue, on East Seventieth, just off Madison. I've got a table booked in half an hour."

"You're on."

They sat in the warm, paneled restaurant, a pitcher of mimosas between them, and drank each other in.

"I don't know when I've been so glad to see anybody," Stone said.

"I'm glad it's me you're glad to see," she replied.

She slipped off her shoe, and, under the table-cloth, rested her foot in his crotch. "Oh, you *are* glad to see me, aren't you?" She rolled her eyes.

"That's not a pistol in my pocket." He grinned.

Her eyebrows went up. "You're supposed to wear a gun all the time, aren't you?"

"That's right."

"Are you wearing one now?"

He nodded.

"So that *could* be a pistol in your pocket."

He laughed. "It could be, but it isn't."

"Where are you wearing it?"

"Strapped to my ankle." He hated the bulge under his coat, hated being careful about inadvertently revealing the weapon.

"You have a badge, too, I guess."

"That's right. I wouldn't be a policeman without a badge, would I?"

"Let me see it."

Stone produced the little leather wallet and laid it on the table.

She flipped it open and ran a finger around the badge. "It's gold," she said.

"A detective's badge is always gold. It's what every cop wants, a gold badge."

The waiter came and refreshed their mimosas from the pitcher, leaning over, eyeing the badge.

Stone flipped the wallet shut and put it back in his pocket.

"I want it," she said.

"Want what?"

"The badge."

Stone laughed and shook his head. "To get that badge, you'd have to sign up for the Police Academy, walk a beat for a few years, spend a few more in a patrol car, then get lucky on a bust or two, and have a very fine rabbi."

"Rabbi?"

"A senior cop who takes an interest in your career."

"Do you have a rabbi?"

"I did. His name was Ron Rosenfeld."

"And he helped you?"

"He helped me a lot. I would never have made detective if not for him."

"Why did he help you?" she asked.

"That's a funny question. Why do people ever help each other?"

"But there must have been some specific reason, apart from just liking you. Did he help all young policemen?"

"No," Stone admitted. He thought about it for a moment. "I think it may have been because he was a Jew and I was such an obvious WASP."

"That doesn't make any sense. Why didn't he help Jewish cops, instead of you?"

"I think because he had been discriminated against when he was a young patrolman, so he felt some empathy with my situation. He saw me getting passed over for good assignments, and it rankled, I guess. Oh, he helped a lot of young Jewish cops, too. It wasn't just me."

"Did he retire?"

"He died. It was a lot like losing my father."

"So who helps you now?"

Stone shrugged. "Nobody. Well, Dino helps me."

"But he's junior to you, isn't he?"

"Yes, but he's more inside than I am. I think he defends me sometimes; I think it's made a difference, too."

"It's a funny situation, isn't it?"

"I guess. I can live with it, though. At least I get to keep doing what I like; I have enough rank to get good cases, and I have a good reputation as an investigator."

"I don't want to pry, but I worry about you sometimes. How are you doing on Sasha? I read the papers."

"The papers were accurate. It's a brick wall; very frustrating."

"Are you getting a lot of pressure from above? Political pressure, I mean?"

"So far, my commander has been able to keep the heat off Dino and me. The taxi murders diverted some attention from us at a good time, but they also took all the manpower we had on Sasha's case."

"Is that hurting your investigation?"

Stone sighed. "Not really; not much. The greater part of the legwork had already been done when the taxi shootings happened. We'd interviewed everybody who had anything to do with Sasha by that time. Dino's going over the reports now, just to be sure we haven't missed anything."

"What's going to happen on the Sasha investigation? I mean, what's likely to happen?"

"We'll get a tip," Stone said. "Eventually. That's

how most cases are solved—never mind all the scientific stuff: fingerprints, DNA matching—most cases are solved because somebody finally tells us something."

Their eggs Benedict came, and they ate hungrily.

When the check came, Stone paid the waiter, then looked Cary in the eye. "Sometimes, in cases like this, the person waits a long time to come forward. Sometimes it's hard to do the right thing."

She kept his gaze for a moment, then looked down at his jacket and frowned. "Where do you buy your clothes?"

She wasn't going to talk to him; not yet, anyway. He glanced at the brown herringbone. "Different places. There are a couple of discount places downtown that have nice stuff, sometimes."

"I said I'd help you furnish the house; I think I'd better start by furnishing you."

"Okay," Stone said, "I guess I could use some furnishing."

"Come with me."

Stone followed her out of the restaurant. She led him briskly around the block to the corner of Seventy-second and Madison and into a handsome stone building. He had seen the place, but he had never been in. It wasn't the sort of place cops bought their clothes.

The store was a wonderland of beautiful things. She led him to the third floor, where she found a rack of tweed jackets. In seconds she had extracted one and helped him into it.

A salesman sidled up. "Our forty-two long fits

you perfectly," he said. "That jacket won't require the slightest alteration."

Stone felt for the tag, but Cary ripped it off and handed it to the salesman. "Never look at price tags," she said. "That's not the way to shop. Buy what's right for you, and worry about the money later. That's what credit cards are for."

She found another jacket, then some trousers, then she started on the suits. He managed to hold her to two, but they were beautiful, he had to admit, and they did fit him perfectly. She shook his wallet out of the old jacket and handed the garment to the salesman. "Send this," she said. "He'll wear the plaid one."

"I guess I should get some shirts," Stone said.

"Downstairs," the salesman said, handing him a credit card chit to sign.

Stone followed instructions and didn't look at the amount. He tried to stop in the shirt department, but she pulled him away.

"They're wrong for you," she said. "We'll get those elsewhere." She hailed a cab. Shortly, they were in a Fifth Avenue department store; she guided him to a shop within the store. "These are English," she said, hauling out a stack of shirts from a shelf, "and they suit you." A dozen shirts later, they were in an Italian shoe store, trying on loafers and featherweight lace-ups.

By the time they reached Central Park, Stone felt like a new man. The mimosas still buzzed in his veins, and the clear, autumn air elated him. Autumn always seemed like the beginning of the year to Stone; New Year's was an anticlimax.

"You look wonderful in that jacket," Cary said.

"I feel wonderful in it," he replied. "I feel wonderful with you."

"That's the way you're supposed to feel," she said. They walked north along the Fifth Avenue side, enjoying the color in the trees, and, at Seventy-ninth Street, she led him from the park. "My place," she said.

The doorman didn't seem to recognize him. On her floor, he glanced at Sasha's door.

"Don't think about that," she said, pulling him into her apartment.

The place was a mirror image of Sasha's, and it was beautifully put together—feminine, without being cloying, beautiful fabrics, good pictures, expensive things. "This is wonderful," Stone said. "You're hired as my decorator."

"You know the best thing about this apartment?" Cary asked.

"What's that?"

"It has a bedroom. And a bed."

"Oh. I'd better have a look at that."

"Yes, I think you'd better," she said, unbuckling his belt.

Later, when they fell asleep, exhausted, it was with his soft penis in her hand. He liked sleeping that way.

When he got home, the following evening, the Saturday mail awaited him. There was a letter from his bank:

Dear Mr. Barrington:

Just a reminder to let you know that your note is due at the end of the month. The note is, of course, adequately collateralized by your house, and I will be happy to renew it, but I must tell you that, with the softening market in large properties, the bank's new lending policy will require a substantial reduction of the principal when renewing. I might be able to persuade the loan committee to accept a reduction of F$25,000. And, of course, there will be $4800 interest due.

The letter hit him like a blow to the belly. He'd borrowed the money to renovate the house, but the banker had promised to keep renewing until he had a buyer. Then he had another thought. He dug out the receipts for the clothing he had bought. The total came to nearly four thousand dollars.

Stone went into the bathroom and lost his lunch.

18

Stone was twenty minutes late to work. When he walked into the squad room, the place went quiet. Dino stood up from his desk and waved Stone toward the stairs.

"What's up?" Stone asked as they trotted up the steps together.

"Leary wants us in the conference room. There's brass here."

"Oh, shit," Stone said.

Down one side of the long table were arrayed the detective squad commander, Lieutenant Leary; Chief of Detectives Vincent Delgado, a slim, rather elegant man in his fifties; and an imposing black man Stone recognized from his photographs, who was wearing the well-pressed uniform of a deputy commissioner. Deputy commissioners were mayoral appointees. Stone didn't know the other man, who looked like a banker, in a pin-striped suit, white shirt, and sober necktie.

"Chief, you already know Barrington and Bacchetti," Leary said.

Delgado nodded, managing a tight smile.

"Commissioner Waldron, these are detectives second grade Barrington and Bacchetti," Leary said unnecessarily.

"I'm glad to meet you, men," Waldron said. "I've heard a lot about both of you."

"Oh, shit," Dino said under his breath, not moving his lips.

"Right," Stone whispered back, Waldron had been a hot assistant DA when he had joined the campaign staff of the mayor, and, after the election, he had been the mayor's first appointee to a law enforcement position. It was said Waldron had mayoral ambitions of his own, since the mayor had let it be known that he would not be running for a third term. Waldron had a reputation for meddling in police investigations.

"And, Detectives," Leary continued, "this is John Everett, special agent in charge of the New York office of the FBI."

Everett, expressionless, nodded sleepily.

"If you'll forgive me, gentlemen," Waldron said to Leary and Delgado, "I'll tell the detectives why we're here."

"Of course, sir," Leary said.

Delgado merely nodded.

Waldron turned to the detectives. "I want to forget what I've read in the reports and what I've read in the papers. I want to hear from you every step that has been taken in the Sasha Nijinsky investigation, from day one. From *minute* one. And don't leave anything out."

Goddamn Leary, Stone thought. If he'd given them a few hours' notice he could have put together some kind of presentation. Now he would have to wing it.

"From minute one," Waldron repeated. "Go."

"Sir," Stone began, "I was proceeding on foot down the west side of Second Avenue at approximately two A.M. on the night of the . . . occurrence. I was off duty. I happened to look up, and I witnessed the . . . Ms. Nijinsky's fall." He was still having trouble calling the event a crime and Nijinsky a victim.

"This actually happened?" Waldron interrupted. "The papers got it right?"

"Mostly, sir." He continued to relate the events of that night. When he got to the collision of the ambulance with the fire engine, Waldron started shaking his head.

"Jesus H. Christ," he said, "that's the goddamndest worst piece of luck I ever heard of."

"My sentiments exactly, sir," Dino said.

Leary and Delgado laughed.

"Go on," Waldron said.

Stone took the man through his and Dino's actions for the rest of the night, then asked Dino to describe the subsequent investigation by the detective squad. Neither detective referred to his notebook.

When they had finished, Waldron spoke again. "Detectives, have you left any avenue uninvestigated?"

"Sir," Stone said, "the detective squad of this precinct interviewed sixty-one witnesses, co-workers, and friends of Ms. Nijinsky and made more than eight hundred telephone calls, all within thirty hours of the occurrence. Since that time, Detective Bacchetti has reviewed each of the interview reports, and he and I have conducted a search of the home and business premises of the possible suspect, Van Fleet."

"Is Van Fleet still a suspect?" Waldron asked.

"Officially, of course, sir. But we haven't got a thing on him, except that he wrote Ms. Nijinsky a great many very polite letters."

"Do you have any other suspects?" Waldron asked.

"No, sir," Stone replied.

There was a brief silence in the room. Nobody seemed to have anything else to say.

Except the FBI man, Everett. "Why didn't you call the FBI?" he asked.

Stone turned to face Everett; he had felt this coming. "Because no federal crime has been committed," he replied. "As far as we know."

"How about kidnapping?" Everett asked.

Chief of Detectives Delgado spoke up. "The lady took a twelve-story dive," he said laconically. "What's to kidnap?"

"Good point," Waldron said.

Everett leaned forward. "Perhaps Detective Barrington would tell us about his terminal velocity theory," he said encouragingly.

Stone felt color creeping up his neck into his face.

"His *what* theory?" Delgado asked sharply.

"Terminal velocity," Stone said, clearing his throat. "It's just a theory, sir. There's nothing really to support it."

"I'd like to hear it anyway," Delgado said.

"So would I," echoed Waldron.

Leary rolled his eyes toward the ceiling.

Stone briefly explained what terminal velocity is and what part it might have played in Sasha Nijinsky's fall.

No one spoke. No one took his eyes off Stone.

"Of course," Dino interjected suddenly, "the lady's gotta be dead. You don't fall twelve stories and write about it in your memoirs."

"We've treated this as a homicide from the beginning," Stone said.

"But you've no evidence of a homicide," Everett said, a little too smoothly. "In fact, the available evidence—the diary—points to a suicide attempt."

"In any case, the lady's dead," Delgado said irritably.

"But Detective Barrington doesn't think so," Everett replied. "Do you, Detective?"

Everybody turned back to Stone.

"I think it's . . . just possible she may be alive," Stone said uncomfortably.

"I think Detective Barrington thinks it's more than just possible," Everett said. "But what counts is, was she alive when she was taken from that ambulance?"

"She may have been," Stone said.

"We know she was alive at the scene of her

fall, because of the videotape evidence Detective Barrington has told us about," said Everett, spreading his hands, the picture of reason. "And the ambulance collision occurred only minutes later."

"It's possible," Delgado said, glaring at Stone.

"All that matters to me, gentlemen," Everett said, "is that she may have been alive when she was taken. Kidnapped. Kidnapping, in the United States of America, is a federal crime."

"Granted," Waldron said. "But, surely, you see our position in treating this as a homicide?"

Everett nodded. "I'm not here for a jurisdictional dispute, Commissioner; honestly, I'm not. But your own chief of detectives has just admitted that Nijinsky may have been alive when she was taken, so I'm calling it kidnapping, for the purposes of investigation, and the FBI is, from this moment, on it. Any objections?"

No one said anything.

Everett stood up. "Well, if you'll excuse me, gentlemen, my purpose here is accomplished. I have an investigation to conduct." He shook hands with those on his side of the table, nodded to the two detectives, and left.

When Everett had gone, Delgado turned to Stone. "Nice going," he said. "Now we've got the feds on our backs."

"If you'll excuse me, sir," Stone said, "I'm glad to have them in. Maybe they'll stumble on something we haven't."

"That's all we need."

Waldron spoke up. "I'm inclined to agree with Detective Barrington," he said to Delgado. "If this

case isn't solved, we can share the, uh . . . credit."
He turned back to Stone and Dino. "Detectives,"
he said seriously, "I think you've done a first-class
job on this, and I want you to know you have my
support. Is there anything you need for your investigation? Anything at all? Just name it."

"We need a break," Dino said.

19

Dino snatched a file off his desk. "Let's get out of here," he said to Stone.

Stone waited until they were in the squad car before speaking. "What do you think?"

"I think we're in the shit," Dino said.

"I don't know; Waldron seemed to be on our side. Said we'd done a first-class job, remember?"

"You trust Waldron?" Dino asked incredulously. "You're so fucking naive sometimes, Stone."

"Look, among the deputy commissioners, Waldron is the best of a bad lot. I mean, we could have drawn that guy who was in advertising before the mayor made him a DC."

"Waldron's a politician, and that makes him dangerous. And I can tell you Delgado is not happy with us for being involved in something that gets Waldron's attention—plus, he blames us for the FBI."

"Come on, Dino, how can he blame us for that? We're lucky we got this far in our investigation without the feds stepping in. Delgado knows that."

"Delgado's Italian, like me," Dino said. "When there's bad news, Italians shoot the messenger, remember? Right now, 'Messenger' is tattooed right across your forehead and mine, buddy."

Stone shook his head. "I think you're overreacting. If we'd made some huge blunder in the investigation, then I think we really would be in trouble, but we haven't done that; we've run it by the book—well, mostly by the book—and we've covered all the bases."

"Well, we haven't covered our asses," Dino said. "The only way we can do that is by making a bust."

"By the way," Stone said, "where are we going?"

"To the network," Dino said, handing him the manila file. "Out of all the interview reports, this is the only one that looked worth doing again."

"Hank Morgan," Stone read from the file. "Makeup artist."

"Look down at the bottom of the sheet."

Stone read the last line. "Subject was nervous, wary, and gave only the briefest answers to questions, without elaboration." Most innocent people, Stone knew, tended to blabber to the cops when questioned, not clam up. There were those who didn't like cops, who were short with them, but this was interesting. "Did you call to say we were coming?" Stone asked.

"Nope," Dino replied.

"Good."

Hank Morgan was casually but elegantly dressed: Italian loafers, brown tweed trousers, a striped silk dress shirt open at the throat, a green cashmere sweater draped over the shoulders, the arms hanging loose. The hair was carefully barbered, the skin tan, the teeth white and even. A handsome character, Stone thought. And a woman, though just barely.

"I'll be the bad cop," Dino said through his teeth, as Morgan led them down the hall. "I hate dykes."

Morgan led them into a room lit by rows of small bulbs around a large mirror. A barber's chair was the only furniture.

"What can I do for you?" she asked, her eyes blinking rapidly.

"We're investigating the Sasha Nijinsky matter," Stone said. "We'd like to ask you some questions."

"I've already talked to two policemen," Morgan said combatively. "I don't feel much like talking anymore."

Dino was on her like a tiger. "Well, we didn't like your answers, *lady*," he snarled at her, "and I don't much care if you feel like talking or not."

"Dino . . . ," Stone began.

"This is an investigation into the disappearance, maybe the death of a human being that you knew and worked with, and we intend to find out what you knew about it," Dino continued, unabated. "We can do it up at the precinct, if you like."

Morgan appeared to wither under this barrage.

Stone tugged at an earlobe.

Dino caught the signal. "Where's the men's room?" he said to Morgan.

"Down the hall to your left," she replied.

"I thought you'd know," Dino shot back as he left the room.

When he had gone, Stone closed the door. "I'd like to apologize for my partner's conduct," he said to her gently. "He's under a lot of pressure on this case—we both are—and he sometimes gets a little worked up."

Morgan looked relieved. "I understand," she said. "It's been a strain on me, too."

Has it? Stone wondered. "I take it you knew Sasha quite well," he said. He had no reason to suppose that; it was a shot in the dark.

Morgan nodded, but did not speak.

"Did . . ." Stone stopped. Another stab. "Were you in love with her?" he asked softly.

Morgan nodded again, and tears rolled down her cheeks.

"I'm sorry," Stone said. "I know how hard all this must have been for you." Yet another stab. "Was Sasha in love with you?"

Morgan wiped a cheek and looked directly at him. "Yes," she said firmly.

"Did she tell you so?"

"She showed me," Morgan replied.

"How long had the two of you been . . . seeing each other?"

"A couple of months," Morgan said, drying another tear. She was composing herself now.

"And when was the last time you saw Sasha?"

"The night before she . . . disappeared." She was calm now, and ready to talk.

"Where did you see her?"

"At my apartment. We always met there."

"Did she stay the night?"

"Most of it. Sasha always left around four. She couldn't be seen . . ."

"I understand."

"Ms. Morgan, do you think Sasha might have been inclined to try to take her own life?"

"I . . . I don't know. She was up and down a lot. She'd have these highs, when nothing could get her down; then she'd sink into these depressions. They never lasted long, but they were intense. She could be difficult to be with during those times. Maybe, in the depths of one of those, she might have . . . impulsively . . . done something. I just don't know."

"Would you characterize these mood swings as manic-depressive?"

"I'm not sure. From what I know about that condition, people who have it are unable to function when they're depressed. Sasha could *always* function, and function brilliantly, no matter what her mood. She had a will of iron."

Stone looked Hank Morgan up and down. She was five nine or ten, a hundred and forty-five, with an athletic, even muscular build. She looked as though she worked out regularly. "Ms. Morgan," he asked, "where were you after midnight the night Sasha fell?"

"I was at home in bed," she replied firmly.

"Were you alone?"

Now Morgan looked away. "No."

"I think I'd better have the name of that person," Stone said.

"Is it absolutely necessary?"

"I'm sorry, but it is. I want you to know, though, that I'll do what I can to keep this information from becoming public. I understand your position."

"Her name is Chelsea Barton. She's a set designer here."

"I'll have to speak with her."

"Her office is the other side of the reception area, on this floor."

Dino came back into the room.

"I think we're about finished here," Stone said. "Thank you, Ms. Morgan. I very much appreciate your cooperation." Dino stepped back into the hall, and Stone followed, then stopped. He turned back to the woman. "Ms. Morgan, was Sasha seeing anyone else that you know of?"

Morgan flushed. "Yes, she was. A man. She would never tell me who, but I had the feeling it had been going on for a long time."

"Do you think it might have been someone she worked with?"

"I honestly don't know. Sasha didn't give much away."

"Thank you again."

On their way down the hall, Stone filled Dino in on his conversation with Hank Morgan.

Dino whistled. "So Sasha swung both ways, huh? How about that?"

"There was nothing in her diary to indicate it," Stone said.

"She had a lot to lose," Dino replied. "She wouldn't have written that down."

They found the office of Chelsea Barton. A rather dumpy young woman looked up from her desk as they knocked.

Stone started to introduce himself.

"Yes," Barton said, interrupting him. "I was with Hank Morgan. All night. Anything else?"

"Thank you," Stone said, "no."

Back in the car Dino turned to Stone. "So, if Morgan is in love with the gorgeous Sasha, what's she doing in the sack with Miss Beanbag the very next night?"

"That crossed my mind," Stone said.

"I think Morgan looks good for it. Pansies are always bashing each other's heads in with hammers, and all for love."

"Lesbians don't fit that mold."

"Still, you see the build on that bitch? Sasha was little, compared to her. I think Morgan could have tossed her, no problem."

"I think so, too. But how are you going to break that alibi? Miss Beanbag looked pretty tough to me."

"She was on the interview list, so we've got her address. I think I'll do a little checking into her whereabouts that night," Dino said. "Maybe I can place her somewhere else."

"You do that, and we might have something for Deputy Commissioner Waldron."

20

The phone was ringing as Stone reached his desk. He picked it up. "Hello."

"Detective Barrington?" a husky voice said.

"Yes, speaking."

"This is Hank Morgan."

"Yes, Ms. Morgan. Did you think of something else?"

"I . . . I lied to you, I'm afraid."

"How so?"

"I was at home alone the night Sasha fell. Chelsea wasn't with me. She said that to protect me, but I realize this is serious, and I don't want to involve her. I hope you'll forget that I didn't tell you the truth the first time; I'm telling you the truth now."

"All right, we'll forget your first statement and leave Chelsea out of it."

"Thank you."

"What time did you get home that night?"

"I worked on the evening news, so it would have been about eight thirty."

"Did anyone see you? The doorman, maybe?"

"I live in a walk-up in the West Village. There's no doorman."

"Anybody else? A neighbor?"

"No. There are only two apartments in the building, and my downstairs neighbor was on vacation."

"Did you go out again for any reason?"

"No. I read until about eleven, then I went to sleep."

"I see. Ms. Morgan, I'd like you to come up to the Nineteenth Precinct to be fingerprinted. It might help us eliminate you as a suspect."

She paused for a long time. "I don't think I want to do that," she said. "I've already talked to a lawyer, and he advised me not to cooperate any further than this."

"That's your right," Stone said. "But I have to tell you that the Supreme Court doesn't consider being fingerprinted to be self-incriminating. We may have to insist."

"I suppose that's your right," she replied. "But I haven't done anything wrong, and you don't have any real reason to suspect me. So I won't be having anything else to say."

"I'm sorry you've decided to do it this way, Ms. Morgan."

"Good afternoon, Detective Barrington." She hung up.

Stone told Dino about their conversation.

"Bingo!" Dino cried. "Let's go see Leary."

"Wait a minute," Stone said. "I just remembered something." He went to the evidence room, dug out Sasha Nijinsky's financial records, and began leafing through her checkbook.

"What are you looking for?" Dino asked.

"I remember some checks Sasha wrote. Here! One . . . two . . . three of them, all made out to Henrietta Morgan! The name meant nothing to me at the time." He totted up the amounts in his head. "Total of twenty thousand dollars over eight weeks, listed as loans. You know what this smells like, Dino?"

"Blackmail!" Dino yelled. "Miss Hank says, 'Pay me, Sasha, or I'll tell all!' Let's go see Leary!"

Leary beamed at them. "I knew good police work was going to break this case." He chortled. "Pick her up right now." He reached for the phone. "I'll call Delgado; he'll call Waldron."

"I don't think that's a good idea, Lieutenant," Stone said, "not yet, anyway. Let's get her up here and hear her story first."

"Get your asses out of here and bring in the dyke!" Leary said, dialing.

"This is insane!" Hank Morgan said, interrupting Stone in his reading of her rights. "You aren't handcuffing me!"

"If you can't afford an attorney, one will be appointed for you," Stone concluded. "I'm sorry about the cuffs; it's department policy." He took her raincoat from a hook on the wall and placed it over her shoulders. "Don't worry, no one here will see them."

"Let's go, lady," Dino said.

"I want to call my lawyer," she said shakily.

"You can call her from the precinct," Dino said. "Let's go."

Stunned into silence, Hank Morgan accompanied the two detectives out of the building and into their car.

"Is there anything you want to tell us before we get to the station?" Stone asked her.

Morgan shook her head. "I want my lawyer," she said.

"Uh, oh," Dino said as they pulled up to the entrance of the 19th Precinct. "What's this?"

"Leakiest precinct in the city," Stone said, slamming his fist against the dashboard in frustration.

A knot of reporters crowded the sidewalk. Television lights went on. Stone and Dino got Morgan out of the car and hustled her into the building, shoving the shouting reporters out of the way.

"No comment," Dino kept yelling.

"I want to call my lawyer," Morgan said, when they were safe from the howling mob.

"Just as soon as we've fingerprinted and photographed you," Stone said, unlocking her handcuffs.

She gave the fingerprints without further protest, then, while Stone had her photographed, Dino hand-carried the prints upstairs. Stone took Morgan into the squad room and put her in an empty cubicle, away from the stares of the other detectives.

Morgan put her face in her hands. "This is so humiliating," she said.

"I'm sorry it had to be this way," Stone replied, "but you've made it harder on yourself by refusing to cooperate."

"I want my lawyer *now*," she said.

Stone handed her the phone, and, hands shaking she dialed a number. Stone noted that she didn't have to look it up. He wondered how many innocent people knew their lawyers' phone numbers off the tops of their heads.

Fifteen minutes passed, and Dino came breathlessly into the cubicle and hauled Stone out.

"Listen to this," he said.

"Was one of her prints in Sasha's apartment?" Stone asked. It would be too good to be true.

"Better than that, pal—we've got a *palm* print—and on the *outside* of the sliding glass door to the terrace. We can put her on the terrace!"

A weak, warm feeling flooded through Stone. "Jesus Christ!" He exhaled. All the work, all the sweat had been worth it. He had not realized until that moment how afraid he had been of this case and what it might do to him. "Let's have another shot at her before her lawyer gets here," he said, heading back for the cubicle.

Morgan was sitting rigidly in the steel chair, her hands clenched in her lap.

"Listen to me, Ms. Morgan," Stone said, pulling up a chair. "You've already admitted to me that you and Sasha were having an affair, and that she was also having an affair with a man; that would make you pretty jealous, wouldn't it? We've got canceled checks showing that Sasha paid you twenty thousand dollars in less than two months; your palm print was found on the terrace that Sasha fell from. We've got all that, Ms. Morgan, and we're going to get more. Now, don't you think it's time you told us about it?"

Morgan's shoulders began to shake, and tears rolled down her face.

Stone thought it was the only moment she had looked feminine since he had met her.

"Oh, God!" she moaned, "I want to tell you . . ."

"Excuse me, gentlemen," a rumbling voice said from behind them.

Stone and Dino turned to see a tall man in a beautiful overcoat standing there.

"My name is Carlton Palmer; I'm Henrietta Morgan's attorney; I know you won't mind if I consult with my client. Alone," he added for good measure.

The two detectives reluctantly gave up the field.

"Shit," Dino muttered. "She was going to confess. We had her in the palm of our hands, and that slick bastard had to show up."

"She had a right to see him, Dino," Stone said. "To tell you the truth, I'd have been uncomfortable with a confession made before her lawyer got here."

"She won't say another fucking word now," Dino complained. "We'll just have to work our fucking balls off, making the case. If we'd had that confession, you and I would have made detective first by tomorrow morning."

"Well, you're right about one thing," Stone commiserated. "She'll never say a word to us now."

Ten minutes later, Palmer came out of the cubicle. "Gentlemen," he said, "my client will answer your questions now."

21

They had moved to the conference room. Tape and video equipment was up and running. Leary had joined them for the big moment.

"I'd like to say something for the camera before you begin," the lawyer said.

Stone nodded.

He got up, walked around to where Hank Morgan sat, placed a fatherly hand on her shoulder, and spoke to the camera. "I am Carlton Palmer, the attorney representing Henrietta Morgan, and I would like this record to show that Miss Morgan is giving this statement voluntarily and of her own free will in a spirit of cooperation with the police." He returned to his seat.

Stone's hands were sweating. "State your full name and address and place of employment for the record," he said to Morgan.

"My name is Henrietta Maxine Morgan; I live at Seventy-one West Tenth Street in Manhattan. I am employed as a makeup artist by the news division of the Continental Network." Her voice quavered a bit, but she was calm.

"Ms. Morgan, have you been advised of your rights under the Constitution of the United States?"

"I have been."

"Are you making this statement voluntarily?"

"I am."

"Have you been subjected to any duress with regard to this statement?"

"No."

"Ms. Morgan, how long have you been employed by the Continental Network?"

"Just over three months."

"And when did you first meet Sasha Nijinsky?"

"Shortly after I joined the network. I did her makeup once, substituting for someone who was out sick, and she began asking for me."

"Did you and Ms. Nijinsky become friends?"

"Yes."

"How long ago?"

"We were on friendly terms from the beginning. We began to become . . . close about eight weeks ago."

"Did you, in fact, enter into a romantic relationship with Ms. Nijinsky?"

"Yes."

"A relationship of a sexual nature?"

Morgan gulped. "Yes."

"Were you in love with Ms. Nijinsky?"

"Yes."

"And was she in love with you?"

"Yes."

"Did she tell you she loved you, in so many words?"

"Yes. Many times."

"Were you aware that, during the same period Ms. Nijinsky was seeing you, she was also having an affair with a man?"

Morgan looked away for the first time. "Yes. She told me so."

"Did she tell you who this man was?"

"No."

"Did she give you any indication, any hint at all as to his identity?"

"No. She referred to him as 'What's-his-name.'"

That rang a bell from Sasha's diary. "How often did you see Ms. Nijinsky outside of working hours?"

"Two or three nights a week; sometimes four."

"Where did these meetings take place?"

"Either at my apartment or at hers."

"And when was the last occasion you saw Ms. Nijinsky?"

"The night before she disappeared."

"Where did this meeting take place?"

"At her apartment."

Stone paused. "Did you not tell me on a previous occasion that this meeting took place at *your* apartment?" •

"I have no recollection of that," Morgan replied smoothly.

Why was she changing her story? What did it matter where that particular meeting took place?

"Did anyone see you in Ms. Nijinsky's building that night?"

"The doorman saw me when we came in together. It must have been around nine o'clock. He was asleep when I left. That was around four in the morning."

"What did you and Ms. Nijinsky do that evening?"

"I helped her pack her things; she was moving to a new apartment in a day or two. We had a late dinner and drank a bottle of wine together." She paused. "We made love. It was a very happy evening."

"And when did you next see Ms. Nijinsky?"

"I never saw her again."

"We'll come back to that. You were taking money from Ms. Nijinsky, weren't you, Ms. Morgan?"

Morgan frowned. "*Taking* money? Certainly not. I borrowed some money from her, and only at her insistence. I was remodeling my apartment, and I ran out of cash. I had some six-month CDs that were not due to mature for another three months, and Sasha said it would be crazy to cash them and lose the interest, and that she wanted to loan me that money to finish the project. It came to twenty thousand dollars out of the eighty that I spent on the project."

This was not going the way Stone had meant it to. "You want us to believe that Ms. Nijinsky just *loaned* you the money—you, a person she had only recently met?"

"I don't much care what you believe," Morgan said coldly. "The money was a loan; I insisted on giving Sasha a promissory note for the amount, although she wouldn't accept interest."

"You're aware that we have Ms. Nijinsky's financial records and that we can search them for this note?" He was faltering now. Why hadn't he gone through those records more carefully?

"That's fine with me. I have a copy, if you need it."

"Ms. Morgan, after the disappearance of Sasha Nijinsky, police experts removed a palm print from the outside of the sliding glass door of her apartment's terrace. That palm print has since been identified as yours. On the *outside* of the door, Ms. Morgan, on the terrace from which Ms. Nijinsky fell. How do you explain that?"

"I told you that I had seen Ms. Nijinsky many times over the past weeks, often at her apartment. In fact, I think I remember when I could have left that palm print. On our last night together, Sasha and I took our wine out onto the terrace. There was no furniture out there, but it was a nice evening, and there was one break in the surrounding buildings where you could see some city skyline. I got something in my shoe, and I leaned against the sliding door while I shook out the shoe. I'm sure that must be that palm print you're referring to."

Leary, sitting next to Stone, was becoming restive.

Stone hurried. "Ms. Morgan, when Sasha told you she was seeing a man—at the same time she was making love to you—how did you feel about that?"

"I didn't like it much, at first, but, as we became closer, I realized that Sasha's sexuality was truly dual—not like mine. When you've gone through what most lesbian women go through to live their lives openly, you become more tolerant of other people's desires. There was a part of Sasha that liked sex with men, and I soon knew I couldn't change that. I told her I understood that, and the subject ceased to be a sore point between us."

This simple, rational explanation stopped Stone. He turned to Leary. "Lieutenant, do you have any questions for Ms. Morgan?"

Leary shook his head slowly. His face was red.

"Detective Bacchetti?"

"Yes, I have a question," Dino replied. His voice was cold and hard.

Stone wanted to stop him, but he knew he could not.

"This is the way it happened, *Miz* Morgan," Dino spat at her. "You fell madly in love with Sasha Nijinsky, and then you found out she was screwing a man, and that drove you crazy, didn't it?" He continued before she could answer. "So then, to get back at Sasha, you started blackmailing her, didn't you? Demanding money not to talk to the tabloids about her swinging both ways. And when she got tired of paying and told you so, there was a fight, and you heaved her off that terrace, didn't you? Isn't that the way it happened, *Miz* Morgan?"

Hank Morgan leaned forward and looked directly at Dino. "You're insane," she said.

Carlton Palmer spoke up, his deep voice resonating around the room. "Gentlemen," he said, "I think that will be all."

22

Leary kept Stone and Dino in the conference room. His face was very red now. "I thought you told me we were going to get a confession," he said, glaring at Dino.

Dino spread his hands. "Boss, how could I know for sure? It felt that way when Palmer said she'd talk to us."

"It did feel that way, Lieutenant," Stone interjected.

"That's a completely unusable tape," Leary said. "Palmer might as well have written and directed it himself."

"She's dirty, Lieutenant," Dino said. "She did it. I can feel it."

"I think so too," Leary said, "but you're going to have to fit her up for it."

"What?" Stone said, alarmed.

"I mean, you're going to have to prove it, get some evidence," Leary said, correcting himself.

"We'll get it," Dino said firmly. "I mean, shit,

Lieutenant, we just got on this bitch. Give us a little time, okay?"

"Okay," Leary said. "I'll give you twenty-four hours to come up with one piece of evidence that will put her in Nijinsky's apartment on that night."

"Lieutenant," Stone said, worried now, "that's unreasonable. Morgan is a whole new development in this case—a promising one, I'll grant you, but we're going to need some time."

"You got it," Leary said. "Twenty-four hours." He turned and walked from the room.

Dino flopped down in a chair. "What now?"

"We'd better get going, don't you think?"

Dino nodded. "Okay, I'll check Nijinsky's records for the promissory note from Morgan."

"I'll check out Morgan's address, see if anybody saw her that night. What are you going to do after you check the records? It won't take you very long."

Dino thought for a minute. "Shoot myself, if the note is there," he said.

Stone drove downtown faster than he usually drove, resisting the temptation to using the flashing light and siren. He parked in front of a fire hydrant on West Tenth Street and put down the visor to ward off tickets.

Hank Morgan lived in a handsome brownstone that had been divided into two duplexes; he wondered how she could afford it. Well, hell, he was only a cop and he lived in a whole brownstone in

Turtle Bay. Must be her daddy's money. He rang the second bell, the one that said VINCENT.

"Yes?" a woman's voice said over the intercom.

"Good morning, I'm Detective Barrington, NYPD. May I speak to you for a moment, Ms. Vincent?"

A pause. "All right, but I want to see a badge through the peephole."

"Of course."

She buzzed him through the outer door, and he held his badge so she could scrutinize it.

She opened the door but kept the chain on. "How about some ID with a photograph?" she said warily.

Stone handed his ID wallet through the opening.

She closed the door, unhooked the chain, and let him in. "Sorry about that, but you can't be too careful," she said.

Ms. Vincent was a pleasingly plump woman in an apron. "I was just about to have some coffee. Can I offer you some?"

"Thanks," Stone said. "I'd like that." He welcomed the opportunity to stretch out his visit.

She led him into the kitchen and gestured for him to take a seat at the breakfast table. When she had poured them both a cup, she joined him.

"What can I do for you?" she said.

"I want to talk with you about your upstairs neighbor," Stone said.

Ms. Vincent's eyebrows went up. "Really? Is Morgan in some kind of trouble?"

"She's helping us with an investigation, and the credibility of witnesses is always important. Also, I wanted to see if there was anything you could add to her information."

"Sure."

He took her back to the night of Sasha Nijinsky's fall. "Did you see Ms. Morgan at all that evening?"

Ms. Vincent thought for a moment. "We were in Bermuda," she said. "My husband's sister lives there, and we go at least once a year."

"Did anyone stay in your apartment while you were gone?"

She shook her head. "Nope."

"How well do you know Hank Morgan?"

"Not very well. We set up this place as condominiums four years ago with some friends. Then the friends got transferred, and they sold the place to Morgan about three months ago."

"Did you know Hank Morgan before that?"

"Nope. Neither did our friends; a real estate agent found her. I was a little worried at first. Shit, I'm still worried."

"Why?"

"Have you met Ms. Morgan?"

"Yes."

"Then I don't have to tell you she's a lesbian."

"No. She was quite frank about it."

"Well, it's not just that she's a lesbian—hell, I don't have anything against gays in general—it's that she's so . . . *involved*."

"Involved in what?"

"Well, she's apparently in two or three organizations about gay rights, and something to do with AIDS—you know those people who did that sit-in in St. Patrick's Cathedral?"

"I know the group."

"Well, she's always doing things like that; she's a real activist, which is, all too often, another way of saying 'pain in the ass.'"

"Why does that bother you?"

"She's always having meetings upstairs, and, believe me, there are some pretty weird people at those meetings. My God, there have been women in this house who should be playing pro football! It gives me the willies. I'm here by myself a lot; my husband travels in his work."

"Have these people behaved oddly toward you?"

"No, it's not that. I'm not really afraid of being raped, I guess. It's just that I'm an Italian girl from Queens, a Catholic, and I'm nervous about things like that. I was brought up to be nervous about things like that."

"Did you ever recognize any of Ms. Morgan's visitors?"

Ms. Vincent grinned. "Yeah, I recognized Sasha Nijinsky, once."

"Was she here for a meeting?"

"Nope, she was alone. I guess that means Sasha was a dyke, too, huh?"

"How often did you see her here?"

"Only once, and then through the peephole. It was her, though. She and Morgan were holding hands." She gave a little shudder.

"Do you remember the date you saw her here?"

Ms. Vincent shook her head. "Not exactly. Must have been a month or so ago."

Stone finished his coffee. "Do you know any of Ms. Morgan's other friends?"

"Nope. We don't socialize. I mean, we're polite to each other, but it's obvious we have absolutely nothing in common, except this house."

"Has Ms. Morgan been doing some work on her place?"

"I'll say she has! She's had builders in the house almost since the day she moved in; she must have done something pretty major to her place. They've stopped coming, though; they must be finished." She paused. "Did I mention that Morgan has a gun?"

"No, you didn't."

"I saw it when she moved in. I ran into her on the front steps—the first time I'd met her—and she was carrying a cardboard box full of stuff, and right on top was this pretty good-sized pistol in a holster. She made some joke about how you can't be too careful in New York."

Stone stood up. "Well, thank you for your help, Ms. Vincent."

"Wouldn't you like another cup?" She seemed anxious for company.

"Thanks, but I have a lot to do today."

Stone left the building and walked up and down both sides of the street. He checked at a bar, a dry cleaner, and a shoe repair shop; all of them were acquainted with Hank Morgan, but nobody had seen her on the night of Sasha's disappearance. He checked his notebook for the home phone number of the doorman at Sasha's old building, called him, and ascertained that Morgan had been there before Sasha's fall. The doorman hadn't seen Morgan that night. Discouraged, he drove back to the precinct.

Dino was at his desk, looking pleased with himself.

"There wasn't any promissory note," he said, grinning. "Morgan lied to us."

"Not necessarily," Stone replied. "Nijinsky might have kept them someplace else."

"Nah," Dino said. "She kept perfect records, and they were perfectly complete. If Morgan had given her a note, that's where it'd be. What did you come up with?"

Stone gave an account of his investigation. "The downstairs neighbor was on vacation, like Morgan said. The lady doesn't like lesbians, but she had nothing to say that would have incriminated Morgan. I had the feeling she wished she'd had something to tell me."

"Morgan's our killer," Dino said. "I can feel it in my bones."

"I can't feel it in mine, Dino. I know how bad we need a bust on this one, but Morgan's just not it. The lady's clean, except maybe on a weapons charge. The neighbor saw a pistol, but Morgan may have a permit."

"I'll check on that, but, take my word for it, the lady's no lady," Dino said. "And she's dirty."

23

On his way home, Stone was stopped in his tracks by a headline in the *Post*: ARREST IN SASHA CASE! He grabbed a copy.

Henrietta "Hank" Morgan, 32, a makeup artist at the Continental Network and a leading activist in lesbian-rights demonstrations, was taken in handcuffs to the 19th Precinct this morning and questioned for more than three hours about the disappearance of TV anchorwoman Sasha Nijinsky. In what a police source described as a "breakthrough" in the investigation, Morgan is reported to have given a detailed statement on videotape, while her lawyer, Carlton Palmer, was present. While the NYPD has not disclosed the contents of the tape, a source has said, "This all but wraps up the investigation." The source would not reveal what the NYPD thinks has become of Sasha.

Ace criminal trial lawyer Palmer said, in a telephone interview at press time, "My client is innocent of any wrongdoing, and the police know that. This entire episode is a perversion of justice."

Morgan, the daughter of a prominent Pennsylvania manufacturer, has been in and out of a dozen makeup jobs in the film and television industry over the past ten years and is known to have been Sasha Nijinsky's personal choice as her makeup artist at the Continental Network.

The story made Stone grind his teeth. The precinct seemed to be leaking from every pore, and whoever had given the *Post* the story had either not known what he was talking about or had deliberately misled the newspaper. There was going to be hell to pay.

The phone was ringing as he entered the house, tripping over a number of boxes in the hallway. The dentist in the professional suite downstairs received packages for him when he was at work and put them inside the front door.

Dino was on the phone. "Leary wants us downtown at the DA's office tomorrow morning at nine."

"What's going on?"

"He didn't say."

A thought struck Stone. "I'm scheduled for a department physical tomorrow morning."

"If you want, I'll do the meeting, you get checked out."

Stone thought for a moment. "I'd better be there, I think. I don't much like the sound of it."

"You seen the *Post*?"

"Yeah. Who do you think is leaking to the press?"

"Could be anybody."

"I guess so."

"I'll see you tomorrow morning." Dino hung up.

Stone turned his attention to the boxes in the front hall. A glance at the labels told him what they were. Shit, he had intended to cancel the clothes orders. How could they have gotten them here so fast? Furious at himself and annoyed by being called to the DA's office for no apparent reason, he ripped through the day's mail and nearly threw away an invitation, thinking it some sort of classy junk mail. It was for dinner on Saturday, at the apartment of Hiram Barker. That should be an interesting evening, he thought. He rang the number, got an answering machine, and accepted, adding that he would bring a date, if that was all right. Well, he thought, sighing, at least he'd be able to dress well for the occasion.

They were at Elaine's, at a small table all the way in the back. It was a crowded night, as usual, and Lauren, the singer-piano player, was straining to be heard above the din.

"Want to go to dinner at Hi Barker's on Saturday night?" he asked Cary.

She nearly choked on her scotch. "No kidding?"

"No kidding. The invitation came in today's mail."

"You're really coming up in the world. Dinner at Barker's is a hot ticket."

"I interviewed him about Sasha, and he said come to dinner sometime. I thought it was just the usual chat."

"I am definitely available," she said. "Now, what am I going to wear?"

"I don't have any problem about what to wear," he said. "All that stuff we ordered came today. You know what you made me spend?"

She waved away his question. "My daddy always said, 'Buy the things you want, and then figure out how to pay for them. Debt is a great motivator.'"

Stone laughed. "Well, I guess I'd better get motivated."

"Come on, sweetheart, that's what credit cards are for. How do you think everybody else in this town dresses?"

"I never did it that way. I never bought anything on a credit card that I couldn't pay for at the end of the month."

"A very stuffy attitude."

"A very necessary one, when you're on a cop's salary."

"I've been meaning to talk to you about that."

"About my salary?"

"About making a lot more money than you are. You've got a low degree, after all; why don't you use it?"

"I never took the bar exam."

"How about a—"

"I know, a cram course. You're as bad as Elaine. She's been at me about that."

"She's right. You're a highly intelligent man, and a highly handsome one, too, I might add. That counts for more than you might think, and not just with women."

"So, I could just quite the force and live on my looks?"

She laughed. "If it were up to me, you could. Does the practice of law repel you so much?"

"Look, I'm thirty-eight years old. I can't just get in line at the big firms with this year's grads and expect to get taken on. 'So, Mr. Barrington, what have you been doing with yourself in the fifteen years between getting your law degree and passing the bar?' 'Oh, I've been arresting drug dealers and investigating murders and other sordid crimes.' 'Wonderful, that experience will stand you in good stead in our estate planning department. Will a hundred thousand a year be enough?'"

She laughed again. "There are other facets of the law besides estate planning, you know."

"Sure there are. You know which ones I'd be qualified for? I'll tell you; I'd be qualified to hang around the criminal courts picking up burglary defenses, drug busts, and drunk driving cases. That's what ex-cops who are lawyers do—they go to night school, get a law degree, and, when they retire, they pick up an extra income by leaning on their old buddies on the force and in the DA's office to go easy on the scum they're defending."

"You underestimate yourself," she said. "Still,

that's an endearing quality in a world where over-confidence is a way of life."

"Let's order," Stone said, picking up a menu.

"I think I'd like you for dinner," Cary said.

"Let's start with a Caesar salad, and go on to the osso buco," he said. "Then we can have each other for dessert."

"I always have room for dessert," she said.

And she did. Stone lay panting in the darkness when she had finished—spent, but still full of desire for her. He had never felt anything quite like it. He was in love with her, but he had been in love before. It was obsession, and that was foreign to him.

She wrapped herself around him. "That was delicious," she breathed, kissing him behind the ear. "I'll want more soon."

"You'll kill me," he panted, "but I can deny you nothing."

"Don't even try," she said.

24

The meeting took place in the district attorney's private conference room, but the DA himself didn't attend. Al Hagler, the chief prosecutor, sat at the end of the table.

Stone had the distinct feeling that this room had not been chosen just because it was available; Hagler believed in effect, and the venue added authority to his position. It was just as significant that the DA was not present, though his presence was felt. The proceedings, whatever they were, had his tacit support, but, this way, he could not be personally tainted by the outcome. It was interesting, too, that Deputy Commissioner Waldron was not in attendance, nor was Chief of Detectives Delgado. It was just Hagler, Leary, Dino, and Stone.

"What have you most recently uncovered?" Hagler asked the room at large.

Leary nodded at Dino.

"There is no promissory note in Nijinsky's files, although they seem complete in every other respect," Dino said. "And Morgan has no gun permit, nor has she ever applied for one."

"Good," Hagler said, looking pleased.

"Why good?" Stone asked. "Just because there is no note in Nijinsky's files doesn't mean it never existed, and what does Morgan's owning a pistol have to do with anything? Nijinsky wasn't shot."

"How do you know that?" Leary asked.

"I saw her," Stone replied. "I didn't see a bullet wound."

"She was covered in dirt, wasn't she?"

"Yes."

"And how long did you see her for?"

"A few seconds."

"Hardly time for a postmortem," Hagler chimed in.

"I heard no gunshot either," Stone said.

"Whether Nijinsky was shot is not relevant to this meeting," Hagler said.

"Just what is the purpose of this meeting?" Stone asked.

"I just wanted to hear from you and Detective Bacchetti before proceeding."

"Proceeding with what?"

Hagler reached into an inside pocket and tossed a document onto the table.

Stone picked it up. "A search warrant for Morgan's apartment? What are we supposed to look for?"

"Anything that might relate to the Nijinsky case," Hagler said.

"On what basis did you get the warrant?" Stone persisted.

"The basis don't matter to you," Leary spoke up. "You just execute the warrant, you and Dino, right?"

Stone shrugged. "Yes, sir."

"Detective Barrington has a physical at ten o'clock," Dino said.

Stone looked at him, surprised. "I can postpone," he said.

"No, no, that's important," Leary said. "You go on and get examined so we can get you restored to full duty." He turned to Dino. "You pick up a uniformed team and conduct the search."

"I'll send an assistant DA with you," Hagler said. "I'd like one of my people on the spot."

"We won't need you further, Barrington," Leary said, looking at his watch. "You go see the doctor."

Stone looked around the table. Everyone seemed to be avoiding his gaze. "All right," he said, standing up. "I'll see you back at the precinct, Dino."

Dino nodded without looking at him.

Stone took his leave feeling shunned, shut out. What was going on?

The doctor took his time getting around to the knee, "Strip down to your shorts," he said. He took Stone's blood pressure, listened to his heart and lungs, looked into his ears, eyes, and mouth, checked his vision and hearing, and a nurse took blood and urine samples. Only then did the doctor turn his attention to the knee. "Swelling seems to be gone," he said, feeling the joint in a gingerly fashion.

"I hardly notice it anymore," Stone replied, not quite truthfully.

"Stand up and give me five half knee bends," the doctor said.

Stone complied, clenching his jaw against possible pain. The exercise went well.

"Now give me five deep knee bends."

This was harder, but Stone managed it. The knee was hurting a little now.

"Now give me five half knee bends on the left leg."

This seemed extreme to Stone, but, again, he managed. Now the knee hurt like hell.

"Get dressed," the doctor said.

"What do you think?" Stone asked, pulling on his trousers.

"You've healed nicely."

"So, I'm restored to duty?"

"Oh, I expect so, but that's not my decision, of course. I'll just make my report; you'll hear from your commander."

"How long?"

"He'll have my report by the first of the week."

"So long?"

"I'll dictate it today; getting it typed is the problem. We've taken some staff cuts this year."

Stone got dressed and called the precinct. Dino wasn't back yet. He went down to the street and hailed a cab. When he arrived at Hank Morgan's building, Dino's unmarked car and a squad car were still outside, and the downstairs door was propped open. Stone ran up the stairs.

The niceties had not been observed. The search warrant was taped to the door, which had been opened with a sledgehammer; the jamb was splintered, and the apartment was a mess. Stone walked through the disarrayed living room and followed the sound of voices to a beautifully designed kitchen. Dino, the assistant DA, and two uniforms sat at the kitchen table, drinking coffee. Knives, silverware, and kitchen implements were scattered around the floor.

"Hey, Stone!" Dino called. "You want some coffee?"

"No thanks. You really tore up this place, didn't you?"

"And look what we found!" Dino crowed, dangling a pistol from his finger by the trigger guard. "Three fifty-seven Magnum, and loaded, too."

"What else?"

"No copy of a promissory note."

"So?"

"And I'll bet she won't be able to come up with it when it counts."

"You all finished here, then?"

"Just about. We'll finish our coffee."

There was a noise from the living room, and Stone turned to see Hank Morgan standing in the doorway, the search warrant in her hand.

"What the hell is going on here?" she demanded, her voice shaking with anger.

"A legal and proper search," Dino said, standing up. "You got the warrant right there."

Morgan turned to Stone, as if she expected she might be able to reason with him. "Just what are you looking for, for Christ's sake?"

Stone shook his head. "I just got here myself, Ms. Morgan, but, I assure you, the search is legal and proper. I'm sorry about the mess."

"So Officers," she said with withering contempt, "did you find anything? A joint, maybe? Or did you plant some cocaine?"

"We don't plant stuff in searches," Dino said, "but we did find this." He held up the pistol.

"That's mine," she said.

"And do you have a permit for it?"

She started to speak, then stopped herself. "I want to call my lawyer," she said.

"You can do that at the precinct," Dino said. He walked over and handed her another warrant. "Right now, you are under arrest for the possession of a firearm without a permit." He began to read her her rights.

Morgan turned to Stone again. "This can't be happening," she said, as if she expected him to make everything all right.

"I'm sorry, but it is happening," Stone replied. He lowered his voice. "And I'd advise you not to say anything further until you've seen your lawyer."

Downstairs, Stone watched as the patrolmen bundled Morgan, now hancuffed, into the squad car.

"You coming back to the precinct?" Dino asked, his hand on the car's door handle.

"Not right now," Stone said.

"How'd the physical go?"

"Okay, I think. He said I'm okay."

"Glad to hear it."

"Dino, where'd you get the arrest warrant for the weapons charge?"

"Hagler had that, too. He came up with it right after you left."

Stone nodded.

Dino got into the unmarked car and drove away.

Stone walked briskly down the street to the corner drugstore and found a phone. He got the number from information, and, when he told the secretary who he was, she immediately put him through.

"Hello, Detective Barrington?"

"Mr. Palmer, Hank Morgan has been arrested on a weapons charge. If I were you, I'd get up to the precinct without delay."

There was a stunned silence from Palmer's end of the line.

"Good-bye," Stone said.

"Thank you, Detective," Palmer managed to sputter before Stone hung up.

Stone walked slowly up Sixth Avenue, not looking for a cab yet. He felt something of the traitor, but he had wanted to do something to redress the balance. He was in no hurry to get to the precinct. He didn't want to be involved in what was gong to happen there.

25

In spite of his lengthy walk, Stone got to the precinct before Morgan's lawyer did. Dino's desk was empty.

"Dino's got the dyke in interrogation room three," a detective at a nearby desk told Stone.

Three had a two-way mirror. Stone walked hurriedly down the hall and let himself quietly into the adjacent viewing room, which was empty. He sat down on a folding chair and took in the scene next door. Morgan was seated at the steel table facing the mirror, with Dino and the ADA on either side of her. She sat rigidly in the uncomfortable chair, gripping the arms. Her knuckles were white. Tears streamed down her face. A tape recorder was on the table.

Stone looked at his watch. She would have been in the interrogation room for nearly an hour. Where was Palmer?

"I want my lawyer," Morgan sobbed.

"You already had your lawyer," Dino replied, "and now you're going to talk to me."

"I have nothing to say to you," Morgan said adamantly, her voice quavering.

Stone could tell she was near breaking. Anything could happen now.

"We've got you cold on the weapons possession charge," Dino said. "That's five to ten, and you won't get sent to a country club. You'll be in there with all the other bull dykes—the muscle freaks, the murderers."

"I have nothing to say," Morgan nearly screamed.

"Let's put the weapons thing aside for the moment," Dino said, his voice kinder. "Let's talk about Sasha."

"I don't want to talk about Sasha," Morgan said. Her head sagged forward until her chin touched her chest. "I don't want to talk about anything."

Dino leaned forward and lowered his voice.

Stone strained to hear him over the speaker.

"Look, nobody's saying you murdered Sasha; I know you loved her, and you wouldn't hurt her on purpose. It was an accident, I know that. You just had a little tussle, and Sasha fell, that's all. You must have felt terrible."

To Stone's astonishment, Morgan nodded slowly. Her face was shiny with tears, and she made no effort to wipe them away.

"That's it," Dino said soothingly, "let it all come out; you're going to feel a lot better when you tell me about it."

Morgan continued to nod but said nothing.

"Look, Hank, tell me about it, and I guarantee

you won't do any time. You had a tussle, and Sasha fell; no judge is going to send you to prison."

At the word *prison*, Morgan's body jerked convulsively. "I don't want to go to prison," she said.

Stone stared at her. The woman was starting to come apart; in another minute she would plead to the Kennedy assassination, if Dino wanted her to.

"I won't let them send you to prison," Dino said, "if you'll just tell me the truth, tell me what happened. It was Sasha's fault, wasn't it?"

Morgan broke down now. The sobbing shook her body, and she made a terrible keening noise. She grabbed hold of Dino's forearm. "I'll say anything you want," she wailed, "just don't send me to prison."

"All right," Dino said, "I'm going to tell you what it was like, and we're going to write it down." He handed her a pen and shoved a legal pad in front of her.

Stone began to feel ill. He wanted to pick up a chair and throw it through the mirror. Then the door to the interrogation room opened, and Lieutenant Leary walked in, accompanied by Carlton Palmer.

"That will be quite enough of this!" Palmer shouted, going to Morgan's side and putting an arm around her. "You've got a lot of nerve pulling this sort of stunt!" he yelled at Dino. "I'll have your badge before I'm done."

"Aw, go fuck yourself, Counselor," Dino said, and walked out of the room, slamming the door.

* * *

Stone found him pacing up and down alongside his desk in the squad room.

"Two more minutes!" Dino said, slamming his fist into his palm. "Two more fucking minutes, and I'd have had her!"

"Come on, Dino," Stone said. "It would never have stood up; you know that. She'd have recanted on the stand, and the jury would have believed her."

"I've still got her for the gun, though," Dino said. "I'll nail her for that. I won't let the DA deal on it either. I'll send her up for it."

"Dino, stop it. You're dreaming. You can't even convince *me* she had anything to do with Nijinsky, so how is the DA going to convince a grand jury, let alone get a conviction? The woman had nothing to do with it." A hard voice behind him caused Stone to spin around.

"Horseshit," Leary said. "You better get with the program, Barrington, or the world's gonna fall on you."

"You mean Deputy Commissioner Waldron?"

"And the chief of detectives, and the district attorney, and *me*, and the whole world. We've got a chance for a good bust on this one, after you've fucked around getting nowhere all this time, and you'd better not get in the way of it."

Stone felt anger rush through him. "That woman had nothing to do with Nijinsky's fall, and you're not going to prove she did. If I thought you could make a jury believe it, I'd testify for the defense myself."

"If you pull something like that," Leary said,

his voice low and cold, "I'll take you out in the alley and shoot you myself." The lieutenant turned and walked away.

Stone turned to Dino. "What about you? Is that how you feel?"

"I'll hold you while he pulls the trigger," Dino said, his voice shaking.

26

As Stone trudged up the front steps of the Turtle Bay house, his downstairs tenant, dressed in a white nylon coat, came out of the professional suite and caught up with him.

"Mr. Barrington?"

"Hello, Dr. Feldstein," Stone said.

Feldstein was a short, stocky, pink-faced man in his late sixties. Stone had always liked him, not least because he had overlooked chronic problems with the downstairs plumbing in return for a reasonable rent. Feldstein thrust an envelope at Stone.

"What's this?"

"It's my notice of leaving, Mr. Barrington. Thirty days, as my lease requires. I'm sorry I couldn't give you more notice, but my wife's recent illness has made me decide to retire. We're moving to Venice, Florida, next month."

The news struck Stone like a spear in the ribs. That was twelve hundred dollars a month of income gone, and he knew he couldn't rent the place again without major improvements, which he could not afford. "I'm sorry to hear you're going, Dr. Feldstein. You've always been a good tenant."

"And you a good landlord, like your great-aunt before you," Feldstein said.

"I wish you and your wife a happy retirement in Florida."

"She'll like the sunshine; she always has."

They both seemed at a loss for words for a moment, then Feldstein shook Stone's hand and walked back down the front steps.

Stone let himself into the house and tossed Feldstein's letter onto the front hall table with the mail. Nothing but bills there, and he didn't bother opening them. He had a nearly overwhelming urge to call Cary; he needed desperately to talk with somebody, but he couldn't forget that technically, at least, Cary was press, and he couldn't let his thoughts escape in that direction. Normally, Dino would be the one to talk to, but he and Dino were on opposite sides this time. He wished his father were still alive.

He changed into jeans and a work shirt and went down to the kitchen. He had hardly cooked anything since the room had been completed, and now all he could manage in his mood was to microwave some frozen lasagna. He had a bourbon while he waited for the oven to do its work. He felt a curious numbness, a distance from reality. Not even the loss of his income-producing tenant, on top of everything else, could penetrate. He simply felt nothing. When the microwave

beeped, he took out the lasagna and ate it immediately, in spite of the instructions to let it sit for
five minutes. His was a simple, animal hunger,
and he didn't care what he was eating or how it
tasted. It was like taking aspirin to make a head-
ache go away. You don't enjoy the aspirin.

He finished the meal and put his plate in the
dishwasher, then poured himself another bourbon and went into the study. The room was spot-
lessly clean now, and an air cleaner was running
to remove the dust caused by the constant sanding by his helpers for the past week.

The bookshelves stood empty and bare of finish, ready for varnish, the first of ten coats he
planned. Tomorrow, the helpers would come back
to sand again. He opened a gallon can of varnish,
selected a brush, climbed the ladder, and started
at the very top, spreading the sealer with long,
straight strokes. It was simple, mindless work, the
sort that he needed for thinking. He let his mind
wander at will over the events of the past days.

Stone knew he was not the first honest policeman to find himself in this position. When a police department had a major crime on its hands,
especially one where the victim was a celebrity,
what it needed was an arrest—preferably, but not
necessarily, of the actual perpetrator. As time
passed without a resolution of the crime, pressure increased on the department to produce results, and after a while the pressure could become
too much for certain of its members. Assignments
were at stake—promotions, careers, pensions—
and policemen, just like everybody else, would

finally act to protect themselves. Stone reckoned that most of the innocent people in prison had been sent there by police officers and prosecutors who reasoned that these victims were, after all, probably guilty of *something*, and better a conviction of an innocent person than no conviction at all.

He had seen it happen, but always from a distance. Now he was involved, whether he liked it or not, and he had a decision to make: he could keep his mouth shut and let Dino, Leary, and their superiors try to railroad Hank Morgan; or he could speak up—go directly to the mayor or the newspapers and create a stink. The first course would protect his job, his career, and his pension; the second would subject him to the contempt that came to any policeman who went against his partner and his department. He would be transferred to some hellish backwater, shunned, ridiculed, perhaps even set up to be killed—sent first through some door with death waiting on the other side. It had happened before. Most of all, he would be separating himself from the work to which he had devoted his whole adult life. He would be a man alone, with enemies, and with no friends or support. It was the law of the cop jungle, and no man could last long on the force when he was subjected to it. It was time for him to decide if he was, after all these years, a cop.

The doorbell rang, causing him nearly to topple from the high ladder. He climbed down, moving carefully, cautious of the bourbon inside him. He went to the front door.

Dino stood there. He was dressed to kill in a new suit, obviously on his way to some girl. "We got to talk," he said.

"Come on in." Stone led him to the study. "The booze is in the kitchen. I've got wet varnish going here; I can't stop." He climbed back up the ladder and started to paint again.

Dino came back with something in a glass with ice. "What are you going to do?" he asked. He didn't have to explain; he knew Stone understood the situation.

"I don't know," Stone replied, brushing on the varnish.

"You know what's going to happen, you go against the grain on this one."

"I know."

Dino still hadn't drunk from his glass. "Stone, you got a lot of time in. A little more than five years, you can walk away with half pay and go practice law, you know?"

"I know."

"You and I got four years in together. You're my partner. I respect you." Dino shook his head. "Jesus Christ, Stone, I love you like you was my brother."

Stone kept brushing. "Thanks, Dino, I knew that, but I'm glad you told me."

"I don't want nothing to happen to you, Stone. I'll feel responsible."

"Dino, whatever I decide to do, it's on my head, not yours. I know the score; I know what can happen. It wouldn't be your doing."

"Well, thanks for that, anyway."

"You're welcome."

Dino stood looking up at him. "Stone, I gotta know what you're going to do."

Stone stopped painting and looked down at his partner. "Dino, I swear to you, I just don't know."

Dino looked down at the floor and shook his head. He set the untouched drink on the floor and left without another word.

Stone heard the front door close. He kept painting, smooth and even strokes. He kept sipping the bourbon.

27

Stone woke at seven and turned on *The Morning Show*. Nothing on the national news. He waited impatiently for twenty-five minutes past the hour and the New York affiliate's news. Nothing. Surprised, he got out of bed and dressed.

His decision had been made while he slept. Over an English muffin, he reflected that he had always wondered what would happen if he had to choose between the right thing and the department. His choice surprised him.

He picked up a *Daily News* at the corner newsstand, expecting another headline about the arrest of Hank Morgan. Nothing. Suddenly, for some reason, the leaks in the precinct had dried up.

The squad room was filling up with the morning shift of detectives, and Dino was already at his desk.

"Hi," he said. "Leary wants to see you."

"I figured," Stone said.

"You decide?" Dino asked.

"Yeah." He turned away and started for the lieutenant's cubicle; he'd let Dino stew for a while before he told him. He knocked on the glass door, and Leary waved him in.

Stone sat down and waited. He'd make Leary ask him.

Leary looked at him for a long time before he spoke. He reached into a large, yellow envelope and extracted a letter. "Stone," he said finally, "the results of your physical came in."

Stone was surprised. "The doctor said it'd be next week."

"It's today."

"Great. The sooner I'm officially back on full duty, the better."

"You're officially retired, for medical reasons."

Stone stopped breathing, stared at Leary, unable to speak.

Leary handed him the letter.

Stone read it.

Detective Barrington has suffered severe, perhaps irreparable damage to his left knee as a result of a gunshot wound received in the line of duty. In spite of extensive surgery and physiotherapy, the knee has not responded to treatment sufficiently to permit a return to active police duty. The prognosis is unfavorable. It is therefore recommended that Detective Barrington be retired from the force with immediate effect and with full line-of-duty disability benefits.

Stone dropped the letter and stared at Leary's desktop, his eyes unfocused.

"You can ask for a reexamination after a year," Leary said, "and, if the results are favorable, apply for reinstatement. Of course, if you were reinstated, that would mean a transfer to other duty and probably a loss of seniority."

That was clear enough to Stone. Don't come back. In a flash, he saw himself floundering through a series of unsuccessful appeals.

"There's no point in appealing this," Leary said, reading his mind. "You're out, and that's it."

"I see," Stone said, for lack of anything else to say.

"Let me have your ID card," Leary said.

Mechanically, Stone removed it from his wallet and handed it over.

Leary took some sort of stamp from a desk drawer, imprinted the card, and handed it back. The word *retired* had been punched into the card. "You can keep your badge, and you're entitled to carry your gun, like you were off duty." He handed Stone a thick envelope. "Here are your papers. Fill out the insurance forms and send them in; you'll still be covered under the department medical plan for life. Your pension will be three-quarters of your highest grade pay, tax free. That's a good deal. There's a check in the envelope for the first month."

Stone couldn't think of anything to say, and he couldn't seem to move.

Leary leaned forward and rested his elbows on the desk. "Look, Stone," he said, not without sympathy, "you're a good investigator, but you're a lousy cop. What you have never understood is that the NYPD is a fraternal lodge, and you never joined. You always bothered people. Being whitebread didn't make it any better; I mean, just about everybody on the force is micks, guineas, yids, spics, or niggers. They got that in common. But you're fuckin' J. Stone Barrington, for Christ's sake. That sounds like a brokerage house, not a cop, and you never even let anybody call you Stoney. A lot of the men respect you—*I* do; but nobody trusts you, and nobody's ever going to. You were never really a cop; you were always a college boy with a law degree and a badge."

Stone took a deep breath and struggled from the chair.

Leary started shuffling papers. "Good luck," he said.

"Thanks," Stone managed to say as he turned for the door.

"And Stone," Leary said.

Stone turned and looked at him.

"Stay out of the Nijinsky thing, you hear me? I don't want to read any of your theories in the papers."

Stone left, closing the door behind him. Numbly, he walked back to his desk. Dino was gone. On top of Stone's desk was a cardboard box containing his personal effects. He looked around the place; everybody was busy doing something.

Stone picked up the cardboard box and walked out of the squad room. Nobody looked at him.

28

The phone was ringing as Stone walked into the house. He picked it up. "Hello?"

"Detective Barrington?"

"Yes?"

"This is Jack Marcus at the *Post*. We're doing a follow-up on the Nijinsky story; does your leaving the force have anything to do with your dissatisfaction with the way the investigation is being conducted?"

Stone was taken aback for a moment. The precinct was leaking again. "I'm leaving the force for medical reasons," he said.

"Weren't your superiors happy about the arrest of Henrietta Morgan?"

"You'll have to ask them about that."

"Do you think Hank Morgan pushed Sasha off that terrace?"

"I don't have an opinion about that. I'm a civilian." He hung up the phone. It rang again immediately.

"It's Cary. It just came over the AP wire."

"That's pretty fast reporting. I only heard myself an hour ago." He had walked home from the precinct.

"Are you all right?"

"I'm okay. Let's have dinner tonight."

"I wish I could. Barron's doing a prime-time special on murder in New York for Friday night. He's shooting every day, and we're editing every night."

"Come over here when you finish tonight."

"I wish I could, Stone; God knows, I'd rather be with you, but you have to understand about my job. I'll be working fifteen-hour days all this week."

"I'm sorry I pressed you; I know the job's important."

"It is, but I'll see you Saturday night for dinner at Barker's."

"Sure."

"Why don't you relax for the rest of the week? Do some work on the house."

"I don't have anything else to do."

"We'll talk about that Saturday. I've got to run now."

"See you."

"Take care."

Stone put down the phone. He could hear the noise of sanding coming from the study. The shelves would be ready to varnish again by late afternoon.

He went upstairs to his bedroom and stood looking at himself in the mirror over the chest of drawers. Nothing seemed different. He unstrapped the gun from his ankle, took the badge wallet from his pocket, and put them both in the top drawer, at the back, under his socks and underwear. As always, he felt naked when he wasn't carrying them. He would have to get used to feeling naked.

He was suddenly overcome with fatigue. He stretched out on the bed, still wearing his trench coat, and closed his eyes for a minute.

When he woke, it was dark outside, and the noise of sanding had stopped. He still felt exhausted, but he struggled out of his trench coat and suit and into work clothes. Downstairs, he repeated his actions of the evening before—ate lasagna, made a drink, varnished. By the time he went to bed, he was drunk.

The next morning, he forced himself, in spite of the hangover, to work out on the exercise equipment; then he took a cab to Central Park and ran twice around the reservoir. It was a clear autumn day, the sort of day he loved in New York, and it lifted his spirits somewhat. He got a sandwich at the zoo and watched the seals cavort in their pool. What would he do tomorrow, he asked himself, and the week and the month after that? He knew how easy it would be to let himself descend into depression.

He finished his sandwich and found a pay phone, which, miraculously, had an intact yellow pages. He found the number and learned that the next bar exam was in three weeks, and the next cram course began the following Monday. He signed up on the spot, giving them a credit card number to hold his place. The thought of sitting in a classroom repelled him, but the thought of doing nothing was worse.

He bought the *Daily News* and the *Times* and looked for news. Hank Morgan had been arraigned the previous afternoon on the weapons charge and had been released on bail, which her father had covered. The *Times* report went no further than that, but a *News* columnist tied her to the Nijinsky case:

> There is little doubt that Henrietta "Hank" Morgan is the chief suspect in the fall of Sasha Nijinsky from the terrace of her East Side penthouse. While everyone connected with the case has declined comment, police sources say that it is only a matter of time before enough evidence will be marshaled for the D.A. to seek an indictment. But an indictment for what? At the moment, there seems to be no proof that Sasha Nijinsky is dead, and even the police have not tried to link Morgan to her disappearance. It looks to this observer that the best the cops can hope for is an indictment for attempted murder, and one wonders how they could get a conviction on even that charge without producing either Nijinsky or her dead body.

It was starting now. The groundwork was being laid for a failure to convict Hank Morgan of anything, the implication being that, even though the police couldn't get enough evidence against her, they knew she was the guilty party. They had solved the crime, and that would get the department off the hook; never mind that Morgan, supposedly innocent until proven guilty, would be branded as a murderer and would live the rest of her life under a cloud.

For the first time, he felt glad to be out of the department. He looked at the photograph of Hank Morgan leaving the court with her attorney, mobbed by photographers and reporters, their lips curled back, screaming their questions. The woman looked terrified, even worse than she had looked in the interrogation room. There was the real victim in all this; Sasha herself had become a secondary figure to the newspapers and television news programs.

Stone forced himself to jog home, and he arrived thoroughly winded.

The answering machine was blinking; he pushed the button.

"Hello, there Det . . . uh, Mr. Barrington. This is Herbert Van Fleet. I was very sorry to read in the newspapers about your retirement from the police force. I hope my mother's letters to the mayor didn't have anything to do with this. She has been a big contributor to his campaigns, you know, and she's known him for years. I don't guess I'll be seeing you in the line of duty anymore—the FBI seems to have taken over, anyway. Can I buy you lunch sometime? You can always get me at the funeral parlor." He chuckled. "I guess you have the number."

Stone gave a little shudder at the thought of having lunch with Herbert Van Fleet.

There was a message from Cary, too. "Sorry I couldn't get over. We worked past midnight, and I was exhausted. I wouldn't have been any good to you. It's all over on Friday, though, and I promise to be fresh and ready for anything on Saturday night. I'll have a car; pick you up at eight?"

There was one more message. "Stone, it's Bill Eggers, your old law school buddy, of Woodman & Weld? I heard about your departure from the cop shop. I'm in LA right now on a case, but I'll be back in the office on Monday. Let me buy you dinner next week? I want to talk about something that might interest you. I'll call you Monday."

Stone spent the rest of the week working furiously on the house, making remarkable progress, now that he had the time. There were five coats of varnish on the bookshelves by the weekend, and they were looking good. He got all the floors sanded with rented equipment and got the tile floor laid in the kitchen. A few weeks more, and the place would start to look like home. A bill came from the upholsterer that put a serious dent in his bank account, and he remembered the letter from his banker and the note, which would be due soon. He tried to put money out of his mind. It didn't work.

Dino didn't call.

29

On Saturday night, Cary turned up not in just a black car but in a limousine. Stone was waiting at the curb, and he slid into the backseat laughing.

He gave the driver the address and turned to Cary. "Are you sure the network can afford this?"

She raised the black window that separated them from the driver and slid close to him. "Don't worry about it. I've been putting in so much overtime, they owe me." She pulled his face down to hers and kissed him.

"There goes the lipstick," he said.

"Fuck the lipstick." She kissed him again and ran her hand up his thigh to the crotch. "Fuck me, too."

"In a limousine?"

"Why not? The driver can't see anything."

"We'll be at Barker's building in three minutes."

"That's just time enough," she said, unzipping his fly.

Before Stone could move he was in her mouth.

She was very good, and he was very fast; by the time the chauffeur opened the door, Stone had already adjusted his clothing, and Cary had reapplied her lipstick.

"You're amazing," Stone whispered as they entered the building. He was trying to bring his breathing back to normal.

"It was the least I could do," she said, "after I abandoned you in what must have been a very bad week."

"I think being alone helped me make the adjustment better," he said, "but I like the way you make up for slights." The doorman took their names and directed them to the elevator.

When the door had closed, she moved close to him. "I wonder how long we have before the elevator reaches Barker's floor?" she said.

Stone leaned down and kissed the top of a breast, accessible above the low-cut dress. "Not long enough for what I have in mind," he said. "By the way, you look spectacular. It's a wonderful dress."

She laughed. "You like cleavage, don't you?"

"The sight of breasts is good for morale."

"You look pretty sharp yourself. The suit suits you."

"I had good advice."

The elevator door opened. A uniformed maid answered the door and took their coats.

"Well, good evening," Hi Barker said, sweeping into the hall from the living room.

Stone introduced Cary.

"You're a fine judge of women, Stone," Barker said, kissing Cary's hand.

"Why, thank you, sir," Cary responded. She turned to Stone. "You didn't prepare me for this man."

"How could I?"

Barker ushered them into the living room, where two other couples and a woman waited. "Meet everybody," he said. "This is Frank and Marian Woodman."

Stone shook their hands. "Mr. Woodman and I have met," he said.

"Oh?" Barker said. "You're better acquainted around town than I thought."

"All in the line of duty," Stone said, "just the way I met you."

"That's right," Woodman said. "Sasha Nijinsky was my client, and Detective Barrington came to see me. Or, I should say, Mr. Barrington. My congratulations; I hear that sort of medical retirement is every police officer's dream."

"Most of the cops I know would rather serve the thirty years healthy," Stone said.

"Oh, the penny just dropped," Mrs. Woodman said. She was a small, handsome woman some years her husband's junior. "You're the detective in the papers."

"I'm afraid so," Stone said.

"You'll have to interrogate him later, Marian," Barker said, pulling Stone and Cary away. "He has other guests to meet." He took them to the other couple. "This is Abbott Wheeling and his wife, India. Stone Barrington and Cary Hilliard."

Wheeling was an elderly man, a former editor of the *New York Times*, now a columnist on the Op-Ed page. He shook hands warmly, and, before Stone had a chance to speak to him, the other woman in the room approached.

"I'm Edith Bonner," she said, shaking hands with both of them. She was tall, on the heavy side, but quite pretty and elegantly dressed.

"Edith is my date for the evening," Barker explained.

A waiter approached and took their drink orders. Bonner excused herself, and Cary pulled Stone to the window.

"It's quite a view, isn't it?" she said, pointing at the United Nations building.

"I hadn't seen it at night," Stone said.

"Do you know who Edith Bonner is?"

"No, the name doesn't ring a bell."

"She's a sort of society psychic," Cary explained. "She's a wealthy widow who does readings of her friends—strictly amateur—but she has quite a reputation."

The Wheelings joined them at the window and admired the view. "Your leaving the force at this particular time has caused quite a bit of speculation," he said to Stone.

"Well, I was scheduled for the physical some time ago," Stone replied. "It was unfortunate that I was in the middle of an investigation at the time."

"I don't mean to interview you, Mr. Barrington . . ."

"Please call me Stone."

"Thank you, and you must call me Ab; everyone

does. As I was saying, I don't mean to interview, and this is certainly off the record, but do you think this Morgan woman had anything to do with the Nijinsky business?"

Stone nodded toward Bonner, who was returning to the room. "Maybe we should ask Mrs. Bonner," he said. "I expect she has just as good an idea about it as anyone assigned to the case."

Wheeling smiled. "You should have been a diplomat, Stone, or somebody's press secretary. That was as neat an answer as I've ever heard, and I couldn't quote you if I wanted to."

The maid entered the room. "Dinner is served," she said. People finished their drinks and filed into the dining room.

Stone was seated between India Wheeling and Edith Bonner and across from Frank Woodman.

"Stone, what are you going to do with yourself, now that you're a free man?" Woodman asked in the middle of the main course.

"I'm returning to the law," Stone said. "It seems to be the only thing I know anything about." He didn't mention that he would soon be cramming for the bar exam.

"Your career as a detective makes for an interesting background for a certain kind of lawyer," Woodman said. "I believe Bill Eggers may have an idea for you."

"I had a message from him this week," Stone replied.

"When he's back from Los Angeles, I hope you'll listen to what he has to say."

"Surely. At this point, I'm certainly open to suggestions."

Edith Bonner, who had been quiet up until now, spoke up. "Mr. Barrington . . ."

"Stone."

"Stone. Of course I'm aware of what you've been investigating recently. I read the papers like everybody else."

"Why, Edith," Woodman broke in, "I didn't know you had to read the papers; I thought you had a direct line to the central source of all knowledge."

Bonner smiled. "You'll have to excuse Frank; he's a very bright man, but his curiosity extends only to the literal—what he can see and hear and touch."

"That's right, Edith," Woodman said.

"What Frank doesn't understand is that some of us see and hear and touch things that are not quite so literal. Do you see what I mean, Stone?"

"I believe I do, Edith, but I have to tell you that my experience as a police officer has made me not unlike Frank. I tend to put my faith in what I can see and hear, and I don't have your gifts with the less than literal."

"I believe I might be able to tell you something about what happened to Sasha Nijinsky," Bonner said.

All conversation ceased at the table.

"Would this be something material, or would it be more . . . ephemeral?" Stone asked, trying to keep the tone light.

Bonner smiled. "I believe you might think it ephemeral," she said, "but I assure you it is material to me. I would not speak if I didn't feel quite certain about what I want to tell you."

"I'm all ears," Stone said.

"I feel strongly that two persons are responsible for what happened to Sasha Nijinsky," Bonner said.

"Well, since two things happened to Sasha—her fall and her disappearance—it seems quite possible that two people could be involved."

"I was referring to Sasha's fall from her terrace," Bonner said, "and only one of these persons was present when she . . . fell."

"That's very interesting," Stone said. It's not very interesting at all, he thought. So much for ESP.

"I warn you, Stone," Barker said, "Edith does not make such statements lightly. You should take her seriously."

"Unfortunately," Stone replied, "I'm no longer in a position to do so, and I have no reason to believe that anyone assigned to the case would be interested in hearing from me about any theory whatsoever. Edith, if you feel strongly about this, perhaps you should contact Lieutenant Leary, who is commander of detectives at the 19th Precinct."

Bonner shook her head. "No," she said, "he wouldn't listen to me. I've done what I can, now; I'll have no more to say on the subject." She returned to her dinner and her silence.

Soon the party moved back to the living room for coffee and brandy. Stone chatted at some length with Frank Woodman and found that he liked the man.

Later, when people made a move to leave, Bonner appeared at Stone's elbow. "There's something I didn't want to mention at the table," she said.

"Yes?"

"Sasha Nijinsky is not finished with you."

"Well, I'm afraid the NYPD has finished with me."

"But not Sasha. There's a connection between the two of you that you don't seem to know about."

"A connection?"

"A . . . well, a spiritual connection."

"But I never knew her."

"Do you think it was a coincidence that you were there when she fell from that balcony?"

"It couldn't be anything else."

"It was no coincidence. You and Sasha are bound together, and you won't be released until she is found and you know what happened to her."

"Edith, I'm going to do everything I can to put Sasha out of my mind permanently."

Bonner smiled. "I'm afraid you won't be able to do that." Then her expression turned serious. "There's something else," she said.

"What's that?"

"I feel that you are, or will be, in some sort of jeopardy, resulting from your connection with Sasha."

"Jeopardy? How?"

"I don't know. I only know that you are at risk, and, if you are not very careful indeed, this thing with Sasha could destroy you."

"Some would say it already has," Stone said. "At least with regard to my career as a police officer." He was near to confiding in her, now, and it surprised him.

"I mean destroy you entirely—mortally. In fact, I have the very strong feeling that your chances of surviving this crisis are poor—certainly, you will not come through without help, and you may not get it."

Stone pushed away the chill that threatened to run through him. "Edith," he managed to say, "I appreciate your concern for me, but please don't worry too much. It's my intention to stay just as far away as I can from the Nijinsky case or anything to do with it."

"You won't be able to do that," Bonner said. She looked away from him. "I'm sorry."

30

Stone was awakened in the best possible way. "You're going to kill me," he said.

"Mmmmmmm," she replied, concentrating her efforts. "It's only fair; you nearly killed me last night."

"I couldn't think of anything else to do," he gasped.

Sunlight streamed into the room, and his blurring vision made the sparsely furnished chamber seem somehow heavenly. A moment later, everything came into sharp focus, and he closed his eyes and yelled.

"You're noisy," she said.

"It's your fault. You made me."

"I want some breakfast."

"You just had breakfast, and I'm not sure I can walk."

She got up and went into the bathroom. Stone heard the water running, and he had nearly dozed off when she came back. She crawled into bed, and, suddenly, there was something icy on his belly.

He yelled again and leapt out of bed. "Jesus Christ, was that your hands?"

"New York City tap water gets very cold in the wintertime," she said. "As long as you're up, could I have an English muffin, marmalade, orange juice, and coffee?"

"I suppose if I get back into bed you'll just attack me with the iceberg hands again."

"Right. But they'll warm up while you're fixing breakfast."

Defeated, Stone got into a bathrobe and went downstairs to the kitchen. He stuck the muffins into the toaster oven, got coffee started, and went to the front door. He peeked up and down the street, then tiptoed out onto the frosty stoop and retrieved the Sunday *Times*. He was back inside before he registered all that he had taken in. He cracked the door again and looked up the block. A plain green, four-door sedan was parked on the other side of the street, and two men inside it were sipping coffee from paper cups. He didn't know them, but he knew who they were.

He went back to the kitchen, got the breakfast together, loaded it onto a cart, and wheeled it into the old elevator, which made the usual creaking noises on the way up.

Cary was asleep, sprawled across the bed, the sunlight streaming across her naked body. He stopped and looked at her for a moment, that length of delicious woman, the flat belly, the swelling breasts with their small, red nipples, the dark hair strewn across the pillow. Slowly, quietly, he sneaked onto the bed and carefully set a glass of chilled orange juice onto a nipple.

"Ooooo," she said without moving. "What a nice way to wake up. Could I have something on the other one, please?"

"You're unsurprisable," he said, setting the orange juice on her belly and returning for the rest of the breakfast. He put the tray on the bed between them while she struggled into a sitting position and fluffed up the pillows.

"I like the sun in the morning," she said. "It's better than blankets."

He drank his juice and reached for the *Times*.

"I get the front page," she said, snatching it away.

He settled for the book review and munched on a muffin.

"Oh, shit," she said suddenly.

"What is it?"

She clutched the front page to her breast. "You aren't at fault here," she said. "You have to get that through your head. This is not your fault."

"What the hell are you talking about?" He tugged at the newspaper, and she gave it up reluctantly.

SUSPECT·IN NIJINSKY CASE IS APPARENT SUICIDE

Henrietta Morgan, a makeup artist for the Continental Network who police sources say was implicated in the fall of television anchorwoman Sasha

Nijinsky from the terrace of her East Side pent-house apartment, last night apparently took her own life in her Greenwich Village apartment.

Ms. Morgan, who was known as "Hank" and who was active in gay and lesbian rights issues in the city, had been questioned about Ms. Nijinsky's fall, then last week was arrested and charged with possession of an unlicensed pistol. She had been released on bail, but sources in the New York Police Department had told the press that Morgan was the chief suspect in the Nijinsky case.

In a late-night statement from City Hall, Deputy Police Commissioner Lawrence Waldron announced that the death of Ms. Morgan had effectively closed the investigation into Ms. Nijinsky's fall. Waldron said that Ms. Nijinsky's disappearance after an ambulance collided with a fire truck while on her way to a hospital was still being investigated by the F.B.I., who are treating her incident as a kidnapping, which is a federal crime.

Stone felt ill. He rubbed his face briskly with his hands and tried to fight back the nausea.

"It's not your fault," Cary said again, rubbing the back of his neck.

He got out of bed, went into the bathroom, and splashed cold water onto his face. Then he thought about the unmarked car downstairs. He went back into the bedroom and got back into his robe. "I'll be right back," he said.

He trotted downstairs to the main hall, retrieved a flashlight from the utility closet, and unlocked the basement door. It took him a minute or so to find the main telephone junction box, and only seconds to find the wires leading from it to a small FM transmitter a few feet away. Angrily, Stone ripped out the wires, then smashed the transmitter with the heavy flashlight. He walked back up to the main floor, then took the elevator upstairs.

"What's the flashlight for?" Cary asked. "It's broad daylight."

"I needed it to find the phone tap," Stone said.

"Somebody's tapped your phone?"

"New York's Finest," Stone said. "Two of them are sitting out in the street in an unmarked car, waiting either to follow me wherever I go or to record my telephone conversations."

"Why?"

"Because they think that when I hear about Hank Morgan's death, I might start talking to the press."

"Stone, I'm confused. If you want me to understand what you're talking about, then you'd better fill me in."

Stone took a deep breath. "This is not something you can discuss with anybody at work."

"Of course not," she said indignantly.

He went back to his and Dino's initial questioning of Hank Morgan and told her everything that had happened since.

"I see," she said when he had finished. "So you think Hank had nothing to do with Sasha's fall."

"Nothing whatever."

"But the NYPD and the DA's office were going to try and railroad her for it?"

"Not exactly; they knew they would never get

a conviction. They just needed a strong suspect to take the heat off the department. Somebody's been telling a reporter or two that Morgan really did it, but they didn't have enough evidence against her for a conviction."

"So everybody would think Hank did it, even though they couldn't prove it?"

"Right. Except it worked out even better than they had planned. They didn't know that she wouldn't be strong enough to handle the suspicion and the publicity; they couldn't predict that she would finally break and kill herself."

"So what happens now?"

"Nothing."

"Nothing?"

"The investigation into Sasha's fall is over. Hank's suicide was as good as a confession."

"But they still don't know what happened to her, do they?"

"No, but the FBI very kindly stepped in and took responsibility for that part of the investigation, so the department is out of it."

"Are you going to do anything about it?"

"What can I do?"

"Go to the press. I can arrange for you to talk with one of our investigative reporters."

"It wouldn't work. There's just enough substance to the evidence against Morgan to justify the department's actions. I mean, I can't prove that she *didn't* do it." He picked up the bedside phone and dialed a number.

"Hello?" Dino said. He had obviously been asleep.

"Dino, it's Stone; I want you to give Leary a message for me."

"What?" He was waking up now.

"Tell him I found the phone tap, and it's now in several pieces, so there's no need to come back for it."

"Stone, what are you talking—"

"Also tell him"—Stone glanced at the bedside clock—"that it's nine forty-five now, and at ten o'clock I'm going to go downstairs and look up and down the street. If the police car is still sitting out there—or if I ever see any cops taking an interest in me again at any time—I'm going to take a full-page ad in the *New York Times* and publish my complete memoirs. Did you get that?"

"Yeah, but—"

Stone hung up the phone and put his face in his hands.

Cary sat up and began massaging his shoulders. "Just take it easy now; you told them off, and that's it. They won't bother you again, and none of this is your fault."

"You don't understand," Stone said.

"Understand what? It's not your fault."

Stone could not look at her, but he told her what he had been telling himself over and over again. "I would have gone along with it," he said. "If they had let me stay on the force, I would have stood by and let them pillory Hank Morgan. I would have done anything to keep my job."

Cary put her cheek against his back. "Oh, baby," she said. "Oh, my poor, sweet baby."

31

Stone filed into the huge room with at least three hundred other aspirants to the bar of New York State, burdened like the rest with course materials, his bank account lighter by the substantial tuition. For eight hours, with a one-hour break for lunch, the instructor drilled the class, and Stone found the lectures to be well organized, to the point, with the fat trimmed away. The volume of material was daunting; when the day ended, he felt as if he'd been beaten up.

Back at home, he called Cary. "I'm near death," he said, "but my incipient corpse is yours for the evening, if you want it."

"I'd love to have it, but I'm stuck again," she replied. "Friday night's ratings were terrific, for a documentary, and we're brainstorming after hours all week to come up with ideas for six more specials."

"Shit."

"I know, but you should be concentrating on passing the bar instead of lusting after me. You can lust after me on Saturday, though. Around here, not even Barron Harkness works on a Saturday."

"You're on. I wish I didn't have to wait so long."

"The law is a jealous mistress, remember?"

"Thank you, Madame Justice Hilliard."

"Until Saturday."

"You'd better get ready for this," he said. "On Saturday, I'm going to tell you I love you." He could hear the smile in her reply.

"It's beginning to sound like a perfect weekend."

Stone hung up, then checked the messages on his machine.

"It's Dino, Stone. I didn't know anything about that stuff that was going on. It was Leary's doing, maybe at the suggestion of somebody upstairs. I just wanted you to know that. Take care of yourself."

"Stone, this is Bill Eggers. I'm stuck in LA for at least another ten days—unforeseen circumstances, I believe the term is. It means all hell has broken loose on my case, and I'm going to be putting out fires until pretty near the end of next week, so we'll have to postpone dinner. You impressed Woodman at dinner the other night, and he isn't easily impressed. I'll call you in a couple of weeks."

"This is Abbott Wheeling, Stone. I enjoyed our conversation at dinner the other night. It occurred to me that, in light of subsequent events, you might be willing to talk about the Nijinsky case for publication. Should you feel that way, either now or at any time in the future, I'd be grateful if you'd call me at the *Times*. I can promise you that your views on the case will get the sort of serious public attention that only this newspaper can command. I won't pester you about this, but please be assured of my continuing interest."

Stone endured a moment's temptation to call Wheeling and tell him everything, but the moment passed, and he returned to putting as much emotional distance as possible between himself and the Nijinsky case and the suicide of Hank Morgan.

He made himself some supper and resumed his varnishing of the bookshelves, trying to let his mind run over the day's lecture. He was surprised at the familiarity of the material after so many years, and he was encouraged to think he might pass the bar exam after all.

On Saturday night Elaine gave Stone and Cary a table next to the piano. Stone liked piano music, and he was particularly enjoying the way Lauren was playing Rodgers and Hart. When they had finished dinner, Elaine joined them.

"Remember that guy, Doc? At the bar awhile back? The diagnostician?"

"Yeah. In fact, I saw a lot of him during the Nijinsky thing."

"We had a weird thing in here with him last night. He was playing doctor with some little girl at the bar, and they left together, and, a minute later, she's back in here, nearly hysterical. She said Doc had tried to muscle her into a van, and she was scared to death."

"Did you call the precinct?"

"Nah, it didn't seem as serious as that. I gave her a brandy and calmed her down; she didn't want to take it any farther. I'm going to throw the bum out the next time he walks in here, though."

"He wrote Sasha Nijinsky a thousand or so letters over the past couple of years."

"No kidding?"

"It didn't get in the papers, but we had a look at his place and where he works. He's an embalmer for a funeral parlor, you know."

"He's not a doctor?"

"Nope. He did graduate from medical school, but the was never licensed. I thought the guy was harmless, but when he starts trying to drag girls into vans, well . . ."

"He's never setting foot in here again," Elaine said emphatically.

In bed, Cary seemed tired and distracted, and their love-making was brief and perfunctory, something that had never happened before. The extra work seemed to be getting her down, and, God knew, Stone was tired himself. Eight hours a day of class and another four of varnishing was wearing him down.

On Sunday morning, Cary ate her breakfast listlessly. "Are you as zonked as I am?" she asked.

"Yeah. It's okay; we're both under the gun at the moment."

"Thanks for understanding. I've been looking

forward to seeing you all week, and now I'm a wreck."

"It's okay, really it is."

"If you don't mind, I think I'll go home and try to get some sleep this afternoon."

He did his best to hide his disappointment. "Next Saturday?"

"Absolutely."

The next Saturday was much the same.

Another letter came from the bank, this time a flat-out demand. Stone, his back against the wall now, called a real estate agent.

"I think it's wonderful what you're aiming at for the place," she said, "but I guess you know what the New York residential property market is like right now. In good times, with the place finished and ready to move into, we might get three, three and a half million for this house. Right now, for an immediate sale, we might be lucky to get three hundred thousand."

Stone was shocked. "Is the market that bad?"

"It is. Listen, you're lucky; at least you'd get something out of a sale. I've got clients with perfectly beautiful town houses who are being forced to sell for far less than they paid, and they're having to pay off the rest of the mortgage out of savings."

Bright and early on a Monday morning, Stone presented himself to be examined for admission to the bar of New York State, along with about fifteen hundred others. Like everyone else, he labored over the questions. There were occasional gaps in his knowledge, but, on the whole, he thought he did well; certainly, he aced the questions on criminal law. Now there was only the waiting.

He got home feeling enormously relieved. He had finished his study for the bar and the varnishing of the library at the same time. Now, if Cary could just get a break in her work schedule, maybe they could . . .

The phone rang.

"Hello?"

"Hi, it's Bill Eggers."

"Hi, Bill."

"How'd you do today?"

"How'd you know?"

"I have spies everywhere."

"Well, I did okay on criminal law, at least."

"Good. How about dinner tomorrow night?"

"Fine."

"The Four Seasons, at eight thirty?"

"Sounds good."

"Don't bring anybody. It's just you and me."

"If you promise not to put your hand on my knee."

"Don't worry, you're not cute enough. By the way, I might have some news for you."

"What sort of news?"

"Let's wait and see."

32

The Four Seasons was busy, as always. The hum of voices from the Pool Room echoed enjoyment of the surroundings and the food, but Bill Eggers had a table in the Grill, next to the bar.

"It's quieter here," Eggers said. "It's crazy at lunch, but at dinner everybody wants to be in the Pool Room. Here, we can talk."

Stone wondered exactly what they would be talking about. This felt something like a job interview, but he couldn't see Woodman & Weld hiring a thirty-eight-year-old novice as an associate.

They had a drink and dawdled over the menu. Eggers seemed in an expansive mood, relieved over the resolution of his Los Angeles case. "It was a bastard," he said. "A bicoastal divorce case of one of our biggest clients. He was claiming New York residence, and she claimed they lived in California—she wanted community property."

"Who won?"

"I did. The LA office is mostly into entertainment work, so I did the dog work while they fronted for me in court. Don't worry about the lady; she's doing very well out of this, but she's not getting the thirty million that community property division would have given her. She's pissed off now, but she'll get used to living on the income from six million."

"You do a lot of divorce work?"

"I'm sort of the firm general practitioner. I have a lot of clients whose personal legal work I handle, and that often leads to divorce work. It's nasty sometimes, but, if you can keep a certain detachment, you can live with it."

"Must be lucrative."

"Not all that much. We only do divorce work for the firm's existing clients, and we don't charge them the earth. In the case of the men, when they see what the wife's lawyer is demanding, they're grateful to us for not taking them to the cleaners; in the case of the women, they're grateful to us for not demanding high fees. That builds client loyalty."

"I should think so."

They ordered their food, and Eggers chose what Stone thought must be the most expensive bottle of wine on a very expensive list. If Stone had been interested before in what Bill Eggers had to say, now he was *really* interested.

Eggers tasted the wine and nodded to the sommelier. When the man had gone, he turned to Stone. "What do you know about Woodman & Weld?"

"Not very much," Stone admitted. "I get the

impression that it's a prestigious firm, from what I read in the papers, but I'm not very clear on why it might be so."

"Good. That's pretty much the impression we like to convey. We see that the people who might need us know a lot more, but we keep a fairly low public profile."

Stone sipped the wine; he thought he had never tasted anything so good. "It's a lovely burgundy," he said to Eggers. "Thank you."

Eggers nodded, pleased that his largess had been noted. "Let me give you the scoop on us. We've got eighteen partners at the moment, and thirty-six associates. That's certainly not big by Manhattan standards, but it's big enough for us to be able to cover a lot of bases. There are seven corporate specialists—we tend to attract companies somewhat below the Fortune Five Hundred level, outfits that don't have huge legal departments; we have four estate planners—that's very important to wealthy individuals—and, just as important, four tax specialists, all Jewish. Nobody seems to take a tax lawyer seriously who isn't Jewish. We're something of a polyglot firm— blacks, women, Irish, Jews, Italians—not unlike the New York Police Department, I expect. That's important to us, because the firm is active in liberal Democratic causes—you'd be surprised how much business comes in that way. Finally, there are three generalists—two of them Woodman and me."

"I liked Woodman when I met him."

"Woodman is a genius, as far as I'm concerned.

He's a client man, first and last; he inspires trust. Also, he has a facility for going into a meeting—corporate, tax, whatever—and immediately grasping the issues involved. Clients think he knows *everything*, which isn't exactly true, but he can give that impression effortlessly. I'd be willing to bet that he could engage you in conversation about a homicide investigation and make you think he was an ex-cop."

Their first course arrived, and they dug in.

"You didn't mention any criminal lawyers," Stone said between bites.

"We don't have a criminal lawyer as such, although you'd be surprised at how much criminal work comes our way. Nowadays, it's the corporate executive or stockbroker who's stepped over the line; also, our clients' kids get into trouble—drugs, rape, sometimes even murder."

"How do you handle that?"

"In different ways. If it's something big, we refer to a hotshot mouthpiece; more often, we bring in a consultant and handle it internally. A client likes it when his own lawyer seems to be in charge. Of course, there's a fine line there; we have to make the judgment on when an outsider best serves the client's needs. We can't afford to make a mistake and underrepresent a client. We're very, very careful in the matter of malpractice, and we've never had a suit against us."

"That seems a good area to be careful in."

"In short, Stone, we're a class act. Every single partner is as good as any lawyer in town at what he does and better than ninety-nine percent of the field. We're low profile, highly ethical, and extremely profitable. I will tell you, in confidence, that no partner in our firm is taking home less than half a million a year, and that's the low end. I made a million two last year, and it wasn't my best year."

Stone sucked in a breath at the thought of so much money and what he could do with it.

"Now that I've stunned you," Eggers said, noting Stone's expression, "let me tell you why we're interested in you."

Somehow, Stone didn't think that he was here to be offered a partnership and half a million dollars a year.

"As I've said, we're taking on more and more criminal and domestic work, without even trying. We've handled some ourselves, farmed out some, and brought in consultants on others, but we're still spread thin. Sometimes we need investigative work done, and we're troubled by the quality of the people available to do that sort of thing. There are some high-class people around, but they charge more than a good lawyer gets; generally, what we see in the investigative area is sleaze—the worst sort of ex-cop, the ones who got the boot."

"You might say I got the boot," Stone said.

"But for all the right reasons," Eggers replied. "We have a pretty good idea of why you were pensioned off." He took a deep breath. "Another thing about investigators, they have a tendency to look wrong for some of the work we give them. They dress badly, drink too much, and sprinkle a lot of 'dems, deezes, and dozes' around their conversation. You, on the other hand, look right and sound right."

Stone shrugged. Eggers was looking for a private detective, and the thought didn't interest him much.

Eggers must have read his mind. "Don't get me wrong, we're not looking for somebody to just kick down bedroom doors, although I wouldn't rule that out. What's interesting about you is a combination of things: you understand how the police department and the DA's office work; you have a fine grasp of criminal justice procedure; you are a highly experienced investigator; and, unusually with all that, you have the background, education, demeanor, and the language skills that will let you fit easily into any upper-level social situation. In short, a client would be perfectly comfortable explaining his problem to you."

"What exactly do you have in mind, Bill?"

"You could be very useful to us; let me give you some typical examples. One: a client's son and heir, who has a three-hundred-dollar-a-week allowance, is, inexplicably, caught selling an ounce of cocaine on his college campus. We need somebody who can show up at the station house, talk to the cop in charge, deal with the DA, and get the charges dropped or reduced to a misdemeanor that the kid can plead to as a youthful offender and that will, in time, be expunged from his record. Two: the kid does something really bad—rapes his date, batters, maybe even murders her. We'll need our own investigation into the events, and we'll need to know how the cops and the DA are thinking. A third: A client suspects his wife of having an affair; we need to know for sure, before we can proceed for him. That's not the whole range of problems that might arise, but it's a good sampling."

"I see." This sounded better than hanging around the criminal courts, picking up burglary and drunk-driving cases.

"Let me lay it out for you. We don't want you to join the firm, as such. Not yet, anyway. What we'd like you to do is set up your own practice, a professional corporation, which would be associated with us."

"You realize I haven't even passed the bar yet."

"Oh, I forgot; that was my news. You passed."

"Now how the hell could you know that? I only took the exam yesterday."

"Friend of a friend had access. He pulled your papers, looked them over, and he reckons you'll finish in the top third, and, since the New York State bar is the toughest in the country, that's damn good. It's not official, of course, but you've got nothing to worry about."

"Bill, this friend of a friend didn't . . . improve my score, did he?"

Eggers looked shocked. "Absolutely not. There's been no tampering here, you don't need to worry about that. I told you, we're an ethical firm. Information was all we were after, and that's all we got; no law was broken; we don't do that."

"Well, in that case, thanks. It's a load off my mind."

"Anyway, as I was saying, we want you to be at our disposal. Of course, you can't actually practice law until your admittance to the bar is official, but you can advise and investigate. In a trial, you can sit at the defense table and whisper into our man's ear. Then, when you're admitted, you can accept cases of your own. We just want priority."

"On what basis?"

"When we hire a freshly admitted associate, the current starting salary is fifty-five thousand. We propose to offer you a retainer of seventy-five thousand dollars annually, against an hourly rate of a hundred and twenty-five dollars."

"What's your hourly rate, Bill?"

"Two fifty to three fifty, depending, but I've been with the firm for twelve years and a partner for eight. Don't misunderstand me, Stone, it's not our intention to keep you at arm's length forever. We're feeling our way, here, with a new kind of association for us. If this works out the way I hope it will, then you would eventually join the firm, and, sometime in the future, a partnership might come into the picture."

"Would you care to be a little more specific about 'eventually' and 'sometime in the future'?"

"No. I can't be. This is simply too new a situation for us. But I'll tell you what I tell our new associates: there are no guarantees, but if you work your ass off for the firm, if you show you can bring in business of your own, and if you can make our clients trust you, then a partnership is almost inevitable. That's what they told me when

I joined, and it was true. Of course, under the terms we're offering you, any new business you bring in will be yours entirely. Then, if and when you join us, you bring your clients with you."

Stone leaned back in his chair and smiled. "Bill, I accept. I'm delighted to accept. And, I'll tell you the truth, this could not have come along at a better time."

Eggers leaned forward. "A cash pinch?"

Stone told him about the situation with the house and his bankers.

Eggers took out a pad and made some notes. "You're being badly treated, and I think we can correct that. May I represent you in this matter?"

"Of course."

"Good. I'll get you an advance against your first quarter's retainer, too."

"Thank you, Bill; that would certainly take the pressure off."

Eggers stuck out a hand. "Welcome aboard."

Stone shook it. "When do I start to work?"

"Tomorrow. We've got a couple of things in-house you can look at and advise on. And I think I'll have an investigative job for you soon."

Stone walked home, not even noticing the light rain. He was employed. He wouldn't have to sell the house. The thought of marriage—suppressed because of his financial condition—broke through into his frontal lobe. He flashed ahead five years: he was a partner at Woodman & Weld; the house was beautiful, and it was his; he and Cary were throwing elegant dinner parties in his elegant dining room; maybe there was a child. Maybe two. Things were suddenly falling into place.

A miracle had occurred. He didn't pause to wonder what it might cost him.

33

When Stone got home, Dino was standing on the front stoop, back against the door, trying to stay out of the rain.

"Hi, Dino," Stone said.

"Hi. Can I buy you a drink?"

"Come on in, let me buy you one."

"Nah, I hate the smell of paint and sawdust. Let's go someplace."

"All right."

They walked silently up Third Avenue to P. J. Clarke's and leaned on the corner of the bar.

"The usual?"

"Fine."

"A Wild Turkey and a Stoly, both rocks," Dino said to the barman. "Make 'em doubles."

They both looked idly around until the drinks came.

Dino held up his glass. "Better days."

Stone nodded and drank.

Dino gulped a quarter of the vodka. "I feel bad about what happened," he said.

"It's okay, Dino. Maybe it was all for the best." He told Dino about his dinner with Bill Eggers.

"That's great, Stone, and I'm happy for you, but it's still not okay with me. You were my partner, and I should have at least warned you what was coming. I didn't know myself until that morning."

"You were my partner, too, and I didn't back you up," Stone said.

"Yeah, but you were right, that's the difference. I was wrong, and because of what I did Morgan croaked herself."

Stone said nothing.

"I took the call," Dino said, blinking.

Stone still said nothing.

"She was in the bathtub, and it looked like the tub was full of blood."

"Jesus," Stone allowed himself.

"She had a straight razor. God knows what she was doing with it, even if she was a dyke. You think she was keeping it in case she grew a beard?"

Stone shrugged.

"She stuck it in right under her left ear and pulled it all the way around, deep."

Stone winced.

"She had guts, I'll say that for her. I couldn't never do that, not in a million years. Pills, maybe. Maybe eat your gun, but you don't die right away when you cut your own throat. It must hurt like all hell, and you got time to think about what you done before you go under." Dino shifted his weight and took another deep pull from his glass. "She left a note."

"The papers didn't say anything about that," Stone said, surprised.

Dino took a folded piece of paper from his pocket and handed it to Stone.

Stone read it.

> I have never harmed another human being in my life. I did not harm Sasha Nijinsky. I loved her, and she loved me, and I would never have done anything to hurt her.
>
> I want my friends to know that this is not a suicide. This is murder, and the police are the murderers.

"You can see why you didn't read about it in the papers," Dino said, taking the note back. He took a pack of matches from an ashtray on the bar, lit the note, watched it burn. "You know something? I went to confession. I didn't go to confession since I was fourteen, but I went yesterday. As part of my penance, I had to tell you this stuff. I didn't do the rest of the penance; I'm not going to. But I wanted to do this part."

"Thanks, Dino, I know what it cost you."

"Don't be so fucking nice about it, Stone. I wouldn't have said a word to you, but I know you won't say nothing to nobody about this."

Stone nodded.

"I always been good at looking out for my own ass," Dino said. "Sometimes I fall in the shit, but I come up smelling like a rose, you know?"

Stone laughed. "I know."

"Nah, you don't know. I made detective first grade today. Ain't that a kick in the balls? I get a promotion I would have killed for—" He stopped and laughed ironically. "Shit, I guess I did kill for it, didn't I?"

"Congratulations, Dino." Stone raised his glass.

Dino drank with him. "They made me deputy squad commander, too. Leary's retiring the end of the year, and I'm getting the job, Delgado says."

"That's great, Dino," Stone said, but it was a statement of sympathy.

"Yeah, get me off the street some, I guess. Teach me a sense of responsibility."

"You'll be good at it. Look out for the politics, though."

"What politics? I'm not going anywhere after that. I'm never going to be chief of detectives—they know it, and I know it. Shit, I never expected to make detective first, to tell the truth. Nah, there's no politics to worry about. I'm bought and paid for. I'll do what I'm told and like it."

Stone couldn't think of anything to say.

"Sounds like I'm feeling sorry for myself, don't it? Well, I am, I guess. I found out how far I'd go to cover my ass, and I feel terrible about it." He tossed down the rest of his drink and squared his shoulders. "I'll get over it, though. In a week or two, or when I get Leary's little cubicle, I'll look around and say to myself, 'Hey, this ain't half bad, you know? These fuckers have to do what I tell 'em now! I'm the fucking boss!' And I'll start to feel okay about it. And come spring, I'll forget

all about Hank Morgan and how she took a bath
in her own blood. I'm good at that—forgetting
what a shit I was about something. I'll forget that
I wasn't the world's greatest detective, too, that I
was lazy and shiftless a lot of the time, that I
didn't give much of a shit about my job. I'll forget
all that, and when the next batch of detective
thirds cruises into the precinct, I'll give 'em the
pep talk, tell 'em how it was when I was scratch-
ing for promotion, how hard I worked on a case,
how many righteous busts I had. I'll be a hard
ass, just like Leary—shit, worse than Leary."

"Sure, you will."

Dino picked up the heavy doubles glass and
heaved it across the bar. The mirror on the other
side shattered, and chunks of glass fell among the
liquor bottles, breaking some of them.

The dozen people standing at the bar and the
two bartenders froze, staring at Dino.

Finally, a bartender, a red-haired, freckle-faced
Irishman who looked right off the boat, spoke up.
"The last one o' dose got broke cost eight hundred bucks, Dino," he said sadly. "And that was
six, seven years ago. They prob'ly went up." He
looked at the mess, shaking his head. "And dere's
the booze, too."

Dino put a fifty-dollar bill on the bar. "That's
for our drinks, Danny," he said calmly, "and the
change is for your trouble. Send me a bill for the
rest."

The bartender nodded and began picking up
glass. The customers went back to their drinking
as if nothing had happened.

Outside, the rain had stopped, and the night had turned clear and frosty. Dino hailed a cab. "Stone," he said, while the cab waited, "I owe you. I'm always gonna owe you. You call me any time you need something. Anytime."

Stone nodded. They shook hands. Dino got into the cab and drove off into the night. Stone walked home thinking that both he and Dino had done all right out of Sasha Nijinsky's trouble.

The only loser had been Hank Morgan.

34

Stone sat in Frank Woodman's large office and sipped strong coffee.

"Stone, I'm very pleased that you're going to be . . . associated with us," Woodman was saying. "I think that, with your help, we can take what has been a nongainful irritant and turn it into a profit center for the firm. That's with you fully on board, of course, after our initial feeling-out period."

"Frank, I should tell you that, for the long term, I'm really more interested in a general practice than solely criminal work, and I'd appreciate it if, after I'm admitted to the bar, you'd consider putting me on an occasional noncriminal case."

"I understand your feelings, and I'll keep that in mind."

Warren Weld, the other name on the door, spoke up. "Are you interested in corporate work, Stone?"

"Not really, Warren. I think I'd prefer to represent individuals."

"That puts you right back in Frank's bailiwick, then." Weld stood up. "If you'll excuse me, gentlemen, I've got a meeting. Welcome aboard, Stone."

They shook hands, and Weld left, leaving only Frank Woodman and Bill Eggers in the room with Stone.

"Bill, you take Stone back to your office, will you? I've got a client coming in." Woodman stood and shook Stone's hand. "I think Bill already has a couple of things for you, Stone. He'll brief you."

They returned to Eggers's office and sat down.

"Frank had a word with your banker yesterday—we keep our trust account at your branch, so we have a little pull there. You're off the hook for the principal reduction they were demanding. You'll still have to make the interest payment, though."

"Thank you, Bill, that's good news."

Eggers handed him an envelope. "And here's ten grand against your retainer."

"You're full of good news," Stone said. "Thanks again."

"Not at all." Eggers looked at his watch. "There's somebody I want you to meet, Stone. He's due in here in ten minutes."

"A client?"

"Son of a client. The father is Robert Keene, of Keene, Bailey & Miller advertising."

"I don't know them."

"The three partners left Young & Rubicam fifteen years ago and set up on their own. Now they're a medium-sized agency well known for good creative work. Warren Weld represents the agency, and I represent Bob personally. Bob Keene is as nice a guy as you'd want to meet."

"And the boy?"

"That's why I want you to meet him. I want your opinion. Bobby Junior is a senior at Brown, and there's a date-rape accusation against him by a girl student. She turned him in to the administration, and, when she wasn't happy with the level of support she got, she added his name to a list of alleged date rapists on the ladies' room wall in her dormitory. Bobby denies everything, and he seems credible. No criminal charges have been filed, yet, but if they are, and, if we feel he's innocent, I want to go on the offensive—sue the girl for defamation, sue the university for allowing his name to remain painted on a bathroom wall, really blast them. And we'll call in a top gun to defend him.

"On the other hand, if he's really guilty, I'll insist that he abjectly apologize to the girl and the administration, and try to avoid criminal proceedings and keep him in school. That would certainly be cheaper for his father, but Bob Senior is willing to do what it takes to defend the boy if he's innocent."

"What does the father think about the boy's guilt or innocence?"

"Oddly, he doesn't seem to have an opinion. I think that, what with the work it's taken to build his business, he hasn't spent a hell of a lot of time with the boy, and they've grown apart. We can't solve that problem for them, but I hope we can give Bob Senior good advice on how to proceed."

"I'll be glad to meet the boy."

"As a cop, you must have gained some insight over the years as to whether an accused man is guilty or not—I don't mean reading the evidence, I mean reading the man."

"I think I have. It doesn't always work, of course. I've been fooled before; so has every cop."

"I want you to question the boy, pull out all the stops, see if you can shake his story."

"You want him cross-examined, as if I were representing the girl?"

"I want him questioned, as if he were a suspect."

The phone on Eggers's desk rang. "Yes? Send him in." He hung up and turned to Stone. "Ready?"

"You be the good cop," Stone said.

"Right."

Bobby Keene was a large young man, whose neck was wider than the top of his head. Stone thought there had been a handsome face in that head once, before the boy had discovered weight training.

"Bobby, how are you?" Eggers said, sticking out a hand.

"I'm very well, Mr. Eggers," Bobby said earnestly.

"Bobby, I want you to meet another lawyer who's helping us out with your case. This is Stone Barrington; Stone's had a lot of experience in this sort of thing, and I think he'll be able to help us a lot."

"Gosh, I hope so." Bobby stuck out a ham-sized hand. "How do you do, Mr. Barrington?"

Stone kept a poker face, shook the hand limply, but did not return the greeting. "Sit down," he said, and it was an order.

Bobby sat, looking worried.

"Tell me about it," Stone said, sounding bored.

"Sir?"

Stone turned to Eggers. "Jesus Christ, Bill, is the kid stupid, or what?"

"Bobby," Eggers said gently, "tell Mr. Barrington what happened on the evening you went out with"—he glanced at a pad on his desk—"Janie Byron."

"Oh, of course, sir. I'm sorry, I didn't know what Mr. Barrington meant."

"Just tell me," Stone said.

"Well, there isn't much to tell. We went to a movie—"

"What kind of a movie?"

"An old one; a John Ford western."

"Downtown, shopping mall, drive-in?"

"Oh, a drive-in, right outside town."

"Then what happened?"

"Well, we got some popcorn, we ate it, we watched the movie, we made out a little."

"Define 'made out.' Exactly."

Bobby retained his earnest tone. "We kissed a few times."

"Did you touch her breasts?"

"Well, yeah, she seemed to want that."

"Oh, she said to you, 'Bobby, please, please grab my tits,' is that how it happened?"

"Well, not exactly."

"Just how did she show you that she wanted you to touch her breasts?"

"Well, when I did, she didn't object much."

"But she did object."

"Well, she played hard to get a little, I guess."

"Then what happened?"

"We started to get heated up a little, and I—"

"Go on, boy, be graphic. We're all grown up here."

"Then she said she wanted to leave, she got all huffy and all, and so I took her back to her dorm."

"Immediately?"

"As soon as I was sure she meant it."

"How long did that take?"

"A few minutes, I guess."

"How many minutes? Exactly."

"Five, I guess."

"Did you lie down on the seat of the car?"

"For a minute or two."

"Did you get your hand in her pants?"

"Yes, sir."

"Did you get your finger inside her?"

"Yes, sir, for a minute."

"Did you get her pants off?"

"No, sir. I didn't do that."

"Why not?"

"Sir?"

"Well, it sounds to me like you were doing real well, there, Bobby; you got at her tits, you got your finger in her crotch, why stop?"

"I guess she didn't want to."

"If she didn't want to, how'd you get your hand in her crotch?"

"Well, I—"

Stone leaned across to Eggers's desk and picked up a legal pad. "It says here you forced her to have sex with you."

"That's a lie!"

"It says here, you ripped off her underwear, pinned her down with your weight, and fucked her against her will."

"It wasn't against her will!"

"So you fucked her, didn't you?"

"No, I . . . you're getting me confused."

"It says here that when she got back to her dorm, her roommate took a cotton swab and collected a semen sample from her public hair and saved it on a glass slide. Her roommate is a biology major. That's your misfortune."

Bobby's eyes widened, and his jaw worked, but nothing came out.

"Do you know what a DNA matching is, Bobby?"

"I . . . well, I read something in the paper about it."

"Give me that lab report," Stone said to Eggers.

Eggers promptly found a sheet of paper on his desk and handed it across to Stone.

Stone looked at the paper, an interoffice memo, and shook his head.

"Listen, I can give you the names of three guys who've screwed Janie Byron," Bobby said. His face was red. "I—"

"I see," Stone said. "So the guys at the frat house are going to back you, huh? They're stand-up guys, so they're all going to go into court and perjure themselves for you and risk going to prison."

Bobby put his face in his hands for a moment.

Stone turned to Eggers. "You can't go into court with this guy, Bill. He can't even convince his own lawyers, how the hell is he going to convince a jury?"

"Bobby," Eggers said gently, "you see what we're up against, don't you? I mean, Mr. Barrington is on *your* side, and he can't bring himself to believe you. Now listen, if you'll just tell us the truth, all of the truth, then we may be able to get you out of this."

"He'll never tell you the truth," Stone said harshly. "He's a lying little piece of shit."

Bobby came half off the sofa, but, when Stone stood up, he sank back. "Can I talk to you alone, Mr. Eggers?" he said plaintively.

"Sure you can, kid," Stone said, heading for the door. "I wouldn't waste any more of my time." At the door, he turned back to Eggers. "I'll tell you one thing, I wish I was prosecuting this one, instead of defending." He walked out, slamming the door behind him.

In the hall, Stone leaned against the door and took a deep breath. Jesus, it had been awhile. Dino usually played the bad cop.

35

Bill Eggers leaned back in his chair and rested his feet on his desk. "That was good work, Stone. The boy has told me everything, I think; I don't believe he actually screwed the girl, though God knows he meant to. He's down the hall in an associate's office right now, writing letters to the girl and the university administration. I think I can negotiate him out of this. The girl wasn't entirely blameless, and she does have a reputation for sleeping around."

"I'm glad it worked out," Stone said.

"Well, you saved his father seventy-five or a hundred thousand in legal fees. Bob Keene will always be grateful to us for that."

"Frank said you had something else for me."

"I do, and this one's sticky. Or, at least, it could be."

"Tell me about it."

"I'm going to have to be a little circumspect in talking even to you about this," Eggers said. "There's a lot at stake, and I'm going to have to proceed strictly on a need-to-know basis, all right?"

"All right."

"I have a client I've known since I was in high school, whose wife is a prominent business-woman. They've never had much of a marriage, but there were a couple of kids, and they stuck it out. Trouble is, the wife has had a couple of affairs. In fact, there've been other men all along, I think, but he's finally run out of patience, and, even against my best advice, he's determined to proceed his own way on this."

"What does he want to do?"

"He wants custody of one of the two kids, the boy, and that means he has to nail her with the other guy—photographs, the works. Actually, he wants a videotape of her in bed with him."

"Do you often proceed this way in divorce cases?"

"No, and I've advised him against this, but he's absolutely determined. He wants a quick, clean divorce with no haggling about money, and, I have to admit, if he gets his little video, there won't be any haggling. The wife has too much to lose to allow a Rob Lowe–type tape to be circulated. If her board of directors so much as got wind of such a thing, she'd be finished. Nobody would ever take her seriously again."

"Well, even in an era of no-fault divorce, I suppose there are still certain advantages to having that sort of evidence. What exactly is it you want me to do? Kick down the bedroom door and film them in living color?"

"I definitely do *not* want you to do that. The firm can't afford to have anybody as closely associated with us as you are be directly involved in such a distasteful affair."

"You mean you want me to find someone else who'll do it."

Eggers grinned. "Right. Someone who can be trusted to be discreet, even if he's caught in the act of doing it. Do you know somebody like that?"

Stone did. The man's face popped immediately into his mind. "Possibly," he said. "But this could get expensive. He's going to have to stalk the lady until he can catch her in the act, and that may not be easy."

"I think it's going to be easier than you think," Eggers said, smiling.

"Oh?"

"My client has been very helpful. His wife's company maintains two apartments in a rather elegant building that specializes in company flats—you know the sort of thing—the out-of-town executive stays in the company apartment instead of at the Plaza. It's supposed to save money for the company, but, mostly, it's regarded as just a perk for the upper-level executive. Anyway, my client has been tipped that his wife has been using one of the company apartments on a rather regular basis for her assignations with her male bimbo—a soap-opera actor no less, and he has thoughtfully supplied us with a key to the apartment." He held up a key.

"Your client has been very helpful indeed," Stone agreed.

"As I said, there are two apartments. My client, as a spouse, also has access to them, and what he is prepared to do, next time he thinks his wife is dallying, is to book your man into the other flat for the night. That gets him access to the building." He tossed the key to Stone. "And this gets him access to the other apartment."

"That's very neat," Stone admitted. "Your client is a very cunning fellow."

"I hope I never have the misfortune to be married to somebody as smart," Eggers said. "Can you think of any reason why this wouldn't work?"

Stone laughed. "There are only a few dozen things that could go wrong," he said, "but it'll be up to our man to handle those. Actually, your client has made it look pretty straightforward. When does he want this done?"

"Within the next few days. Next time the lady says she's working late, he'll call, and it's on. Can you find your man in a hurry?"

"I'll make some calls."

"Let me know what he wants for a fee. I'm authorized to go to ten grand." Eggers reached behind his desk and pulled out a fat aluminum briefcase. "My client has even supplied us with some very neat, lightweight video equipment." He began to laugh. "It belongs to the wife."

Stone had to laugh with him.

Teddy O'Bannion was a thick-set, gray-haired man of, maybe, fifty-five, who had been unfortunate enough to be chosen to take the heat for his precinct a few years back, when one of the periodically instituted crime commissions was going about its work of rooting out corruption in the police department. The evidence allowed against him had been slim, and he had simply been dismissed from the force without prejudice, which allowed him to collect a twenty-year pension, in addition to the very nice monthly stipend his old companions on the pad still paid him.

Teddy could easily pass for your typical out-of-town businessman, in the city for meetings. He looked around the house carefully, obviously trying to figure out how Stone could afford it. "Jesus, Stone, the pad must be bigger than ever," he said, wonderingly.

"I inherited it, Teddy, from a great-aunt, and now I have to spend the rest of my life scrambling to keep it."

"Whatever you say, lad."

Stone handed Teddy a stiff scotch. "I've got a night's work for you. There's five grand in it."

"How many children and dogs do I have to murder?"

"It's a straightforward bedroom job, that's all."

Teddy laughed aloud. "Straightforward? Shit, the last bedroom job I did, the woman flew out of the bed and nearly bit my ear off!"

"Those are the risks you take, Teddy."

"That they are, lad. What's the setup?"

Stone explained about the apartment building. "There are only two apartments to a floor; you'll be booked into 9-B. The wife will be across a vestibule in 9-A. You let yourself in—late, I'm advised—find the bedroom, wake the occupants, and take their picture." He opened the aluminum case and showed Teddy how the camera worked. "You switch on the light; the camera is autofocus, so you just point and shoot. Make sure you get good shots of both faces, and show us a little flesh, if you can. The juicier the better."

"I think I understand your needs," Teddy said. "And I've used this camera before. Is there anything else I should know?"

Stone shook his head. "If there's trouble, don't hurt anybody; if you're apprehended, say nothing and call me. My client will cover any costs. If a case against you comes to anything, there'll be another five thousand for you, if you do the right thing."

"Don't worry, I'm not getting myself apprehended, and if I do, I'll take the rap. Nobody'll trace me back to you. Can I get a look at the place ahead of time?"

Stone shook his head. "I don't want the concierge to see you twice. I'll look it over myself."

"That's okay with me."

"Good. When you've done the job, take a cab to P. J. Clarke's and have a drink at the bar. Make sure nobody's after you. I'll be there, and, when I'm sure you're clear. I'll leave an envelope above the urinal in the men's room with the five grand in it. You go in immediately after me, leave the camera case, take the money, and go home. That's it."

Teddy nodded. "Sounds fine."

"I don't want you recognized, Teddy. What can you do about that?"

Teddy put on his hat, took a pair of heavy, black-rimmed glasses from his coat pocket, put them on, then produced a fat cigar and stuck it in his mouth, distorting his face.

Stone laughed. "Good. Simple and good. Oh, and wear your best suit. You want to look prosperous."

Teddy nodded. "When is it?"

"Probably this week. Stay loose, and I'll give you as much notice as I can. You can pick up the camera stuff here, on your way." Stone gave him a hundred-dollar bill. "Here's cab fare."

Teddy shook his hand at the door. "Thanks, Stone. I'll do it right for you."

Stone hadn't the slightest doubt he would.

36

"Your name is Willoughby," Eggers said. "Just check in with the concierge, and he'll give you the key to 9-B. I gave you the key to 9-A, but be careful, there may be somebody in residence."

"Okay," Stone replied.

"I take it you found your man."

"I did. He's waiting for my call."

"Looks like Friday night."

Stone breathed a sigh of relief. He hadn't wanted this to interfere with his Saturday night with Cary. "All right. When will we know for sure?"

"Maybe not until that day. You sure you have to go to the building yourself?"

"Yes. I don't want my man seen there more than once, and, anyway, I'm in no way at risk today."

"Okay, it's your call."

The building was a small postwar apartment building in the East Sixties that had been refurbished for its current purpose. An elderly man in a blue suit was behind the desk.

"Good afternoon," Stone said. "My name is Willoughby; I believe I'm expected."

The man consulted a list. "Yes, Mr. Willoughby, you're in 9-B. You just need it for the afternoon, I believe?"

"Not even that. I just needed a place to do a little work, and they were kind enough to offer me the apartment."

The man produced a key. "To your right as you leave the elevator. Do you have any luggage?"

"Just my briefcase," Stone said, holding it up. "Is there anybody using the apartment next door? I may have to do some shouting on the telephone." He smiled.

"Shout all you like," the man said. "9-A is empty at the moment."

Stone thanked the man and went to the elevator. When he got off, he put an ear to the door of 9-A and listened for a long moment. No sound. He let himself into 9-B and looked around. The place was handsomely, if impersonally furnished, with good upholstered pieces and one or two antiques. There were two bedrooms, a master and a smaller one, and two baths. After a quick look around, he went next door and let himself into 9-A.

The apartment seemed to be a mirror image of the other, but there was a difference. 9-A had been lavishly done to someone's particular taste, and probably by a very expensive designer. The furnishings were richer and more distinctive than those in 9-B, and the art on the walls was probably a part of the company's collection of expensive paintings. He checked both bedrooms and decided that the master was where the assignation would take place. There was a gorgeous, canopied bed, with a matching silk bedcover, and every stick of furniture in the room dated from the eighteenth century, Stone reckoned. He was about to reenter the living room when he heard the front door open and close.

Oh, shit, he thought, trying to think of some plausible reason why he should be in the apartment. There was a rustling of what sounded like paper bags, followed by a feminine cough. He looked around the bedroom for someplace to hide, should the woman come his way. Her footsteps on the carpet told him she was doing just that.

He ran on tiptoe across the room and practically dove behind the bed. She came into the bedroom, then he heard the hollow click of the bathroom light being turned on. Please close the door, he said to himself, be modest. She did not. He peeped above the edge of the bed and saw it standing wide open and her shadow against the door. There was the sound of water running, then the toilet seat being raised. The water continued to run while she peed. Sitting on the toilet, she would be facing the bathroom door, he knew, so he could not make a run for it. He arranged himself more comfortably and waited.

The woman came out of the bathroom, and he could hear her footsteps approaching the bed. Stone pressed himself closer to it. He heard the rustle of the silk bedcover being turned down and the creak of the springs as the woman lay down.

Stone lay motionless for the better part of a half hour, while the woman tossed and turned, then finally settled down for her nap. When her breathing told him she was sound asleep, he stirred from his position as silently as possible, wincing at the cramps that had formed in his legs. He slipped off his shoes and started for the bedroom door. As he approached the door he glanced back at her, just as she stirred, her back to him. He froze until he was certain she had not actually awakened. Then he made his way across the deep Oriental carpet in the living room to the front door, where he spent several seconds turning the knob as silently as possible. As he closed the door, he saw two large shopping bags from Bergdorf Goodman lying next to a living-room chair.

A moment later, he was back in 9-B, running cold water over his face in the master bathroom. He had done some undercover work in his time, but nothing in his police career had ever prepared him for being a second-story man. Now he knew that burglars are just as frightened as their victims.

He let himself out of the flat and left the building before the lady next door finished her nap.

At home, there was only one message on his answering machine: "Hi, it's me. I'm sorry you aren't in; I wanted to hear your voice. And now I have to go to a production meeting, so you can't even call me back. I'm so looking forward to Saturday; I want to hear this important news of yours—and it must be important, if you want a table at Lutèce. I booked that, which was no problem. Barron goes there all the time, and they know me. After dinner, and after hearing your news, I'm going to make you the happiest man in New York City, I promise. I've missed you so. Until Saturday night, my love."

Stone felt the sort of glow that comes with a double brandy. Saturday night was no longer the loneliest night in the week; it was the only night in the week.

The phone rang. "Hi, it's Bill. We're on for Friday. My client reckons they won't be in the apartment until near midnight."

"Right. I'll let my man know."

"Stone, my client says that this is likely to be the only shot we're going to get at this, so tell him not to fuck it up, okay?"

"Don't worry, he's as steady as they come."

He hung up and called Teddy. "It's Friday night," he said. "I've cased the place already, so be at my house at nine, and I'll brief you and give you the camera."

"Looking forward to it, lad," Teddy said.

"And, Teddy, no booze that night, all right?"

"Lad," Teddy replied, sounding hurt, "I only drink *after* work."

Stone hung up the phone feeling a certain order in his life. There was money in the bank, and he had handled his first assignments for Woodman & Weld in a way that was earning their confidence.

He allowed himself to be troubled for a moment about the ethics of what he was doing, but he brushed the thought aside. An errant wife deserved whatever came her way. Stone was on the side of the angels—or, at least, on the side of the wronged party, his client.

He put the last coat of varnish on the library shelves that night, then slept the sleep of the righteous.

37

Late Friday morning it started to snow. The big flakes floated straight down, with no wind to blow them into drifts, and, gradually, the city grew silent as traffic decreased and the noise of what was left was muffled by the carpet of white.

As delighted as a child, Stone forgot working on the house and trudged up to Central Park, where he watched children sledding and building snowmen. As it started to get dark, he hiked down Park Avenue, watching the lights come on and the taxis and buses struggle through the deepening snow. By the time he got home, twelve inches had fallen on the city, and it seemed to be getting heavier. Then it occurred to him that Teddy O'Bannion lived in Brooklyn. He grabbed the telephone.

"Don't worry, Stone"—Teddy chucked—"the subway is just down at the corner, and I can get a cab from your place. I'll start early, so I'll be sure to be on time."

Stone hung up relieved. The thought that he

might have to replace Teddy on this mission had never occurred to him, and even the possibility made his knees tremble.

In the study, he pulled the drop cloths off the crates holding his books—his and his great-aunt's and his father's and his mother's. He estimated there were more than two thousand of them. He took them from their boxes and began arranging them carefully on the shelves. This was a job he would not want to do again. He arranged them by category—art books, fiction, philosophy, politics, biography—and alphabetically by author. It was slow going, and he often had to shift books to keep them in order.

At eight o'clock, he fixed himself some dinner and ate it at the kitchen table, watching the news on CNN.

When he had finished his dinner, he returned to the arranging of the books and became so absorbed in the job that it was nine forty before he realized that Teddy O'Bannion had not arrived.

Worried, he called Teddy's number. It was busy, and it remained busy during his next ten attempts. He called the operator and had the number checked: out of order, she would report it. What was going on?

At ten thirty, he began to face the reality that he was going to have to walk into Apartment 9-A and take videotapes of a strange woman and man in bed together. The thought made his bowels weak. He wished he had not eaten such a large dinner. Teddy's phone number still would not ring.

At a quarter to eleven, Stone realized that he

would have to shower and change, so that he would be presentable to the doorman at the apartment building. He hoped to God it would be a different doorman; he couldn't afford to be seen twice by the same man.

In the shower he ran over what might go wrong. The couple wouldn't be there—that was the best thing that could happen. The man would overpower him and call the police—that would end his relationship with Woodman & Weld, and he would end up in court, if not in jail. The man would produce a pistol from a bedside drawer and . . .

The doorbell rang as he stepped out of the shower. He got into a terry-cloth robe and raced down the stairs. Teddy O'Bannion stood, knee deep in snow, on the front stoop.

"Jesus, I'm sorry, Stone," he began. "There was a fire in the subway station at the corner, and it knocked out not only the trains but every phone in the neighborhood, including mine."

"Come on in, Teddy," Stone said, nearly trembling with relief.

"I'm double-parked out there," Teddy said, brushing snow from his coat. "I had to come in the wife's Jeepster. Good thing I had something with four-wheel drive, but if still took me an hour and a half from the Brooklyn Bridge."

Stone pointed him at the camera case. "Look that over while I change."

When he came back down, Teddy was impatient to go. "I'm not going to get a cab in this," he said.

"I'll come along and wait for you in the car," Stone replied.

Five minutes later, they were grinding slowly up Park Avenue. Stone turned into the right street and stopped the Jeepster a few doors down from the apartment building. "You'd better hurry," he said to Teddy. "You don't want to run into these people in the lobby and let them get a look at you."

Teddy reached inside his coat and produced a nine-millimeter automatic pistol. "Don't worry," he said, grinning, "I'm ready for anything."

Stone grabbed at the pistol. "Are you crazy, Teddy?" Then he laughed. The thing was a water pistol, albeit an extremely realistic one. "What the hell are you doing with this?"

Teddy took the water pistol back. "I'll explain later," he said, getting out of the car. "Keep the motor running, no matter how long it takes."

"Don't worry, I don't want to freeze to death." Stone handed him the key to 9-A.

Teddy pointed at the car phone. "I'll call you, if I can, when I have some results." He closed the door and trudged through the snow toward the building, finally disappearing into the entrance.

Stone turned the radio to a jazz station and settled down to wait. Five minutes later the car phone rang.

"Hello?"

"They were in before me, but I think they're still awake. I can hear music and voices, if I put a water glass against the wall."

"Take your time," Stone said. "We've got all night, if necessary."

"It won't take that long," Teddy said. "In my experience, people who are fucking illicitly don't waste much time getting down to it." He hung up.

Stone turned the heater up a notch, pushed the seat back, and made himself comfortable.

A sharp rapping against the window woke him. He was momentarily disoriented, and, by the time he figured out where he was, the rapping came again on the window. The car's windows were blocked by a blanket of white, and, when he rolled down the driver's side window, snow fell into the car.

"Teddy?" Stone said to the figure outside the car.

"What's up, here, mister?" a voice said.

Jesus, a cop. "Oh, Officer, I'm just waiting for a friend," Stone said, scrambling around in his sleepy mind for a story.

"You been here half hour, pal," the cop said. "Let's see your license and registration."

"Well, to tell you the truth," Stone said, "there's somebody in there with my wife, and I mean to find out who it is. She thinks I'm in Chicago on business." This was fairly close to the truth.

The cop shook his head. "Listen, pal, let me give you some advice. Go to Chicago, and forget about it, then come back and forgive her. You don't want to know who the guy is."

"I'm not breaking any laws, am I—parked

outside my own house?" Stone tried to sound annoyed.

"I guess not," the cop said. "I won't wish you luck, though." He turned and waded away through the snow.

Stone took a few deep breaths of fresh air before he raised the window. He looked at his watch: ten past midnight. Teddy had been in there less than an hour. He arranged himself again and settled down to wait, switching on the windshield wipers to clear the snow. As he did, Teddy walked out of the apartment building and started toward the car. He didn't seem to be in much of a hurry.

"Get in, and let's get out of here," Stone said, opening the door for him.

"No hurry," Teddy said. "Nobody's going to be following me. Not for a while, anyway."

"Tell me what happened," Stone said, guiding the Jeepster up the block through the deep snow.

"You can hear pretty good with a glass against the wall, you know."

"So what did you hear?"

"I heard the music for a while, and their voices, and then I heard the voices move away, so I figure they'd gone to the bedroom." He shifted in his seat to get comfortable. "Now, there are two ways you can do this," he said. "One, you can wait for them to go to sleep and then wake them up. That's good enough, really; I mean, you got them in bed together, right? But the best way is to catch them doing the actual horizontal bunny hop. That way, there's no talking their way out of it."

"So, what happened?"

"You can hear pretty good with a glass against the wall," Teddy said again, maddeningly. "I could hear them talking over the music. I reckoned they were sitting in front of the fireplace. But then I heard them move away, so I figure they're headed for the bedroom, right?"

"And?"

"I was right. That's where they were going. So I wait, maybe three minutes, and I go in."

Stone's heart was in his mouth. "Teddy, for Christ's sake, tell me what happened."

"I'm telling you, Stone; just be patient. Anyway, I leave the camera case and my shoes outside the door, I unscrew the bulb in the vestibule, and I go in real easylike with my key, and, right from the front door, I can hear them going at it, you know?"

"Teddy, spit it out. Did you get the shot we need?"

"So, what I do is, I switch on the camera, but not the light, so I'm recording sound, right?"

"All right, Teddy, go on, give me the gory details."

"Then I tippy-toe to the bedroom door, and there they are in the moonlight. I think it's probably good enough without the light."

Stone was alarmed. "You didn't use the light?"

"So I run a few feet with just the moonlight. The lady's on top, she's really taking a ride on the guy, you know? And they're building up to it. Both of them are sounding like something at the zoo, no kidding. So, I'm grinding away in the moonlight, and they're grinding away in the bed, and I can tell things are coming to a head, so to speak, so I wait until just the right moment, when they're both bellowing like seals, and I hit the light!" Teddy was sounding absolutely delighted with himself.

"Thank God you hit the light." Stone breathed, his heart pounding.

"Now, tell me, Stone, what's your first reaction, somebody suddenly shines a bright light on you?"

"Oh, shit," Stone said. "I'd throw up a hand to shield my eyes. You didn't get their faces?"

"Stone," Teddy said, sounding hurt, "you underestimate me." He held up the water pistol. "That's where this came in."

"You shot them with a water pistol?" Stone asked, baffled.

"Right. I mean, here you got these two naked people, they're on top of the covers, and they're throwing their hands across their faces to shield their eyes or to keep me from photographing their faces, so with one hand, I give 'em a shot or two with the water pistol, aiming at tender spots like the armpit or the ribs, and, what do they do? Why, they grab at the places I squirted them, don't they? And they leave their faces exposed, just long enough for me to record them for posterity."

"Great! Then what happened?"

"Then the guy, who's on the bottom, remember, tosses the lady in the air, and he starts for me. But I'm outta there, filming all the way, of course, and outside the door I got this little hook that goes one end over the doorknob and the other end hooked to the door molding, so the guy can't open the door from the inside, right?"

"Wonderful," Stone said.

"So, I ring for the elevator, and, while it's coming, and while the guy is trying to break down the door, no doubt bruising his shoulder pretty badly, I slip into my shoes, stick the camera back into its case, and then the elevator comes, I ride down and walk right out of the building. To make it even nicer, the doorman is asleep!"

"Perfection," Stone said. "Teddy, you're a wonder."

"Of course, our guy is going to have to call downstairs and get the doorman to open the door for him, and that's going to be just a little embarrassing for him."

Stone pulled up in front of his house. He reached into a pocket and handed Teddy a thick envelope. "Five thousand, as agreed," he said.

"I thank you, sir," Teddy said, glowing. He handed over the case. "Your camera, and your videotape."

Stone got out of the car, and Teddy drove away. He let himself into the house and called Bill Eggers.

"Jesus, Stone, I haven't slept a wink. How'd it go?"

"It went perfectly, absolutely perfectly."

"You've seen the tape, then?"

"Well, no, I haven't; I don't have a VCR. But my man says he got it all, and he's a good man."

"You gave him the five grand without seeing the tape?"

"Take it easy, Bill, it went well, believe me."

"I hope so, for all our sakes. Meet me at the office at nine tomorrow morning, and we'll have a little private screening."

"All right, but don't worry, Bill. It went well."

"If you say so," Eggers said. "I'll see you in the morning."

Stone wearily got undressed and went to bed, but it was his turn not to sleep. If he'd known where to get a VCR in the middle of the night, he'd have gone out and gotten one. He hoped to God that Teddy O'Bannion's confidence in his own work was not in any way misplaced.

38

Before leaving the house, Stone shoveled the steps and the sidewalk in front. The weatherman had said there had been eighteen inches of snow over-night, and Stone believed it. He could not remember such silence in the city.

There were no cabs to speak of, and, since the sun was shining brightly anyway, Stone hiked the distance to the offices of Woodman & Weld, walking in the paths broken by buses and the odd cab with chains. The only people in sight seemed to be those who had come out to play. He passed more than one group of adults building snowmen or throwing snowballs at each other. That, and the memory of a task well accomplished, made the day seem festive.

He arrived a little early and waited in the lobby for Eggers. When the lawyer arrived, he introduced Stone to the security guard and had him put on the list for after-hours entry to the Woodman & Weld offices.

"Jesus," Eggers said as they rode up in the elevator, "I hope your man did this right. If we don't have what we need on that tape, it's going to put my client in a very awkward position. I mean, his old lady will be on her guard, and she could make it tough for him."

"My man says he got it," Stone said, "and that's good enough for me." At least, until we see the tape, he thought. It was not going to be good for his position with the law firm if the tape was not good.

Eggers unlocked the front door and relocked it behind them. "Take that stuff down to the small conference room," he said to Stone. "That's where our video system is. Third door on your right. I'll be with you in a minute."

Stone went to the conference room, unsnapped the camera case, took out the camera, and pushed the reject button. The cassette fell out into his hand. He turned to the wall of video equipment but wasn't sure which piece of equipment to use.

Eggers came in. "Pretty impressive, isn't it? We tape depositions, and we have other capabilities, too. You'll see in a minute." He took the cassette from Stone, inserted it into a machine, and flipped a number of switches. Snow filled the screen of a large monitor, then the picture snapped on.

"Here we go," Stone said, sitting down and resting his elbows on the conference table. "Hey, your camera worked pretty well in the low light. Listen."

The sound of two people making love came faintly from the bedroom. The camera moved slowly, smoothly across the living room to the bedroom door. The moonlight was as Teddy O'Bannion had described it, bright as day. The figure of a woman was clearly visible, and she was moving rhythmically in sync with the noises heard a moment before. She was sitting on a man, who was also clearly visible, though neither of their faces could be made out.

"This is sensational!" Eggers said wonderingly. "Hang on a second." He picked up a remote control and froze the frame, then he walked to the wall of equipment and turned on another piece of gear. There was a whirring noise, and, a few moments later, a color photograph slid out of the machine. Eggers looked at it approvingly, then handed it to Stone. "Very artful, wouldn't you say?"

"You're right," Stone said. "It's a beautiful shot, but the faces are shadowed."

"He did turn on the goddamned light, didn't he?"

"Yes, but later; hang on."

Eggers started the tape again. The lovemaking was growing in intensity, and the couple's voices rose with it. Then, at the moment when both seemed to be reaching a climax, the floodlight came on. Instinctively, both the man and the woman threw up a hand to shield themselves from the light. Eggers froze the frame again and made another print.

"This is where the water pistol comes in," Stone said.

Eggers stopped what he was doing. "Water pistol?" he asked incredulously.

"That's how my man gets shots of their faces," Stone replied. "Watch."

Eggers started the tape again and pressed the slow motion button. A jet of water could be seen to enter the frame and strike the man in the chest. His hand started down. Another jet struck the woman just below the armpit, and her arm followed, too.

"There! That's it!" Eggers shouted, freezing the frame. "That's our shot!" He ran to the printer and pressed the button again.

Stone froze to his chair, unable to move, unable to speak. The man's face had surprised him, but the woman's rendered him nearly catatonic. The man was Barron Harkness; the woman was Cary Hilliard.

"Perfect, perfect!" Eggers yelled in triumph, shoving the print in front of Stone. "You can have that for your scrapbook." He pressed the button for another print. "The cat's out of the bag now, though. I'm sorry for my little subterfuge, but I guess you recognize the guy. His wife is my client."

Stone was unable to speak. His eyes ran up and down the two forms frozen on the screen. Harkness was clearly furious, Cary terrified. Her breasts shone with sweat in the bright light, the nipples erect; her lips were swollen and her eyes round with fright.

"Let's see the rest!" Eggers cried. "Here we go!" He started the tape again.

Harkness reared up in the bed, upsetting Cary from her perch atop him.

"Jesus, the guy's hung!" Eggers said admiringly. "And look at the tits on that broad! Shit, I don't blame the guy!"

The camera backed out of the room as Harkness rose from the bed and came after it. In the nick of time, the front door closed, and the camera wobbled out of control. Teddy's hand could be seen applying his latch to the knob and the molding.

"An absolute goddamned Academy Award winner!" Eggers yelled, jumping out of his chair and doing a little dance. "Gotta call my client; she's waiting on tenterhooks." He grabbed a phone and started dialing. "Stone, you win the Oscar for best producer," he was saying.

Stone willed himself to move. He shoved the photograph into his overcoat pocket and got shakily to his feet.

"Hello, Charlotte? This is Bill Eggers. My dear, your settlement is assured!" Eggers crowed into the phone. "I'm going to come over to your house right now and show you the videotape that's going to do it. Hang on a minute . . ." Eggers looked up to see Stone leaving the room. "Stone, where are you going?"

Stone didn't reply. He continued down the hallway to the reception room and straight to the waiting elevator. Riding down in the car, he tore at his collar; he couldn't seem to get enough air. Ignoring the security guard's pleas to sign out, he rushed into the street, gulping the cold air, trying to keep his breakfast down. He stumbled through the deep snow, gasping for still more air. After a while, he slowed to a walk; a little while later, he found himself inside his house, leaning against the front door, weeping.

When he had calmed himself a little, he noticed the blinking light on the answering machine. There was only one message.

"Stone, darling," she said. "I've had a little family emergency, and I'm going to have to go to Virginia to see the folks for a few days. I'm leaving this morning, so I'm afraid I can't see you tonight. I'll call you when I get back. Take care."

39

The rest of the weekend was awful. Stone felt ill and stayed in bed, getting up only to make soup and bring in the newspapers. He couldn't concentrate on the papers, and, for the first time in months, the house did not intrude into his thoughts. He thought of nothing but Cary.

He tried to think of something else, but nothing worked. Sunday sports on television were a blur; the news meant nothing; he couldn't keep his mind on the book review or the Sunday magazine. The crossword puzzle worked for a few minutes, but every time he stopped to think, Cary popped into his head—Cary and the awful photograph in his overcoat pocket.

She had lied to him from the beginning; the married man in her life had always been Harkness; Stone had been just a diversion. As Sunday wore on, Stone began to find a way to deal with his thoughts of her; he hardened himself, belittled the weeks they had had together, made her unimportant. By Monday morning a scab was beginning to form on the wound. He would force it to heal.

On Monday morning a gossip columnist in the *News* had the story:

> The Barron Harknesses are calling it a day, after more than twenty years together and two children. We hear the ice age crept up on the marriage long ago, and the split is just a final acknowledgment of reality.
>
> Insiders say that Barron is being uncommonly generous, that Charlotte Harkness is getting both the house in Easthampton *and* the ten-room Fifth Avenue digs, where Barron has long been chairman of the cooperative's board.
>
> We hear, too, that as part of their agreement, a certain other apartment owner has to leave the building immediately, surely a new wrinkle in divorce settlements.
>
> Since Barron has never been seen squiring ladies around town, speculation on his paramour centers on the Continental Network—insiders figure it must be somebody at the office. Watch this space.

Stone threw the newspaper at the wall, then concentrated on forming the scab again. The phone rang.

"Hi, it's Bill. I just wanted to let you know that the outcome of Friday night's little opus has been most satisfactory for my client."

"I read the item in the news," Stone said. "I'm

happier than you know that it worked out so well for her." He did his best to mean this.

"Woodman is delighted, too. He was very, very nervous about your being involved in something like this, and it's unlikely he'll want to do it again soon, but he asked me to express his gratitude."

"Tell him I was glad to be of help."

"I've got nothing on my plate at the moment that I might need you for, so take it easy for a while. Why don't you take a vacation? The islands or someplace?"

"Thanks, but I've got a lot more work to do on the house; I'll use any free time for that. I have to get an office together, too."

"Right, whatever you say. I'll let you know when I have something else for you."

Stone hung up and glanced out the window. A moving van had pulled up outside, and furniture was being loaded into it. Feldstein was moving out of the downstairs professional suite. That suited Stone fine; he'd need the space now.

For the rest of the week, Stone turned his attention to the study. When the books had all been unpacked, dusted, and arranged on the shelves, he waxed the floor, then unrolled the beautiful Aubusson carpet that had come back from cleaning. He got the old desk, now refinished, back in its place, then hung two of his mother's paintings, along with some of his great-aunt's pictures. By Saturday, the room gleamed, but it looked as though someone had always lived in it.

Stone spent a month on the professional suite,

ripping out the partitions Feldstein had installed for his treatment rooms, hiring a plumber to replace the old pipes, ducting the new central heating into the space, and stripping and refinishing the original oak paneling. He finished up with a reception room and two offices, plus a storeroom for a copying machine and supplies. He had a discreet brass plate made for the front door that read THE BARRINGTON PRACTICE. He would install it when news of his passing the bar exam came.

He began thinking about a secretary, but, before he could place an ad, Bill Eggers came up with someone who wanted to return to Woodman & Weld after raising children. She was a plump, motherly woman named Helen Wooten, very bright and capable, and she suited his needs perfectly. Not having much else for her to do yet, he put her in charge of his personal finances and the construction costs on the house. She began saving him money immediately.

Bill Eggers arranged a three hundred-thousand-dollar mortgage on the house that let him pay off his old bank loan and gave him the funds to complete work and furnish the house and office.

Three months passed. Cary never called.

Every couple of weeks he had dinner with Dino, usually at Elaine's. Elaine liked Dino; he made her laugh.

"Stone," Dino said one evening, "you're not going to believe this."

"What?"

"I'm thinking of getting married."

"You're right, I don't believe it."

"A girl from the neighborhood. We know each other since grammar school."

"I don't believe it."

"Mary Ann Bianchi, a good Italian girl."

Stone turned to Elaine. "He's hallucinating."

"I think you're right," Elaine said. "It must be the Sambuca; he's had too much."

"I kid you not," Dino said. "Will you stand up for me, be my best man?"

"I know what this is," Stone said to Elaine, "it's an elaborate practical joke. I'll turn up for the wedding, and the whole 19th Precinct will be there, laughing like hell, because I believed this ridiculous story."

"Stone, I swear to God, I'm doing it. We already got the church booked. I bought her a ring, for Christ's sake."

"You stole it from the evidence room."

Dino looked wounded. "I paid cash money. I know a guy in the Diamond District."

"This means you can't bring any more girls in here, Dino," Elaine said.

"Don't worry, Mary Ann would kill me in my sleep. She's Sicilian."

"You're in a lot of trouble," Stone said, "but sure, I'll stand up for you."

"It's a week from Sunday," Dino said.

"That's moving pretty quick," Elaine said.

Dino shrugged. "So, it'll be a seven-month kid,

so what? Happens all the time in my neighborhood."

Elaine waved at a waiter. "Bring a bottle of champagne, the good stuff. Dino's got a lot to celebrate, here."

They celebrated.

Elaine looked at Stone closely. "You're looking almost human these days," she said. "A few weeks ago you looked like death."

"Hard work on the house," Stone said. "I'm getting used to it."

"He's getting over the broad," Dino said.

"Ahhhh," Elaine said.

"You're right," Stone agreed, "I am." And he was, except for an occasional spear through the heart, when he thought about her. He had stopped thinking at all about Sasha Nijinsky and Hank Morgan.

On the Friday morning before Dino's wedding, Stone received a letter. He recognized the handwriting immediately.

Dear Stone,

Please pardon the familiarity, but, although we've never met, our lives have been so intertwined that I feel you are a friend.

I'm sorry that my problems at least indirectly resulted in your leaving the police force, but I understand that you are now doing well. I saw your name in the *Times*, on the list of those who had passed the bar exam.

I think, perhaps, the time is coming when we should meet. Maybe you would come to dinner sometime soon? It would be so nice to meet you, at last.

I'll be in touch.

Best,
S.

40

They sat at a table in the little room in back of the bar at Clarke's. The mirror behind the bar had been replaced; everybody seemed to want to forget the incident, and Dino was obviously welcome.

"You're looking better," Dino said. "You put the girl behind you for good?"

"What else can I do?"

"We've all been there, Stone, believe me. Thank God that's all over for me."

"I'd like to think so, Dino."

"Believe me, it's over. When you marry a Sicilian, it's for life, and that can be short if you fool around."

"How are things at the office?"

"Looks like we got *two* serial killers on our hands."

"The taxi killings, I guess."

"That's one of them. It's the most trouble, too, because every time another cabbie gets greased, the rest of them go bananas and block a major artery for the day."

"I read about it. Any suspects?"

"Negative."

"What's the other case?"

"That one's even weirder. We got two men and two women in the past seven weeks who just went *poof*. Right off the street."

"Where?"

"Everywhere. All over Manhattan."

"No bodies?"

"No nothing."

"What do they have in common?"

"Fuckall. The women were twenty-six and thirty-two; the men were thirty-seven and thirty-nine. The guys were a stockbroker and a Porsche salesman; the women were an advertising art director and a VP at a cosmetics company."

"No ransom notes?"

"Nope. They only got one thing in common I can see."

"What's that?"

"They're good looking, all of them. Good dressers, real prime-time yuppies."

"Where were they last seen?"

"Leaving work; restaurant; leaving exercise class; jogging in Battery Park."

Stone shrugged. "Good luck, Dino."

"I'm going to need it. What're you working on at the law firm?"

"A fairly juicy one. A client—chairman of an electronics firm—is accused of beating up a high-class hooker in the Waldorf Towers. Looks like it'll go to trial, and I'll assist in the defense."

"They're not giving you nothing to try yourself, huh?"

"Not yet. I think they expect me to come up with my own. Any ideas?"

"I'll keep it in mind, tell a couple of the guys. You never know."

Stone took the letter, in a plastic envelope, from his pocket. "I've got something to show you." He handed it over.

Dino read it and stopped chewing his salad. Then he started again and swallowed. "So? Who's 'S'?"

Stone stared at him, unbelieving. "Come on, Dino, you read her diary; don't you recognize the handwriting?"

"Can't say that I do," Dino said, concentrating on the salad. "I never had much memory for handwriting."

"I didn't expect this."

"Expect what? You expect me to recommend reopening the investigation based on this?" He tossed the letter back across the table.

"I didn't expect you to stonewall me."

"I ain't stonewalling you, Stone. You come up with something substantial, and I'll go with you on it."

"Substantial? A letter from a dead woman isn't substantial?"

"Where was it mailed?"

"Penn Station."

"Any prints? I know you checked."

Stone held the plastic holder at an angle and pointed. "Three. Will you run them against what we found in her apartment?"

Dino looked skeptical, then shrugged. "Okay, I'll do that. It may take a few days; the records have probably left the precinct."

"As soon as you can. And will you have the handwriting analyzed?"

"Against what?"

"The diary, the other stuff in evidence."

"The case has been cleared. I expect all that stuff has gone back to her estate, to her family, by now."

"Dino, if I can get a good analysis done, and the prints turn out to be hers, will that be enough for you to reopen?"

"Tell you the truth, I don't know. I'd have to go to Delgado; he'd have to go to Waldron; he might even have to go to the mayor. The thing is, even if an analyst says it's her handwriting, even if the prints are hers, what have we got to go on? We can't trace the letter. It looks like pretty ordinary stationery to me; it was mailed in the biggest post office in the city. What could we do?"

"We'd know she's alive." He pushed the letter back across the table. "That's a start."

Dino laughed and shook his head. "You still got a hair up your ass about that, ain't you? All that crap about cats bouncing off concrete and walking away. You know, if I had come to *you* with that kind of a theory, you'd have kicked my ass."

Stone laughed. "I don't know, Dino, I think I'd have given your idea a hearing."

"I gave your idea a hearing," Dino said.

"For about fifteen seconds."

"That was all I needed."

"Okay, okay, but will you have the lab look at the paper and anything else they can find?"

"All right, but I'll have to get somebody to do it on his own time. If word got around about this, I'd be pounding a beat, pronto."

"Thanks, Dino."

"I'll owe somebody a favor, too."

"I'll owe you one."

They paused outside the restaurant.

"One forty-five, Sunday, at the church?" Dino said. "You got the address?"

"I've got it."

"Tuxedo. I'll pick up the rental."

"I own one."

"We're coming up in the world, aren't we?"

"I've actually used it a couple of times. A firm party, that sort of thing."

"I'll see if I can have something for you on the letter by then. Otherwise, it'll have to wait till after the honeymoon."

"Where you going?"

"Vegas—where else?"

"Sounds great. I'll see you Sunday."

"You ever been to an Italian wedding?"

"No."

"You got an experience coming."

Dino turned out to be right.

41

Frank Woodman was at his desk, dictating something into a recorder, but, when he saw Stone at the door, he waved him in. "How are you, Stone?" he said, pointing at a chair.

Stone sat down. "I'm fine, Frank. There's something I want to ask you about."

"First," Woodman said, "there's something I want to say to you, and I'm sorry I didn't seek you out and say it sooner. Stone, only Bill Eggers, Charlotte Harkness, and I have seen that tape, and I'm the only one who knows you knew Cary Hilliard. I want you to know that it won't go any further than that."

Stone nodded. He couldn't think of anything to say.

"You did a fine job for us, and I'm sorry the result had to cause you pain."

"Thank you, Frank."

"Enough said about that. What can I do for you?"

"I was wondering if you have the effects of Sasha Nijinsky that the NYPD took."

"They sent them back to me a couple of weeks ago. After going through them myself, I sent them to Sasha's father."

"I see."

"Why? Did you want to see them again?"

"Yes, I wanted to get a look at her handwriting again."

"Why?"

Stone handed Woodman a copy of the letter.

Woodman read it through twice, and his expression revealed nothing. "What do you make of this?" he asked at last.

"I'm not entirely sure what to make of it. A friend of mine at the 19th Precinct is getting it looked at by the lab, but I wanted to compare the handwriting to something of Sasha's."

"That's no problem," Woodman said, rising and going to a file cabinet. "Sasha didn't type. She told me once that she refused to learn, so that she wouldn't get shunted aside into 'woman's' work." He flipped through a folder, extracted a letter, and handed it to Stone. "She did all her correspondence by hand."

Stone laid the two letters side by side on the desk, and both men bent over them. Woodman produced a magnifying glass, and they examined them closely.

"They're a lot alike, I'd say, but the one sent to you looks a little cramped," Woodman said.

"The lines are not as straight, either," Stone added.

"This is over my head," Woodman said, picking up the phone. "Sophie, please find the name of that handwriting man we used on the mineral rights case last year, then see if you can get him over here right away." He hung up. "When did you get this, Stone? It's not dated."

"Friday. It was posted the day before at Penn Station."

"It must be some kind of crank who read your name in the papers as being associated with the case."

"That seems more than just possible. Still, there's the handwriting."

"I suppose someone who knew Sasha might have had a letter of hers and used that to make a forgery."

"But why?"

"Maybe someone who isn't satisfied with the outcome of the case. A lot of people aren't; I'm one of them. Maybe someone's just trying to get you interested again."

"The letter certainly had that effect," Stone said.

The phone rang, and Woodman picked it up. "Good," he said, then hung up. "Man's name is Weaver. His office is only a couple of blocks away; he's coming over." Woodman looked uncomfortable for a moment. "Stone, I get the impression that you are at least considering the possibility that Sasha might still be alive. Is that right?"

"Yes," Stone replied. "I think it's just possible." He explained the circumstances of Sasha's fall and his terminal velocity theory.

"Jesus Christ," Woodman said.

* * *

Weaver was a tall, thin man in his sixties. He looked at both letters carefully. Woodman had folded the letters so that the signatures did not show. "This is a Xerox copy, I presume," he said, holding up Stone's letter.

"Yes, I don't have the original at the moment."

"I'd like to see it, but it probably wouldn't make much difference in my opinion."

"What is your opinion, Mr. Weaver?" Woodman asked.

"I'd say there's about an eighty percent chance that the same person wrote both letters."

"Why can't you be sure?" Stone asked.

"Well, the similarity in the shaping of the letters is profound, but there's anomaly that could mean it's a forgery. You see, here, the spacing in the more recent letters is closer; it has a cramped quality. Its lines aren't as straight, either."

"We noticed that," Woodman said. "Could there be some other reason than forgery for the difference between the two letters?"

"Well, yes. The recent letter doesn't have quite the vitality of style that the earlier one exhibits. That's a common trait of forgeries, but it often turns up, too, when the writer is ill or injured or is convalescing." Weaver held his right elbow close to his side and demonstrated. "A person who is weakened or in pain would characteristically hold his arm in like this, restricting the movement of his hand. This would especially be true in the event of injury—say, a broken arm or ribs.

That could quite easily account for the cramped nature of the second letter."

Stone and Woodman exchanged a look. Woodman raised his eyebrows.

Weaver continued. "In my experience, this characteristic of what you might call the 'wounded writer' would be more evident in the writing of a woman, but both these letters were, of course, written by a man."

"By a man?" Stone asked, incredulously.

"In my opinion, yes; definitely," Weaver replied.

"Anything else you can tell us?" Woodman asked.

"That's about it, I think, though I would like to see the original of the second letter."

Woodman escorted the man to the door. "Thank you, Mr. Weaver, and please send me your bill." Woodman came back to his desk and sat down. "This is the goddamndest thing I ever heard," he said.

"Frank, are you certain that Sasha, herself, wrote you this letter?"

Woodman went back to his file and extracted a small sheet of paper. "I watched her write this," he said. "She was sitting where you are now."

Stone picked up the paper. It was the address and phone number of Sasha's new, Fifth Avenue apartment. He compared the note with the first letter, then the second. "The handwriting seems identical to me," he said, handing Woodman the papers.

"Me, too," Woodman said, poring over them.

"Now, why would Weaver think the writer was a man?"

"Well," said Woodman, "for a lady, Sasha always had incredible balls."

At home, Stone built a fire in the study, poured himself a drink, and stretched out on the leather sofa before the fireplace. He sipped the drink and cast his mind back over the events surrounding Sasha Nijinsky's dive from the terrace, letting them run through his mind without hindrance, comparing one event with another, listening to fragments of conversation from people he had interviewed. Something nagged at him, something he should be remembering. The phone rang.

He reached out to the extension on the coffee table. "Hello?" he said.

"Hello."

Stone tightened his grip on the phone. Images flew before his eyes—a breast, a wrist. He felt her body against his, her hair in his face, her legs locked around him, her mouth on his penis.

"I want to see you," she said.

Stone wanted to speak, but his throat tightened.

"I want to see you tonight," she said.

He made a huge effort to control himself, to make his voice work, to tamp down the rage and hurt inside him. It didn't work. He hung up the phone.

He lay on the sofa through what should have been dinner, until past midnight, waiting for a knock on the door or another call. Neither came.

42

Dino Bacchetti and Mary Ann Bianchi were married at San Gennaro's Church in Little Italy on Sunday. Stone had never worn a tuxedo at two o'clock in the afternoon, but he stood as best man for Dino, and he was impressed with the elaborate and somber Roman Catholic ceremony. Dino kissed his bride, and the wedding party began moving back down the aisle, the happy couple leading the bridesmaids and groomsmen.

Near the back of the church, Stone glanced to his right and stopped in his tracks. Cary Hilliard was sitting in the back pew, bundled in a mink coat. Somebody behind Stone stepped on his heels, and he moved on with the wedding party. Stone was trapped on the front steps of the church as the party posed for photographs, then the group was bundled into limousines and driven to a restaurant for the reception, so he did not see what became of Cary.

The restaurant was not large, and two hundred happy people were crammed into it, singing, dancing, and generally raising hell. The only non-Italians, besides Stone, were the Irish, Puerto Rican, and black cops who worked with or for Dino. Stone kissed the bride and was surprised at the enthusiasm with which she responded.

He shook Dino's hand. "Well, you did it," he said, laughing.

Dino looked supremely happy. "You goddamned right I did, *paisan*."

"Speaking of *paisans*," Stone said, nodding at a group of severe-looking people across the room, "who's that?"

"That's Mary Ann's people," Dino replied. "Her old man's a capo in the Bonanno family. Well respected."

"No kidding?"

"No kidding."

"Why do they look so . . . unhappy?"

"Because their most beautiful daughter got knocked up by a cop, that's why. The old man's really pissed off. If I wasn't Italian, I'd be at the bottom of Sheepshead Bay with a concrete block stuck up my ass."

"Dino, you better be very, very good to that girl," Stone said gravely.

"Don't worry." Dino took an envelope from his inside pocket. "Here's your report on the letter," he said. "I don't want to hear about it again, okay?"

Stone put the envelope in his pocket. "Okay."

"Guess who sent us a real nice piece of silver?" Dino said.

"Who?"

Dino nodded. "The very beautiful lady over there," he said.

Stone followed Dino's gaze and found Cary standing on the opposite side of the dance floor.

"See you later, pal," Dino said, and vanished.

Stone stood and watched her make her way across the dance floor toward him. Under the mink coat, she was wearing a very short silk dress that made her legs seem longer than he remembered. Stone's mouth went dry.

She took his hand and led him onto the floor; the band was playing something romantic and Italian; he followed her dumbly. They began to move together; she laid her head on his shoulder and kissed him on the neck.

"God, but I've missed you," she said.

Stone was unable to say anything; he put his hand inside the coat and pulled her to him. The familiarity of those curves pressed against his body made him light-headed, and he lost himself in the music and the feel of her. Her cool hand was on the back of his neck, her fingers in his hair, her tongue played at his ear. The music continued—a medley—and she seemed to become more and more a part of him. Suddenly, she stopped dancing.

"Come with me," she said, tugging at his hand.

He followed her across the dance floor, through the crowd, along a wall to a door. She opened it, looked in, then pulled him inside with her. They were in a small office—only a desk, a chair, and an old sofa. She closed the door and locked it.

"Where have you—"

"Shhhh," she whispered, throwing the mink coat onto the sofa and snaking an arm around his neck. "Don't say anything." She was unzipping his trousers; in a moment, she had him in her hand.

After that, things happened effortlessly. They were on the sofa, on the luxurious coat, his trousers around his knees, her legs around him. She wasn't wearing underwear. They both gave themselves to the moment, made it last, then came with a roar of blood in the ears, her cries mixing with the music, loud through the thin walls.

They lay limp in each other's arms for a few minutes, then Cary found a toilet off the office, and Stone tried to make himself presentable again. She was a long time in the john, and, when she came out, Stone was reading the lab report.

"What's that?" she asked, putting a hand at the back of his neck and reading over his shoulder.

Stone handed her the letter without comment.

She read it, and her eyes went wide. "Sasha's *alive?*" she asked, stunned.

"It would seem so," Stone said, reading the report. "An expert says it's almost certainly her handwriting, and her fingerprints are on the letter." He read on. "They were very clear, because she had olive oil on her fingers—extra virgin olive oil, according to this."

"It doesn't seem possible," she said, incredulously.

"No, it doesn't," he replied. "Nevertheless . . ."

She walked over to the sofa and retrieved her

coat, seemingly lost in thought. "That means she's going to be able to identify whoever pushed her off that balcony, doesn't it?"

"I hope so. I wonder why she hasn't done it already."

Cary slipped into her coat and walked to the door, unlocking it.

"You're leaving? When can I see you?"

"I'll call you," she said. "I've left my job, and I'm staying with a friend. Don't worry, we'll see each other. You'll see me sooner than you think. Pay no attention to what you hear."

"What am I going to hear?" he asked.

She ignored his question; her brow was furrowed. "There's something I never told you," she said. "I should have told you a long time ago." She seemed to be wrestling with whether to tell him now.

"What is it?"

She looked at the floor. "Barron wasn't on that airplane from Rome."

Stone stared at her. "But Dino saw him . . ."

She looked up at him, then slipped through the door. "Dino didn't do his job," she said, then closed the door behind her, leaving him alone in the room.

Stone went to the bathroom and splashed some cold water on his face, his mind racing. Then he rejoined the crowd and found Dino, who was making his way out of the party with Mary Ann. He could see the car outside, festooned with tin cans and old shoes.

"Dino, when you went to the airport to meet Barron Harkness's plane, did you actually see him get off?"

"Stone, c'mon, okay?" He kissed an old lady on the lips.

Stone managed to stay alongside him. "You didn't actually *see* him, did you?"

"I checked the manifest, all right? Hey, Cheech, how you doin'?"

Stone bodily prevented a fat woman from squeezing between them. "Dino, you didn't *see* him."

"Stone, I'm leaving on my honeymoon; gimme a major fucking break, will you?"

Stone stopped moving, and the crowd surged past him. He watched Dino carried along by the crowd to the car, then he was driving away, waving.

43

Late in the evening, as Stone was drifting off to sleep, the telephone rang. He fumbled for it. "Hello?"

"Mr. Barrington?" The voice was vaguely familiar.

"Yes?"

"This is Herbert Van Fleet."

Stone looked at the clock. "Jesus Christ," he muttered under his breath. "What is it?"

"I know I must have awakened you. I'm very sorry."

"What do you want, Mr. Van Fleet?"

"I want to retain you."

"Retain me?"

"I understand that you are practicing law now."

"Yes, that's right, but why do we need to talk about this at eleven o'clock on a Sunday night? Can you call my office number tomorrow morning?"

"I'm afraid it's more urgent than that. I've been arrested."

Stone sighed and swung his legs over the side of the bed. "What were you arrested for, Mr. Van Fleet?"

"Please call me Herb."

Annoyed. "What were you arrested for, *Herb?*"

"They're calling it attempted rape. They want to arraign me in a couple of hours, in night court."

"Where are you now?"

"I'm in a place called the Tombs. They let me make this one call."

"You're going to need to raise bail, Herb. Can you lay your hands on some money?"

"How much money?"

"I should think that, with no previous arrests, the judge might want as much as twenty-five thousand dollars in cash, or you can put up ten percent and some property to a bail bondsman. You won't get the ten percent back."

"I've got about forty thousand dollars in a money market account," Van Fleet said.

"That should do it," Stone said. "All right, Herb, I'll represent you at the arraignment. My fee for that will be a thousand dollars. If you want me to represent you after that, we can talk about a further retainer."

"All right, that's acceptable."

"I'll meet you at night court." Stone hung up, oddly elated. Herbert Van Fleet was a strange person, but this was the first time somebody had asked Stone to represent him, his first client outside Woodman & Weld. It promised to be a fairly lucrative representation too. He began to get dressed.

Night court was a zoo. Every prostitute, vagrant, and petty criminal arrested during the past few hours would be arraigned there, and the crowd was colorful and noisy. From the back of the huge courtroom, Stone could barely hear the judge, who was shouting.

Stone counted. Standing before the bench, looking at the floor and shifting their weight from one foot to the other, were twenty-four Chinese men, all neatly dressed in business suits. He took a seat down front and listened, curious. The men had been gambling in the basement of a restaurant in Chinatown, only a few blocks away, and an old lady next door had turned them in. Their Anglo lawyer, in unctuous tones, was explaining to the somewhat amused judge that his clients were all respected members of the community, businessmen out for an evening of diversion. They were not criminals, not really, and were very sorry to have disturbed the old woman's sleep. The judge released the men on their own recognizance.

Stone got up, introduced himself to the bailiff at the door to the holding cells, and, shortly, Herbert Van Fleet appeared, in handcuffs. Stone sat him down in one of the little rooms set aside for consultation with attorneys. "All right, Herb, tell me exactly what happened."

Van Fleet sighed. "I was at the Tribeca Grill,

having a drink, and I got to talking to this girl. I offered her a ride home—she said she lived in the West Village—and, on the way, we were getting sort of friendly, and—"

"Exactly what do you mean by 'getting sort of friendly'?"

"We were holding hands, and she was sitting close to me. We stopped at a traffic light on Sixth Avenue, and we kissed."

"Did you put your hands between her legs or on her breasts?"

"Yes, on her breasts, and she seemed to like that. It was when I put my hand down the front of her dress that she became difficult."

"Difficult?"

"She started screaming at me. I didn't realize how drunk she was until that moment. She started to get out of the van, and I tried to persuade her to calm down, and then she started screaming for help."

"Were you fighting?"

"I had hold of her wrists and was talking to her, trying to get her to calm down, when a police car pulled up alongside us at the light, and she jumped out of the van and started screaming hysterically about how I had tried to rape her."

"Did you ever get your hand on her breast—inside her dress, I mean?"

"Yes, but just for a minute."

"Herbert, is that all that happened? Is there any more? I have to know if I'm going to be able to give you a proper defense."

"I swear to you, that was all there was to it. If

the police car hadn't just happened to show up, it would have been all over in a minute. She would either have calmed down, or she would have gotten out of the van. This whole thing about attempted rape is completely crazy. Oh, I forgot, the policemen gave me a breath test—made me blow up one of those balloons."

"Did they indicate what the results were?"

"No, I asked them, but they didn't answer."

"Did they give the girl the same test?"

"I don't know, I didn't see them do that. They put me in the back of the police car while they were talking to her and calming her down."

"All right, you go with the officer back to the holding cell, and, when they bring you before the bench, I'll be waiting for you."

Van Fleet stuck out his hand. "Thank you for coming, Stone; I really appreciate this. I didn't want to get my mother involved, you know?"

"I know, Herb. Maybe we can deal with this without her knowing about it; we'll see."

When the charges were read against Herbert Van Fleet, Stone pointed out to the judge that Van Fleet had no record of arrests or of criminal activity, that he was gainfully employed in a supervisory position, and that he was a responsible member of the community. He mentioned also that the woman making the complaint was unharmed, unless she had a hangover, and that there were no witnesses to support her complaint. He asked that Van Fleet be released on his own recognizance. The judge thought for about three seconds, then set bail at ten thousand dollars and ordered the release of Van Fleet's vehicle. An hour later, Stone and Van Fleet met in front of the courthouse, and Van Fleet thanked him profusely.

"What happens next?" Van Fleet asked.

"If you want me to represent you, what I'll do first is to try to prevent the case going to trial. The district attorney might offer us a deal, but I don't think we'd take it. If what you've told me is the truth, and there were no witnesses to any of this, then it's your word against the girl's. In fact, it sounds to me as though the police officers should have dealt with this on the spot, just put the girl in a cab and sent her home, then lectured you and let you go."

"I'd like you to represent me," Van Fleet said.

"All right; my fee will be ten thousand dollars, including tonight's court appearance—that's if I can negotiate this without a trial. If we have to go to trial, I'll represent you on the basis of two hundred dollars an hour, with a guaranteed minimum of twenty-five thousand dollars, which will include any previous pretrial negotiations. And my fee will be payable in advance, as is customary with criminal cases."

Van Fleet thought for a moment.

"Of course, I'm sure you can find another lawyer who will do it for less, and you're free to retain anyone you wish. At the moment, all you owe me is a thousand dollars." Stone watched the man think. He didn't mention that he knew of the altercation outside Elaine's some months before, and he thought that Van Fleet might be guiltier than he was admitting.

"All right, that's acceptable," Van Fleet said finally. "I'll give you a check for ten thousand dollars right now."

Stone nodded and watched while Van Fleet wrote the check. They shook hands. "I'll call you as soon as I find out which assistant DA your case has been assigned to, and after I've had a chance to talk to him."

"Good night, then, and thank you again for coming down here and getting me out."

Stone watched the man walk to his van and drive away, then he caught a cab uptown.

Later in the week, Stone visited the offices of the district attorney and found the assistant DA assigned to Van Fleet's case. She was a rather plain young woman named Mendel. She offered him the other chair in her tiny cubicle, then flipped quickly through the file.

"Your client is a potentially dangerous man, Mr. Barrington," she said. "If the police had not arrived on the scene, chances are this young woman would have been raped."

"Come on, at a traffic light?" Stone said derisively. "This was nothing more than a quick grope, and the girl encouraged it."

She glanced at the file again. "Your client had been drinking."

"But he wasn't even over the limit for driving, was he?" Stone asked, taking a stab. "And what was the girl's blood-alcohol content?"

Mendel snapped the file shut. "I can't discuss that."

"Come on, Ms. Mendel, the police didn't even test her, did they? How is that going to look in court?"

"I might be able to reduce to simple battery," she said. "Your client, as a first offender, wouldn't do any time. I'd recommend counseling and community service."

"How long have you been on the job?" Stone asked.

"That's not relevant to this discussion," she replied primly.

"As little time as that, huh?" She had probably been a member of the bar longer than he had, but she didn't know that. "Look, if this went to trial, I'd blow you right out of the water. In fact, I could insist on going down the hall to the chief prosecutor right now and get this one tossed, but that would embarrass you and take up my time. Please don't think I'm patronizing you, but I want to give you some advice. The traffic is too heavy in this office to give your time to anything but cases you have a real chance of winning. This one is a nonstarter, and we both know it. Why don't you just drop charges now—you have that authority—and let's save ourselves for something worth going to trial on?" He smiled.

"Oh, shit, all right," she said, tossing the file on her desk. "But I'm going to take it out of your ass when I do get you into court." She smiled seductively.

Stone thanked her and fled the premises. Back

in his new office, with Helen typing in the reception room, he called Van Fleet and gave him the news.

"Oh, thank you so very much," Van Fleet breathed into the phone. "I can't tell you what a load off my mind this is."

"Glad to be of help, Herb," Stone said, "but let me give you some advice. Stop picking up girls in bars. This was a close call, and, if you keep it up, you're going to get in trouble. I don't want to see that happen."

"Don't worry, Stone," Van Fleet said. "You won't have to defend me again."

Stone hung up and reflected on what an easy ten thousand dollars he had made.

Helen came into his office. "A Ms. Hilliard called while you were on the phone. She dictated this message to me."

Stone read the message:

Please meet me in the lobby of the Algonquin Hotel at four o'clock this afternoon. Don't disappoint me.

Stone felt an involuntary stirring in his crotch. The hell with her, he thought; he wouldn't do it.

44

Stone arrived at the Algonquin at four on the dot. The Japanese had bought the hotel, as they had seemed to buy nearly everything else, and had restored the lobby. It was beautiful, he thought, gazing at the polished oak paneling and the new fabrics. He looked around for Cary; she had not yet arrived. He snagged the headwaiter and was given a table. He ordered a drink and waited.

Five minutes later, a bellman walked among the tables calling, "Mr. Barrington, message for Mr. Barrington!"

Stone accepted an envelope and tipped the man. It was a hotel envelope, and inside was a plastic card with a lot of holes punched in it. A number had been written on it with a marking pen. He paid for his drink and walked to the elevator. Sweat was beginning to seep from his armpits and crotch, and he was breathing a little faster than he normally did.

The room was at the end of the hall. He inserted the card in a slot, there was an audible click, and the door opened into a nicely furnished sitting room. The door to the bedroom was closed, and he opened it, letting a shaft of light into the darkened room. He closed the door behind him and took off his overcoat. There was a slit of light from under the bathroom door and the sound of water running. Breathing harder now, Stone began ridding himself of his clothes.

When she opened the door, the bathroom light illuminated her from above for just a moment. She was wearing only a terry-cloth robe, and it fell open. She switched off the light and crossed the room to him. Somewhere along the way, the robe disappeared.

He rolled off her and sprawled on his back, panting and sweating. It had been the third time in two hours; he hadn't known he was capable of that. In the time since he had entered the room, neither of them had spoken a word that had not been connected with what they were doing to each other.

She handed him a glass of water from the bedside. He drank greedily from it, then handed it back.

"Turn on a light," he said. "It's on your side."

"No."

"I want to see you."

"No."

"Why are we doing this in a hotel room? I have a home; you could have come there."

"It would have been an unnecessary risk," she said.

"Risk? What risk?"

"We can't be seen together."

"Cary, for Christ's sake! I think you owe me some sort of explanation for your behavior."

"My father always said to me, 'Never explain, never apologize.'"

He got angrily out of bed and went into the bathroom. He peed, then turned on the light and looked at himself in the mirror, his hair awry, his face streaked with sweat. He found a facecloth and cleaned himself, brushed his hair with his fingers, rinsed his mouth. When he came out of the bathroom, she was dressed and pulling on a coat. A silk scarf was tied around her hair.

"Cary, stay here and talk to me."

"I can't."

The photograph of her and Harkness in bed together was still in his overcoat pocket. He felt an urge to thrust it into her face, but he held back. It disgusted him that he still wanted her, but he did, and he could not afford to push her further away.

"Did you check on the Rome flight?" she asked casually.

"Yes. Dino didn't see Harkness. His name was on the manifest, though; that means someone used his ticket."

"Probably a crew member." She was buckling the belt of her trench coat.

"I can't prove he wasn't on the airplane, and, if he wasn't, then I can't prove where else he was. Not without your help."

"I can't do that."

"Why not? If he murdered her, don't you want him caught?"

She went into the bathroom and began putting on lipstick. "There's something else you could look into, though."

"What's that?"

"Sasha gave him a very large amount of money; I'm not sure how much."

Stone remembered the funds missing from Sasha's accounts. "Could it have been as much as two million dollars?"

"Yes. She wanted it back, and he couldn't come up with it."

Motive, he thought. Finally, a solid motive. Harkness borrowed the money, then lost it somehow—gambling? Bad investments?

"Why did she give him the money?"

"To invest. Barron thinks of himself as God's gift to Wall Street. Wall Street thinks of him that way, too; he's lost millions in his time." She put her makeup back into her purse and snapped it shut.

"How can I get in touch with you?"

"I told you before, you can't. I'll call you soon." She was in the living room and opening the front door before he could move to stop her. She paused there and looked back. "You were wonderful," she said. "You're always wonderful." She closed the door behind her.

He nearly went after her, then remembered he was naked.

* * *

When he got home, there was an invitation in the mail, postmarked Penn Station:

The pleasure of your company is requested for dinner,
Saturday evening at nine.
A car will call for you at eight thirty.
Black tie

A handwritten note was in a corner:

I so look forward to meeting you.
S.

45

Stone spent a good part of the night restless in his bed, wondering how he could use the new information Cary had given him about Barron Harkness. He found a possible answer in the television column of the following morning's *New York Times*:

BARKER GETS LATE-NIGHT SHOW

Hiram Barker, the writer and social gadfly, has landed his own interview show, Sunday nights at 11:30 P.M., on the Continental Network, beginning this Sunday. Barker, contacted for comment, said that negotiations had been going on for several weeks and that he expected to be able to attract guests who did not ordinarily give interviews.

Stone picked up the phone and called Hi Barker.

"Hello, Stone, how are you? I hear good things about you from Frank Woodman."

"I'm very well, Hi. I see in this morning's *Times* that you've landed a television show."

"That's right. In fact, I had hoped to interview you about the Sasha business."

"It's a little early for that, I think, but you may remember that when we first met I agreed to tell you what I knew first, in return for your help."

"I remember that very well indeed, dear boy, and that's an IOU I intend to collect."

"Well, I'm not ready for you to publish just yet, but I am ready to start telling you what I know about the case."

"I'm delighted to hear it."

"How about lunch today?"

"You're on. Where?"

"The Four Seasons at twelve thirty?"

"Fine. Use my name; you'll get a better table."

"There's just one thing, Hi."

"What's that?"

"If I'm going to tell you all, you're going to have to do the same."

"But I thought I already had, Stone." Barker sounded wounded.

"You held something back, Hi, something important, and today I want to know all about that."

"Hmmmm," Barker said, "I wonder if you're fishing."

"Today, I'm catching," Stone replied. "See you at lunch."

He was fishing, indeed. He didn't know what Barker was holding back, but he figured there must be something. Most people held back something.

* * *

Stone arrived first, and Barker's trip to their table was slowed as he stopped at half a dozen others to greet their occupants.

"I love this place," Barker sighed as he slid his bulk into a seat. "It's just so . . . *perfect.*"

"I'm glad I chose it," Stone said. He ordered a bottle of wine.

"All right," Barker said when their lunch had come, "you first."

Stone began at the beginning and took Barker through his investigation of the Nijinsky case. He glossed over the business with Hank Morgan's suicide to protect Dino, and Barker didn't call him on it. When he had finished, Barker looked skeptical.

"Then you're still nowhere on this?"

"Not quite nowhere," Stone replied. "I have some new information."

"Tell me, dear boy."

"I've learned that Barron Harkness wasn't on the airplane from Rome."

Barker's eyebrows went up in delight. "And how did you learn that?"

"I must protect my source."

"So now you'll have him arrested?" Barker seemed thrilled at the prospect.

"No. I can't prove he wasn't on the airplane. His ticket was used, so his name appears on the manifest."

"How about questioning the flight attendants? Surely, they would remember such a celebrity."

"Not necessarily. Months have passed. The flight attendants might testify that they don't remember seeing him, but they couldn't credibly swear that he was not on the plane."

"Hmmmm. I see your problem."

"There's something else. Sasha gave Harkness two million dollars to invest, and he was having trouble returning it."

"Now *that's* very interesting."

"Yes, but again, I can't prove it. The money seems to have been laundered through a Cayman Islands bank, so there's no paper trail. The only person who could testify to the transaction is Sasha, and she's not available—at least, not yet."

"Not yet? You sound as if you think she might still be alive."

Stone took Barker through his terminal velocity theory.

Barker looked doubtful. "That's pretty far-fetched, Stone. I think you're grasping at straws."

Stone took the note and the invitation from his pocket and put them on the table.

"Jesus H. Christ," Barker said. He took out his glasses and examined the note carefully. "I've had a couple of letters from Sasha in the past, and that certainly looks like her handwriting."

"An expert says it almost certainly is," Stone said. "What's more, her fingerprints were on the note."

Barker forgot about his food. *"Her fingerprints?"*

"I kid you not."

"Well, if Sasha is alive, and if you are having dinner with her on Saturday night, then you'll soon have her testimony about Harkness."

"If she's alive, and *if* the dinner isn't some sort

of elaborate hoax perpetrated by some demented Sasha fan. I can't depend on that to nail Harkness. I need your help."

"I would be absolutely delighted," Barker said, grinning. "Barron has never been one of my favorite people. What is it you want me to do?"

"I want you to invite him to be your first guest on your new television show."

"And?"

Stone told him.

Barker chuckled as he listened. "I *love* it," he said.

"That's even better than writing about it in *Vanity Fair,* isn't it?" Stone asked.

"Oh, I could do that, too," Barker said, laughing. "Print *all* the details." He laughed again. "You know, I'm going to see Barron this afternoon at a social event. I'll corner him there and get him to agree to do the show. He's never given personal interviews, you know."

"I'd heard that. Now, Hi, it's your turn. I want to know what you didn't tell me about Sasha."

Barker looked at Stone appraisingly. "I've underestimated you," he said. "I wouldn't have told anybody in a million years, but now you've trapped me."

Stone sat back and waited.

"There is one promise I must extract from you," Barker said.

"What's that?"

"If Sasha is alive, you will never tell a living soul what I am about to tell you. If you find out she's dead, then I'll tell the world."

"All right, I agree." Suddenly, Stone knew what he was about to hear.

"This really has no relevance to your investigation, at least I can't imagine how it could be relevant, but who knows?"

"Come on, Hi, tell me."

"It came out in my research. I do a great deal more research for my profiles than anybody imagines. I use only a fraction of what I learn, but I learn *everything*." Barker leaned forward and wagged a finger. "You must never let me do a profile of you, if you have anything to hide."

Stone sat back and relaxed. Barker was going to stretch it out.

"At the time I was researching the Sasha piece, I knew a fellow in the American embassy in Moscow. I asked him to get me a copy of Sasha's birth announcement and fax it to me, along with a translation. Her father was a member of the academy and a very famous writer in the USSR, so I knew there would be an announcement in *Pravda* or *Izvestia*. And there was." He paused for effect.

"Go on," Stone said.

"And what do you think the baby was named?"

Stone let Barker have his moment. "I can't imagine."

"The baby was named Vladimir Georgivich Nijinsky." Barker rested his chin on his folded hands, looking pleased with himself.

"A boy's name? But when her family came to America six years later, all the pictures showed a little girl. What about the passport?"

"They had no passports. They were thrown out

of the Soviet Union and given asylum here. They had no records of any kind, not even birth certificates. The Soviets refused to supply them. The State Department, as was usual at the time, issued them documents based on sworn statements from the parents."

"And Georgi Nijinsky swore that little Vladimir was a girl named Sasha?"

"Precisely. I never got the whole story—God knows, I would never have asked Sasha—but I surmise that, from birth, the little boy exhibited female traits, and the parents accepted that and raised him as a girl. I did find out that they took her to Morocco on a six-week vacation when she was twelve, and I believe she must have had hormone treatments and a sex-change operation at that time. After all, the onset of puberty was at hand, and people would have begun to notice if little Vladimir wasn't developing breasts, et cetera." Barker looked at Stone closely. "You don't seem particularly surprised. I thought I would knock you right out of your chair with this story."

"I figured it out when you began to tell me, but I had the advantage of an important clue."

"What was that?"

"The handwriting expert who compared this note to a sample of Sasha's writing said that both letters were written by a man."

"Oh, that's a wonderful touch for my *Vanity Fair* piece!" Barker crowed. Then he became serious. "But tell me, Stone, what happens if neither of these things works—if Sasha isn't alive, and if Barron refuses to do my show?"

"Well, I have an ace up my sleeve—my source for the information about the flight and the money. This would be a reluctant witness, but a subpoena can work wonders, especially if the witness may be an accessory to the crime because of withholding information."

Barker looked down at the table. "Stone, I know you were seeing Cary Hilliard—you brought her to my house, remember? Might Cary be your source?"

Stone played cagey. "Why do you ask?"

"I didn't want to bring this up; I got the impression at that time that you and Cary were close."

"You could say that."

Barker's voice was sympathetic. "Stone, I have to tell you that Barron Harkness and Cary Hilliard are being married this afternoon, at three. I was invited to the wedding."

Stone took a quick breath. "I wasn't," he said.

"And, Stone, after they're married, Cary can't be subpoenaed to testify against her husband, can she?"

"No," he said.

46

The carpet layers took up much of Stone's time on the afternoon of Cary Hilliard's wedding, but his mind was not on the work. He walked through the house looking for the thrill that usually came when he thought about its completion, but it did not come.

He mustered his defenses and thrust the thought of Cary into a corner of his mind from which he was determined not to let it escape. Instead, he thought about Barron Harkness, of his every contact with the man, their every conversation, trying to remember something that would help connect him with Sasha's fall.

He told himself that his desire to nail Harkness had nothing to do with the loss of Cary, but, when he looked at his watch and saw that it was a little after three, he fantasized that he was interrupting the ceremony at the point where the minister asks for reasons why the marriage should not take place. "Reverend," he would say loudly from the back of the congregation, "I am here to arrest the groom for murder. I should think that sufficient cause for the wedding not to take place." For some reason, in his fantasy, he spoke these words with an English accent.

He used an old technique for when he was stumped on a case—go back to the beginning and review possible suspects. But in his attempt to incriminate Barron Harkness, he came up dry. There was only one other conceivable suspect, now that Hank Morgan had removed herself from the scene: Herbert Van Fleet. But, in spite of his obsession with Sasha, Van Fleet had come up clean. Dino didn't think so, he remembered, and Dino's instincts were often good; but, for that matter, so were his own, and he could not bring himself even to dislike Van Fleet, strange as he was.

Then, he remembered something else odd about Van Fleet, though it did not seem connected to Sasha. Van Fleet had finished medical school but had been rejected during his internship as "unsuited for a medical career." That was the statement Dino had read to him, something one of the investigative teams had turned up, a statement from somebody at Physicians & Surgeons Hospital, where Van Fleet had served his abortive internship.

When the carpet layers had finished, Stone retrieved his badge from a dresser drawer and caught a cab uptown. Dino was still on his honeymoon, he reasoned, and there was nobody he could turn to for the original record of the investigation, so he would have to do this himself. Anyway, it kept his mind off Cary.

The hospital was the most prestigious of its kind in the city, having treated the great and near great for more than a century. There was as much cachet attached to checking into Physicians & Surgeons as there was to moving into a Fifth Avenue apartment.

"Can you tell me who is in charge of interns?" he asked at the front desk.

"The chief resident," a young woman replied.

No good. The chief resident would not have been at the hospital long enough. "And who does he report to, ultimately?"

"The chief of medicine," the young woman replied. "His name is Garfield. Did you wish to see an intern, sir?"

"No, I just need some information, and I think the chief of medicine is the person I should see."

"Well, his office is on the fifth floor, but I shouldn't think he'd see you without an appointment."

"Thanks, I'll just have a word with his secretary. By the way, how long has Dr. Garfield been chief of medicine?"

The woman shrugged. "I've been here for twelve years, and he had the job when I arrived. Since Adam, I guess."

Stone took the elevator to the fifth floor and followed the signs. The chief of medicine occupied a spacious corner suite, and two secretaries guarded his door. Stone showed the badge to one of them. "My name is Barrington. I'd like to see Dr. Garfield."

"I'm afraid he's in a staff meeting at the

moment, and he has another appointment immediately after that," the woman replied, unimpressed.

"Would you please take him a note saying that I'm here and that I would like to see him? This is a serious matter."

The woman seemed uncertain, but she disappeared through a door for a minute, then returned. "Dr. Garfield will be finished with his staff meeting in just a few minutes. He asked that you wait."

Stone took a seat and picked up a magazine.

Shortly, a tall, elderly man dressed in a long white coat appeared in the reception room. "I'm Garfield. What can I do for you?"

"I wonder if we could talk privately?" Stone asked, glancing at the two secretaries.

"I suppose so," Garfield said, striding toward his office door, "but I haven't got a hell of a lot of time."

"This won't take long," Stone said, following him.

The doctor did not sit, and he did not ask Stone to. "Well?" he said impatiently.

"I'm inquiring about a former intern at this hospital named Herbert Van Fleet," Stone said.

Garfield didn't reply immediately. "There was somebody here about him a few months ago," he said finally.

"Well, somebody's here again, Doctor, and it's important."

"Why is it important?"

"Let's just say that it's in connection with a serious crime."

"What do you want to know?"

"Were you in charge when Van Fleet was interning here?"

"I was."

"Why was he terminated from his internship?"

Garfield stared at him for a moment. "Am I going to end up testifying in a court of law about this?"

"That's unlikely," Stone said. "This is purely for background."

"It's about the Nijinsky woman, isn't it?"

"I can't say, sir."

"Well, Mr. Barrington, you'd better say, if you want to get anything out of me. I read the tabloids, from time to time, and I'm aware that you are retired from the police department."

Stone tried to keep from showing embarrassment. "That's true, sir."

"Then why are you flashing a badge around here?"

"Retired officers are allowed to keep their badges."

"I don't have to talk to a retired detective, you know."

"I know that, sir, but I think the information I'm asking for could be important."

"You don't have the slightest notion of whether it's important, do you? You're just curious."

"To tell you the truth, sir, I am. I couldn't break

this one when I was on the force, and it bothers me that it's no longer being investigated."

"The Morgan woman didn't do it, then?"

"No, sir, she didn't."

Garfield sat down behind his desk and waved Stone to a chair. "Let me explain something to you, Mr. Barrington. This is a very highly regarded institution of healing, and we get some very well-known people in here as patients."

"I'm aware of that, Doctor."

"It's conceivable that if the information you're asking for got into the papers, there could be . . . repercussions for this hospital."

"I assure you, Doctor, nothing you tell me will become a part of any public record, and I certainly won't pass it on to the press."

The doctor looked at Stone thoughtfully. "I'd like to know what happened to Sasha Nijinsky myself," he said.

"So would I, Doctor; that's why I'm here."

"All right, but if it ever comes up, I will deny I ever told you any of this."

Stone nodded. "I understand."

Garfield took a deep breath and began. "This happened, what—twelve, thirteen years ago?"

"That sounds about right."

"You have to understand that interns, like everybody else, have their own little . . . eccentricities. I have seen year-end pranks pulled that would stand your hair on end—cadavers in the cafeteria, you know? We try to be a little tolerant of these things—after all, these young people are under a lot of pressure, and they don't get much time off—but we keep a close eye on them, all the same. I've had alcoholics, drug addicts, nymphomaniacs—all sorts of problems exhibit themselves, and, usually, with a little counseling, we can keep the offender in the program, maybe make a fine physician out of him later on. We're not out to wreck careers, here; these kids come to us with eight years of higher education, and they've worked hard. But we have to draw the line somewhere."

"Where did you draw it with Herbert Van Fleet?"

"Van Fleet was one of our brighter interns," Garfield said, placing his feet on his desk, unwilling to be hurried. "He finished, I don't know, sixth or seventh in his med school class at Columbia, and he exhibited an inclination toward pathology. Might have been good at it, too; unfortunately, that was not the only inclination he exhibited." He paused.

"Go on, Doctor," Stone encouraged.

"Van Fleet appeared to be attracted to sick people."

"That seems like a desirable quality in a physician."

Garfield shook his head. "I'm not making myself clear," he said. "I mean he exhibited a sexual attraction for the ill. Women, that is. He seemed very uncomfortable with male patients, didn't like to touch them. One of his professors at Columbia told me that, as a med student, he had refused to work on a male cadaver, except when forced to study the genitalia. My guess is that he was suppressing homosexual, or at least bisexual, tendencies, and that he had difficulty accepting these tendencies or dealing with them."

"How did this attraction to ill women manifest itself?"

"The chief resident noticed that he was spending a lot of extra time with young women patients, especially those recovering from injury or surgery, looking frequently into the rooms of these patients. If someone else was in attendance, he'd leave; he'd wait until they were alone before he visited them. The nurses noticed him, and there were jokes about it. The patients always seemed to be those who had IV's running. We started to keep a watch on him, surreptitiously.

"About that time, we had a very well-known actress in here as the result of an automobile accident. She had to have extensive reconstructive surgery done on a hand, and, as you can imagine, the reaction among the interns to the presence of this famous and beautiful woman was startling. A lot of them suddenly exhibited a keen interest in surgery of the hand. Van Fleet, in particular, was attentive.

"Then one night, only a few hours after a surgical procedure, a nursing supervisor walked into the woman's room and found Van Fleet on top of her."

"On top of her?" Stone asked, unbelieving.

"He'd taken a syringe of morphine from a drugs cabinet, injected it into her IV, which immediately put her to sleep; then he had removed his clothes, had removed *her* clothes, and he was . . . copulating with her."

"Jesus Christ."

"Indeed. I was summoned from my bed and told the circumstances. The actress was still sleeping peacefully, and Van Fleet, as you might imagine, was distressed at having been caught in the act. While they were waiting for me to arrive, he threatened the nursing supervisor if she reported him. She did, of course, and I made short work of young Dr. Van Fleet."

"I can imagine."

"The nursing supervisor cleaned up the patient and put her clothing in order, and no more was said about it. I should have called the police, I suppose, and had him charged with rape, but you see the position I was in: the papers would have had an absolute field day, the actress would have sued us—and won—and this hospital would have been done irreparable harm as a result."

"And the actress never knew?"

Garfield shook his head. "I lived in fear for months that she would turn up pregnant—she didn't, thank God. I'm not sure what I would have done if that had happened." Garfield sighed. "You see why I'm concerned that this go no further."

"I do, and I promise you it won't."

Garfield stood up and slipped out of his white coat. "I'm afraid I'm going to have to run now." He got into his suit jacket. "I hope this story might somehow help you."

"It might, Dr. Garfield, and I thank you for

confiding in me." He shook the doctor's hand and turned to go.

"Mr. Barrington," Garfield said, "whatever became of Van Fleet? What's he doing now?"

"He's a mortician," Stone said.

Garfield gave a little shudder. "How very appropriate," he said.

47

When Stone woke on Thursday morning, his first thought was that only three days remained until Sasha's dinner party. His second thought was that there was someone in his bathroom.

It could be only one person, he knew; she had a key, and she knew the code for the security system. He was flabbergasted and revolted that she should be in his house only days after her marriage, but his revulsion vanished when she came out of the bathroom.

She was naked, and the sight of her body had always had a powerful effect on him. It came to him at that moment that he was lost; that she could, if she wished, lead him around by the cock for the rest of his life. So this is obsession, he thought, as she silently slid under the sheets and drew close to him. He gave himself to it.

"You know this was a completely disgusting and immoral thing to do, don't you?" he asked when they had finished and lay panting in each other's arms. He was not joking.

"Of course, my darling," she replied. "That's why it's so much fun."

"Has anyone ever completely satisfied you?"

"You satisfy me, for a time, but to answer your question honestly, no. At least, no man ever has. I knew a girl in college who could satisfy me longer than anyone. She was only twenty, but she knew everything about pleasing a woman, because she was a woman, I suppose."

"Do you still see her?"

"No. She committed suicide our senior year, shot herself with a pistol borrowed from a boy we knew. She left a note saying she had done it for me, because she knew she could never have me, and she wanted to prove she really loved me. The housemother in the dorm found the note and showed it to me, then destroyed it."

"How did you react to that?"

"I was elated. It did wonders for my self-esteem, that someone could love me so much. I never loved her, of course, I just liked having her make love to me."

"You don't make love, Cary. You merely fuck."

Cary raised herself on an elbow and looked at him. "Do you really think so?" she asked wonderingly.

"Yes."

She nodded. "You're right, I think, but I do fuck surpassingly well, don't I?"

"You do," Stone said; then he fucked her again.

When they had exhausted each other, she lay on her back, her breasts pointing at the ceiling. "You think it's terrible that I'm still fucking you, now that I'm married," she said.

"Yes. And it's just as bad that I'm still fucking you."

"You wait. One of these days, perhaps before very long, you'll get married, but you'll still want to fuck me. And believe me, my darling, you will. Because I'll never let go of you."

"Yes," he said, "I will." Whenever she wanted him, for as long as she wanted him.

On Thursday nights at Elaine's, the big table across from the bar was kept for the guys—the regulars who had been coming for years, whom Elaine had fed when they were broke, the starving writers who might not have made it in New York without the nurturing and bonding that went on in an uptown neighborhood saloon. They wandered in and out during the evening, bitching about their agents and the promotion budgets for their most recent books, moaning about the pitiful advance sales and the huge reserve for returns on their royalty statements.

There were guys who were getting a million dollars a book now—sometimes more—and others who were getting twenty-five thousand and pretending it was two hundred. There were guys who had given up on writing fiction and were churning out screenplays for the movies and television, and there were guys who were doing it all—books, magazines, television series—the works. They were bonded by the common knowledge that nobody—not their wives, sweethearts, or publishers—believed they really worked for a living, and, sometimes, they weren't too sure of that themselves.

Stone often sat with the bunch these days, and he liked them. He wasn't exactly sure he was working for a living either, so they had something in common. Most Thursday nights, somebody would bring a girl, and they were always smart and pretty. Stone envied them their girls.

This Thursday night, drained of desire by Cary, relaxed, and depressed, Stone got drunk. He had three Wild Turkeys before dinner—which was, in itself, a big mistake—drank most of a bottle of wine with his pasta, and, when Elaine said she was buying, couldn't resist a Sambuca or two. He switched to mineral water for a while, until he felt steadier, then started on cognac. By the time he and a couple of other guys closed the place at 4:00 A.M., he was ambulatory, but only just.

He walked carefully from the place, uncharacteristically gave the bum on duty a buck, and thought for a minute about whether he should walk. He usually walked; it was good for the knee and for the gut, but tonight walking seemed out of the question. He flagged a cab, gave the driver the exact address, explaining that he wished to be driven to the door, not to the corner, then hunkered way down in the backseat and tried to keep from passing out. That was what he was doing when the shooting started.

They had pulled up to the light, and the cabbie had decided he felt like talking. "You follow baseball?" he asked, half-turning toward the backseat.

Stone was trying to answer him when there was a sound like a watermelon being dropped from a great height, and the driver's face exploded, leaving a huge hole spouting blood. As Stone hit the floor of the backseat, the screech of rubber on pavement told him the shooter was on his way.

Stone scrambled out of the cab, and, operating instinctively, yanked the left side door open, shoved the dead driver aside, and got the cab in gear. A block and a half ahead, a van was roaring away. Stone stood on it. He switched the blinking caution lights on, leaned on the horn, and streaked off down Second Avenue after the van.

There was almost no traffic on the avenue at 4:00 A.M. "Where the fuck are the blue-and-whites?" he demanded aloud, suddenly aware that he was now cold sober. "Where are you, you sons of bitches?" The cab was new, and he gained on the van for a minute, until the driver realized he was being pursued. Still, Stone was keeping pace a block behind. He wasn't sure he wanted to get any closer, since he wasn't armed; all he wanted to do was to attract a blue-and-white or two. He tried to make out the license plate on the van and failed.

At Forty-second Street, the van hung a left and nearly turned over. "That would be good," Stone said, "turn the fucking thing over and save me some trouble!" Good luck, too. On Forty-second Street a blue-and-white was parked in front of an all-night joint, the cops drinking coffee from paper cups. Stone glanced in the rearview mirror as he passed and saw the cups go out the windows on both sides and the car start after him.

The van turned left again and started up First Avenue, keeping all four wheels on the ground this time. Stone managed a wide four-wheel drift and made up a few yards on him. The blue-and-white was doing even better; it was faster than both the van and Stone's cab. At Fifty-seventh Street, the blue-and-white overtook Stone, and the cop in the passenger seat was waving him over. Stone shook his head and pointed ahead. "No! Get him! Get him! He's the cab killer!" The cop didn't seem to understand, but the driver floored it and went after the van. Stone followed. At Seventy-second Street, another blue-and-white joined the chase. At Eighty-sixth Street, the van driver made his mistake. He started a turn to the left, then saw a hooker crossing the street. He wavered, missed her, then, too late, tried to get the van around the corner. It teetered on two wheels, then went over and slid twenty feet on its side, coming to rest against a parked car.

"This is one for Scoop Berman," Stone cackled, skidding to a halt behind a blue-and-white. "I wonder where the little guy is tonight."

The little guy came out of the driver's window, holding an impossibly large pistol equipped with a silencer. He popped off one shot, which shattered the window of a blue-and-white, then a returning fusillade knocked him back inside the van.

Four cops approached the van warily now, three pistols out in front, another with a riot gun. They hesitated, then the bearer of the shotgun crept around the front of the van and peered in through the windshield. The shotgun went off, and Stone made it around the van in time to see the cop reach into the cab through the hole he had blown open and remove Scoop Berman's pistol.

The cop used the butt of the shotgun to clean out a larger area of the windshield, and with help, pulled Scoop out of the van onto the pavement.

"You the cabdriver?" a cop asked Stone as they crowded around Scoop.

"No, the passenger. The driver's in the front seat, there, missing most of his head."

"Well, we finally got the fucker," another cop said. "That's cabbie number six he's offed. We'll get a fucking commendation for this one." He pulled out his notebook. "Let's have your name," he said to Stone, "and we'll want a statement from you."

"My name's Barrington. I was fourteen years on the job, detective second, most recently out of the 19th."

"I know you," another cop said. "You were Dino Bacchetti's partner."

"Right."

"Let him write out his own statement," the cop said to his colleague. "He'll do it better than you."

"I know this guy," Stone said, nodding at Scoop.

"His name's Berman; he's a free-lance television cameraman. You want me to talk to him?"

"Yeah," said the cop. "If you know him."

Stone went and knelt over Berman. "Scoop, how are you feeling? An ambulance is on the way."

Scoop was gutshot, twice, and there was blood around his lips. His eyes focused. "Hey, Stone," he said. "I thought you was out to pasture."

"I was, buddy, but I was in the cab."

Scoop looked worried. "I'm sorry about that," he said. "You okay?"

"I'm okay. Scoop, did you shoot the other cab-drivers?"

"Yeah, the bastards always got in my way when I was on a story. Other cars would get out of the way, you know? But not hacks, the sons of bitches."

Stone turned to a cop, who had a notebook out. "You get that?"

"Yeah," the cop said. "You know, I wanted to shoot a few cabbies myself, at times."

"Stone," Scoop said.

"Yeah, Scoop?"

"There's something I never told you. I shouldda told you, but I didn't. I wanted it for myself."

"What's that, Scoop?" He could hear the ambulance approaching.

"The night Sasha took her dive, remember?"

"You bet I remember."

"I was there, remember?"

"I remember. You got her on tape. It was a good job."

"There was a guy on the scene had these black glasses, with tape on them."

"I remember. His name is Van Fleet."

"That's right. He works on stiffs."

"Right."

"I think he knows something. I think he saw who tossed Sasha, or something. He was acting funny at the scene. I tried to find him after I showed you the tape, but he was gone. I bought him a drink later, tried to get it out of him, but he wouldn't talk to me."

"Okay, Scoop, I'm glad to know that. Thanks."

The ambulance screeched to a halt, and two men came with a stretcher. Stone stood up to let them at Scoop, and, as he did, he saw Scoop's eyes glaze over and his head fall to one side. A paramedic produced a stethoscope and listened to his chest.

"This one's had it," he said to a cop. "No ticker at all, and, with those kind of holes in him, he ain't gonna resuscitate, believe me."

"Ah, shit," the cop said. "I wanted to see him stand trial."

"No, it's better this way," Stone said. "All neat and tidy; you got your confession."

Later that morning, when Stone finally got into bed, he discovered he was drunk again.

48

On Friday, Stone sat down and thought about his options. He should have gone to the FBI, he knew, when he got the first letter. Their kidnapping case was still open and would remain open until there was some sort of resolution, but they had already conducted their own investigation of Van Fleet and had turned up nothing. Neither had their search of his loft produced anything, and they were unlikely to find Stone's new information compelling. Anyway, his years as a police officer had made him very nearly constitutionally incapable of going to the FBI for anything.

He could, too, have gone to the police, maybe approached Delgado directly, but it had already been made abundantly clear to him that the police hierarchy considered the case closed and did not want it reopened. If he could deliver Van Fleet and Sasha, handcuffed together, Delgado might listen to him, but not otherwise.

His best alternative was Dino. Dino was even less anxious than Delgado to reopen, because he didn't want to piss off his superiors, but Dino was his friend, and he still felt guilty about the treatment Stone had received from the department. The trouble was, Dino was in Las Vegas. Stone called Dino's mother and learned that he was due back from his honeymoon sometime the following day. Stone heaved a sigh of relief. Dino wasn't going to be easy, but at least he would be in town.

The phone rang.

"Stone. It's Hi Barker."

"What's happening, Hi?"

"I got him. He's mine for the Sunday-night show. Is there anything else I should know before I interview him?"

"I told you everything at lunch. I'll leave it to you how to handle him."

"Will you be there?"

"I'll be there with a cop," Stone said. "Where do I go?"

"We're broadcasting from what the network calls the 'executive studios,' on the top floor of their headquarters building on Seventh Avenue. You know the building?"

"Yes."

"I'll leave your name with the security guard— and what's the name of your cop?"

"Bacchetti. What time?"

"Be there at a quarter to eleven, sharp, and go straight to the control room and stay there. We go on the air, live, at eleven thirty, and I don't want Barron to see you."

When Stone hung up, he was starting to feel excited.

At noon Saturday, Stone called Dino's new apartment in the West Village. A woman answered.

"Hello?"

"Is Dino back in town yet?"

"No, who is this?"

"This is Stone Barrington."

"Oh, yes, we met at the wedding. This is Mary Ann's mother. I'm just over here tidying up a little so the place will be nice when they get in."

"What time are they due, Mrs. Bianchi?"

"I'm not sure exactly. They were supposed to come home last night, but Dino was on a winning streak, and they missed their plane. He said they'd get whatever flight was available today. Dino wanted Sunday to rest before going back to work."

"I see. Mrs. Bianchi, would you write a note to Dino and ask him to call me the moment he gets in? Say that it's important."

"Okay, I'll tack it to the door, so he'll be sure to see it."

Stone thanked her and hung up.

The day droned on with no word from Dino, and Stone began calling every hour on the hour. There was no answer. At seven thirty, he got out his tuxedo and began to get dressed. At eight, he called Dino again and still got no reply. At eight thirty, the doorbell rang. Stone thought about it for a moment, then he retrieved his badge and gun from the dresser drawer and strapped on the ankle holster.

When Stone opened the front door, a limousine was at curbside and a mustachioed, uniformed chauffeur stood on the stoop. Stone asked the chauffeur to wait. He went to the living-room phone and called Dino's number again.

"Yeah?" Dino—sleepy, exhausted.

"Dino, it's Stone, hang on." He ran back to the front door. "What address are you taking me to?" he asked the chauffeur.

"Sorry, sir," the man said, with what seemed to be an Italian accent, "I can't tell you; it's supposed to be a surprise. I'm not supposed to wait either; I've got a schedule to keep. If you can't come now, I'll have to leave."

"I'll be right with you," Stone said and ran for the phone again. "Dino."

"Huh?"

"Listen to me now. I need your help."

"You listen to me, Stone. I've hardly had any sleep for the past three nights, you know? Now, I'm going back to bed; you call me tomorrow."

"Tomorrow may be too late, Dino. Sasha has invited me to a dinner party."

"Oh, Jesus," Dino moaned, "will you ever let go of that? I told you I don't want to hear about it again."

"I've got some new stuff on Van Fleet, Dino, and he may be mixed up in this thing tonight."

"I told you, I don't want to hear it."

"Dino, I need some backup. I don't even know where I'm going."

"I suggest you call nine-one-one when you get there, Stone. I'll call you when I'm coherent. In the meantime, fuck off!" He slammed down the telephone.

Stone ran back to the front door to see the chauffeur heading for the car. "Wait!" he called out, locking the door behind him. The chauffeur came wearily around the car and opened a door for him.

The limo was an old one, sixties vintage, but well cared for. The upholstery was well-worn velour, and black velvet curtains were drawn over the side and rear windows. "Come on," he said to the driver, "where are we going?"

"Sorry, sir," the driver said cheerfully and raised the glass partition between his compartment and the rear seat.

Stone found himself looking into a mirror. He picked at the side curtain; it was sewn or glued down. He immediately felt that he had walked into a nineteen-forties B movie. Bela Lugosi would be waiting for him at his destination. He decided to sit back and enjoy the experience. For a few minutes, he tried counting the left and right turns and estimating his position, but he became disoriented. The car seemed not to stay long on any street, not taking any avenue up or downtown, as far as he could tell. He found a light and glanced at his watch from time to time. They had left his house at eight thirty-two.

At exactly nine o'clock, the car stopped, and Stone could hear a garage door being raised. He was being taken indoors without getting out of the car first, and he didn't like it. He tore at the side curtain, but by the time it came loose he could hear the garage door winding down again.

The chauffeur opened the left-hand door for him, and, as he got out of the car, Stone saw another door leading off the garage. The chauffeur opened that one for him too, then quickly closed it behind him.

Stone looked around. He was in a nicely decorated vestibule with one other door, probably leading to the street. He tried that door and the one behind him; he was locked in. There was nowhere to go but up. An open elevator awaited him, and there was only one button. He pressed it, and the elevator rose slowly, creaking, reminding him of the one in his own house. Old. The elevator stopped, and the door opened.

Stone stepped out of the car into another vestibule, much like the one downstairs. There was an elegant, gilded mirror and a vase containing a large flower arrangement resting on an antique table. A hallway led away from the vestibule, and from that direction he could hear a murmur of conversation and the tinkle of silver against china. They had apparently started without him. A woman's laugh rose above the talk, then subsided. Was that voice familiar?

Stone walked slowly down the hallway and emerged into a very large, rectangular room, which had been divided into two areas. Ahead of him was a living area, with two leather sofas facing each other before a fireplace, in which a fire merrily burned. Soft chamber music came from speakers somewhere. There was something familiar about the room. To his left was a dining table set for eight, and, apparently, Stone was not the only one late for dinner, for three places were empty. The conversation was louder now.

A woman in a backless dress sat with her back to him, a man next to her, and a couple faced him from across the table. Both the men were in evening clothes. At the end of the table, to his right, dressed to kill, her elbow resting on the table, her hand holding a glass of wine, her face turned to greet him, smiling invitingly, was Sasha Nijinsky.

Stone took a step forward and opened his mouth to speak. Instead of what he had intended to say, a scream burst from his lips. A searing pain had thudded into his buttocks; his back arched, his knees bent, and he fell heavily onto the polished hardwood floor, his body convulsing.

He had only a moment of consciousness to grasp that Sasha and the other people at the table were immobile; were glassy eyed; were, of course, dead.

49

Stone came awake slowly. His first sensation was that his ass was on fire; the second was that every joint, every muscle in his body hurt like hell. His vision was cloudy for a moment, and he blinked his eyes rapidly to clear it. He became aware that he could not move.

He was naked. His shoulders lay on a hard table, his hands were bound behind him, and his feet were tied and suspended from a block and tackle above him, which raised him half in the air. Instinctively, he squirmed, tugging at his bonds, but they were too tight. His hands were numb.

He could move only his head, and he craned his neck to see as much as he could. He was in a long, narrow room; the walls and ceiling were covered in white tiles, aged and cracking. Two overhead bulbs were protected with steel screens. The tabletop was made of metal and sloped from head to foot. There was a faint chemical smell, something he couldn't identify.

He craned his neck farther. Near the other end of the room, just at the edge of his vision, was a vertical object, but he could not swivel his head and eyes far enough to make it out. He tried the bonds again, trying at least to stretch them enough to allow the flow of blood to return to his hands. No luck.

Minutes passed, and he wracked his brain for some other means of escape. He found that by manipulating his shoulders he could creep sideways on the table, but it became apparent to him that, since his feet were elevated, if he slipped over the edge, his head would strike the floor very hard. He stopped moving and waited.

Perhaps twenty minutes passed before he heard a scraping noise somewhere behind him, followed by hollow footsteps striking the cement floor. The chauffeur appeared, upside-down, the collar of his uniform hanging open. He reached up and ripped the mustache from his upper lip.

"There, thatsa better," he said in his Italian accent. Then he laughed.

"Herbert?" Stone said.

Van Fleet laughed again. "Didn't recognize me, did you?"

"No, I didn't. Listen, Herb, could you loosen whatever you've got around my wrists? The circulation has stopped."

"Sure," Van Fleet said. He grabbed Stone under the arms, lifted him, and flipped him over on his stomach. He fiddled with the bonds.

Stone's ankles hurt now, but he could feel the blood flowing back into his hands. "Thank you," he said. "Now, could you turn me back over, please?"

Van Fleet turned him over on his back again. "Are you cold?" he asked solicitously.

"No, it's quite warm in here. Where am I, exactly?"

"You are in what used to be part of a kosher meat-processing plant. It runs along one side of my loft, and it is accessed by moving the refrigerator in my kitchen, then removing a panel from the wall." He laughed again. "Neither you nor the FBI were able to figure it out."

"It's very clever, Herb. Now, can we talk about what's going on here?"

Van Fleet stepped forward and began feeling around Stone's neck.

"Don't do that," Stone said, irritably. He didn't like the man's hands on him.

Van Fleet took his time at whatever he was doing. "Sorry to disturb you," he said. "Just to rest your mind, I have no sexual interest in you. I don't like men that way."

Stone was relieved to hear that, but not much.

"How much did you take in before I used the stun gun?" Van Fleet asked.

"So that's what it was."

"That's right. Something like fifty thousand volts, but only for a few milliseconds."

"That was enough."

"It was, wasn't it?"

"To answer your question," Stone said, "I took in a number of corpses sitting at a dining table."

"Let's not refer to them that way, please," Van

Fleet said. "They are my friends, and, if they could hear you, they'd be very upset."

"As you wish. How did you get, uh, meet these people?"

"Oh, here and there. You might say I picked them up around town. They're all very interesting people who do interesting work. I find that interesting work makes an interesting person, don't you?"

Stone realized that he had now solved the disappearance of Dino's yuppies, not that it mattered much. "Sure, I think that's true. But, somehow, I don't think they make very interesting conversationalists at the moment."

"You're quite wrong," Van Fleet said. "I know you think of them as dead, but they're not, you know. In fact, I've given them a whole new kind of life. It's a technique I've developed myself, over the years, one I refined both in my work at the funeral parlor and in my previous job, at the Museum of Natural History. They remain as supple as when they were alive, in the usual sense of the word."

Stone could think of nothing to do but keep the conversation going. Besides, there was more he wanted to know. "Tell me about Sasha, Herb."

"Ah, Sasha." Van Fleet sighed. "She is the centerpiece of my little dinner party of course. Everybody likes a celebrity at the table. Adds spice to the evening."

"Was she alive when you brought her here?"

"I told you, they're all alive," Van Fleet said emphatically. "Please don't make it necessary for me to mention that again, or I will terminate this conversation immediately."

"I'm sorry," Stone said. "I meant alive in the usual sense of the word. What I meant to ask was, after her fall and the ambulance wreck, what sort of condition was she in?"

"Well, when I took her out of the wreck," Van Fleet said, "she was in very poor condition, indeed. The fall had broken some bones, but, oddly, not the skin. The traffic accident had done somewhat more damage. It took me quite a long time to bring her back to her present condition."

"Was she . . . breathing when you took her?"

"Amazingly enough, yes," Van Fleet said. "In fact, I believe that, if not for the traffic accident, she might have continued to breathe. As it was, she lasted only a few days, in spite of the very excellent medical care she received from me."

Stone winced at the thought of Sasha alive for days with this creep. His terminal velocity theory, though, had panned out, sort of. "Who wrote me the letter?" Stone asked.

"Oh, Sasha did—with my help, of course. She wrote me two letters, you know, when I first began writing to her, so we had something to help us with her handwriting."

"Why did she have olive oil on her hands?"

"Oh, you noticed that, did you? Well, I wanted an agent that would make a good fingerprint, and, since I was in the kitchen at the time, the oil was handy."

"Herb, we have to talk seriously now. We have to get you some help."

"Help?" Van Fleet sounded surprised. "I don't need any help. I've done all this work on these people alone, without any help at all. And it was pretty good work, don't you think? Let me explain it to you. I'll skip the technical parts, but have a look." Van Fleet took hold of the table and dragged it until Stone was facing down the room, then he put a hand under Stone's head and raised it, so he could see.

At the other end of the room was the object Stone had not been able to make out before. The body of a young woman hung by its heels, the fingertips just brushing the floor. She had been opened with one long incision from her pubic hair to her sternum, and the abdominal cavity had been emptied. "Oh, God." Stone breathed. He turned his head away.

"Oh, I'm sorry, I didn't mean to upset you," Van Fleet said, turning Stone back to his original position. "I was going to take you through the process, but if you'd rather not . . ."

"I'd rather talk," Stone said. "When I said you needed help, I didn't mean with your work."

"Oh, you mean a psychiatrist. That was suggested to me once, a long time ago."

"By Dr. Garfield?"

Van Fleet walked around Stone so that he could look at him. "What do you know about Garfield?"

"Oh, Dr. Garfield and I had a long chat about you the other day, Herb. He told me about your internship, about why you didn't complete it."

Van Fleet bristled. "This is not an amusing conversation," he said. "I hope when you're at the table you can find something more interesting to talk about." He turned and walked out of Stone's line of vision, then seemed to leave the room.

At the table? Stone began to sweat, then, almost immediately, to shiver.

Van Fleet returned. "Sorry, I had to get my instruments. Since you're going to be such a boring conversationalist, I may as well start work on you now."

"Wait a minute, Herb," Stone said quickly. "We have more to talk about."

"Do you think you can refrain from referring to past unpleasantness?"

"Oh, yes. I'm terribly sorry about that; it was rude of me."

Van Fleet dragged a stool over and sat down facing Stone. "All right, what would you like to talk about?"

"Tell me about the night Sasha fell from her balcony."

"Oh, that. I've told you about taking her from the wreck of the ambulance. Before that, well, I left Elaine's a bit after you did, I guess, and, on the way home, I thought I'd drop by Sasha's building. I often did that on the way home, just to catch a glimpse of where she lived. When I turned into the block, I could see the doorman through the glass front of the building. He was asleep in a chair, and I saw somebody walk right past him into the building, and he never woke up.

"I found that very interesting, so I parked the van and went into the building. I just walked right past him, and he never turned a hair. I took the elevator up to the twelfth floor—I knew Sasha's apartment number from my research—and, to my surprise, her door was open. I had just planned to leave a little present and go, but there was that open door. I couldn't resist.

"I crept into the apartment, and I could hear these angry voices from out on the terrace. I peeped out there, and she and this other person were having a knock-down, drag-out fight, and, all of a sudden, Sasha was just dumped over the railing.

"I jumped back behind the door, and I could hear this other person rummaging around the room, looking for something, I guess. That went on for a minute, then I heard the elevator start up, and I guess the . . . well, the murderer heard it too, and ran. I heard the fire stairs door open, then the elevator door open, and I heard somebody running down the stairs.

"I peeped out the door, and the doorman was standing at the top of the stairs, looking down, so I just popped into the open elevator and rode down. I got out on the second floor and tiptoed down the stairs. When I saw you get back into the elevator, I left the building, got into the van, and drove around the block to where Sasha was. The ambulance arrived about that time, and I followed it. I wanted to see which hospital Sasha was being taken to, so I could send flowers.

"Then, wham! That fire truck came out of nowhere, and the ambulance got hit. You know the rest."

"Herb, who threw Sasha off the balcony?"

Van Fleet shrugged. "Nobody I knew," he said.

"Can you describe him?" Stone asked.

Van Fleet started to speak, then stopped. "No, I don't think I will," he said petulantly. "You were unkind enough to bring up the past, so I don't think you deserve to know, at least not yet. Later, if you're nice, you can bring it up at dinner, and maybe I'll tell you." Van Fleet stood up, reached down, and picked up his case. He set it on the stool, opened it, and took out a large scalpel. "Don't worry, I'm very good at this; it'll be absolutely painless, I promise."

Stone had thought about dying before, but never in such close proximity to the event. Would his whole life flash before his eyes? Would it be less painful if he just relaxed and let it happen? He discovered he could not give in to it; he would go down fighting, with what meager resources he had left. "Wait a minute, Herb!" he said. "There's something I have to tell you."

"You can tell me at the dinner table," Van Fleet said, sliding his hand under Stone's chin and pulling it up to extend his neck.

Stone jerked his head free. "It's about Sasha!" he said, and watched Van Fleet's face.

Van Fleet showed interest. "What about Sasha?"

"Something you don't know about her, something important. I wouldn't want to say this in front of her at the table."

"What is it?"

"You like guys, don't you, Herb?"

"What do you mean?" Van Fleet replied indignantly. "I'm no queer. I like women."

"What about your relationship with the men at the table?" Stone asked.

"You have a filthy mind," Van Fleet said. "I have no kind of *relationship* with anybody at the table. Except Sasha, of course. We have a perfectly normal sex life."

Perfectly normal? Stone laughed aloud. "Come on, Herb, you're as queer as a three-dollar bill." Words were all Stone had left to fight with, and he was at least going to get in a few punches before this maniac slaughtered him.

"That's a lie!"

"Then why do you think you like fucking Sasha so much?"

"Sasha's a woman, you idiot," Van Fleet said. "We have a heterosexual relationship!"

"Sasha's not a woman, Herbert. I found out. When she was born in Russia, her parents named her Vladimir, because she was a boy. They raised her as a girl, though, and, when she was twelve, she had a sex-change operation in Morocco!"

"You're insane!" Van Fleet cried.

"You're fucking a guy, Herbert, you goddamned faggot!" Stone screamed. "All this time you've been fucking a guy's corpse, a dead guy, Herbert!"

Van Fleet was making animal noises now, and spittle had formed on his lips. He raised the scalpel over his head, and his voice became a howl.

Stone braced himself, baring his teeth. He'd bite the bastard's arm off, if he could.

Then a huge noise filled the room, echoing off the tile walls, and, simultaneously, a hole appeared in Van Fleet's throat; a moment later, the noise came again, and another hole appeared under his right eye. Van Fleet reeled backward and disappeared from Stone's view.

Stone was nearly deaf from the noise, which was now settling into a constant ringing in his ears.

Then Dino walked into Stone's view and looked down at him. "Jesus, Stone," he said, shaking his head. "How do you get yourself into these situations?"

50

"Well, I always told you Van Fleet was dirty, didn't I?" Dino said. He and Stone were sitting facing each other on the sofas in front of Herbert Van Fleet's fireplace.

Stone was dressed again and was rubbing his ankles where they had been bound. "Jesus, Dino, I guess I should have just listened to you all along," he said sourly. He took a large swig of Van Fleet's bourbon.

"I wouldn't have recognized this place," Dino said. "He's sure done a lot to it since we were here before."

"I didn't recognize it either," Stone said. "I didn't remember the garage door in the building. I had no idea where I was. How did you figure it out?"

"You mentioned Van Fleet; that was all I had to go on. I had to take a tire iron to the downstairs door, or I would have been up here sooner."

"How much of my conversation with Van Fleet did you hear?"

"Most of it, I guess. I had to duck out when Van Fleet came back to the kitchen to get his tools."

"Well, why did you wait so fucking long to stop the bastard?"

"I wanted to hear it all. Anyway, you were in no trouble; I wasn't going to let him carve you up."

"I wish I'd known that. He gave me about the worst hour of my life."

Dino picked up the phone on the coffee table. "I guess I'd better call it in."

"No!" Stone said, snatching the phone away from him.

"Look, Stone, I'm beat. Between screwing Mary Ann twice a day and shooting craps all night every night, I'm coming apart. Let's get this over with."

"You can't call it in, yet. We still don't have the guy who tossed Sasha off the balcony, and, if he finds out Sasha's dead, he'll feel safe."

"It's Harkness, then?"

"Damn right, and, if you'd done what I asked you to at the airport, we might have had him long ago."

"Come on, Stone, his name was on the manifest; let's not go over old stuff again, okay?"

"All right, let's not. But tomorrow night, Hi Barker is going to have Harkness on his TV show, and I mean to see him nailed, right there on television. I want you to be there to bust him."

Dino thought for a minute. "I gotta cover my ass some way, here, in this place."

"Do this: seal the place, and put a blue-and-white outside to make sure nobody disturbs the scene."

"Not until I get the medical examiner in here. We can't just let Van Fleet's corpse rot for a couple days, you know."

"Look, we have no solid evidence against Harkness, and, unless Barker can force some admission out of him on the air, we'll never get him. If somebody in the ME's office leaks this to the press, we're cooked; we'll never get him."

"Too bad you pissed off Van Fleet when you were on the table in there. He might have given us Harkness."

"He might have given us Harkness anyway, if you hadn't blown him away."

"What was I supposed to do? Stand there and watch the ritual slaughter? Shout 'freeze!'? What if he didn't freeze? You're pretty fucking ungrateful."

"Ungrateful? I've dragged you kicking and screaming through this whole thing, and now, when you turn up at the last possible minute, like the cavalry, you want gratitude?"

"That's the second time I've taken out somebody who wanted to kill you, and, come to think of it, you didn't thank me the first time either!" Dino was standing up now.

Stone stood up too. "If you'd been a little quicker the first time, I wouldn't be hobbling around on this knee, and I'd probably still be on the force!"

"Yeah, instead of a tax-free pension and a big-time law practice! I really did you a fucking disservice, didn't I? And, now, you got the cabbie killer, you cleared four murders, and you're going to bring down Barron Harkness—all in one week! It's a rough life you're gonna be living, ain't it, Stone?"

Stone opened his mouth, then shut it. Then he started to laugh. So did Dino. They sat down again and laughed until they were exhausted.

"Okay," Dino said, "you get out of here." He handed Stone his car keys. "I know a guy in the ME's office who can keep his mouth shut. I'll get him to check Van Fleet into the morgue as a John Doe, then I'll seal this place until Monday morning."

"Okay. You meet me tomorrow night at ten forty-five sharp at the Continental Network headquarters building on Seventh Avenue. We'll go up to the studio control room together. And have a blue-and-white waiting downstairs."

They both got up and walked toward the door, passing the dining table where the five mute conversationalists still carried on.

Dino walked over to Sasha's corpse and ran the back of a finger along her cheek. "Soft as a baby's ass," he said. "I wonder how the son of a bitch did it?"

51

Stone could not concentrate on the Sunday papers. Oddly, he gave little thought to the events of the night before. What he thought about was the evening ahead and what it might mean to him.

From the point of view of solving the case, he was unconcerned about proving the guilt of Barron Harkness, but, he was convinced, his future happiness depended upon that proof.

Throughout his adult life, it had been Stone's habit to go out with one woman at a time. Some of these affairs had been important—marriage had been discussed, although it had never happened. Others were less important, even unsatisfactory, but he had usually stuck with them for a time, because it was easier.

But now he was in love, with all that implied; he had not so much as thought of another woman since the moment he had met Cary. She had consumed his body and his mind from the beginning, and, when she had suddenly disappeared from his life, he had clung to the belief that there was a reasonable explanation for her conduct, if he could only know it. Now, on this late-winter Sunday afternoon, with a high wind howling around his house, he sought that explanation and found it.

From the beginning of their relationship, Cary had urged him to improve his position in life, to leave the police force and practice law. He had steadfastly refused even to consider this. Then, when he had been, in rapid succession, kicked off the force and offered an opportunity by Woodman & Weld, he was suddenly in a position to offer her what she wanted. It was at that moment, before he had had a chance to tell her what the future held, that she had returned to Barron Harkness.

It had always been Harkness, he now believed. When she had told him of her long affair with a married man and had disguised his identity, it was Harkness she was protecting. Then, in despair of Stone's ever getting anywhere, she had returned to Harkness, and Stone had, himself, made it possible for her to marry him, by making Harkness's divorce inevitable. Now she had the position and money she coveted, although she still loved Stone. He was certain of that. Why else would she still be sleeping with him?

All that remained to correct this situation was to put Harkness away for attempted murder. Hounded by publicity, Cary would seek shelter with Stone, who would now have the means to give her the life she wanted. That result was what he wanted of tonight's events. Dino could have the bust—it was his anyway. All he wanted was Cary, in his life and in his bed, all the time. Tonight, he would go as far as necessary to make that happen.

Dino was late. There was nothing new about this, but Stone waited impatiently in the lobby of the network building, afraid that Harkness would arrive before Dino did. Dino arrived at eleven, and Stone hustled him into an elevator.

"Jesus, Dino," Stone said as the car rose, "I thought that, just this once, you would be on time."

"Stone, I made it, didn't I? Don't I always make it?"

"Is there a car downstairs?"

"They're ready and waiting, don't worry."

"This is your bust, Dino. I don't want any of it."

"Thanks," Dino said. "Maybe it'll help take the curse off the Morgan thing."

"I hope so."

The elevator doors opened, and an anxious Hi Barker awaited them. "You're late," he said, and he was sweating. "Barron just arrived downstairs and is on the way up. Come with me." He led them to the control room door and ushered them in. "Jimmy," he said to a man wearing a headset, "these are police officers. I don't want Harkness to see them."

"Don't worry, Hi," Jimmy replied. "I've got a light on the glass partition that will make a reflection; Harkness won't be able to see into the control room."

"Good," Barker said. "I've got to go and meet him now. Anything else you want to tell me, Stone?"

Stone shook his head. "If you get into trouble, I've got an ace up my sleeve. I'll send you a note."

Barker nodded, then fled.

Stone looked around the control room; it was a smaller, simpler version of the one he had seen months ago at the news division. The executive studios, he had learned, were a couple of sets designed for small-scale interviews, like *The Hi Barker Show*. The backdrop of the set was simply the New York City skyline, looking south, as seen from the sixty-fifth floor, their current level. The exterior windows were of nonreflective glass, and the view was spectacular.

Hi Barker appeared on the set, followed by Barron Harkness and, to Stone's surprise, Cary. He hadn't expected her to be here. Harkness looked flushed, and he tripped on the carpeting and nearly fell as he stepped up to the platform where his seat would be.

"They must have been out somewhere before this," Dino said. "This is going to be even easier, if he's a little drunk."

Stone nodded. He watched as Harkness sat down and had a microphone clipped to his lapel. Hi Barker was flitting about, putting his guests at ease; Cary was given a folding chair just out of camera range. The whole group was no more than twelve feet from where Stone stood. "You're sure they can't see us?" he asked the director.

"Not a chance," Jimmy replied. "I checked it out earlier."

Two other people, a man and a young woman, came into the control room now and took seats on either side of Jimmy, paying no attention to Stone and Dino. "Ten minutes," the woman said, looking up at a clock above the row of monitors.

Stone watched the monitors as cameras were pointed at Barker and Harkness. For a moment, a camera rested on Cary, sending Stone a pang of desire. She looked beautiful and serene in her mink coat.

"One minute," the young woman said, jostling Stone from his reverie. He had been fantasizing about life after Barron Harkness.

"Ten seconds," she said, then counted down from five. Jimmy pushed a button, and lively music filled the control room.

The man next to Jimmy leaned into a microphone. "From the executive studios of the Continental Network, high above Manhattan, we bring you the premiere of *The Hi Barker Show.*"

A camera moved in on Hi Barker. "Good evening," he said amiably. "We're off to a flying start with this new series. Our aim is to bring you guests who don't often appear on programs like this one, and our guest tonight is one who, although he appears on television five nights a week, rarely talks about himself. I welcome my old friend, Barron Harkness. Good evening, Barron."

"Good evening, Hi," Harkness said, managing a smile. "I'm glad to be here . . . I think. It's been a long time since I let myself in for the sort of grilling I ordinarily hand out to others, and I'm not sure I'm looking forward to the experience."

Barker laughed. "You're not trying to get my sympathy, are you, Barron? I think you know how to take care of yourself in a clinch."

Smart, Stone thought. Set him up as somebody who can't be sandbagged on television, then sandbag him. He watched as Barker skillfully put Harkness over the jumps, starting with his early career, and occasionally interjecting a sharp, almost rude question about the newsman's behavior on some occasion. Harkness fenced well, and he was beginning to relax. Twenty-five minutes of the program passed in this vein, with Barker increasingly pressing Harkness for his personal views on politicians and events. Then Barker paused and sorted through his notes for a moment.

Now we begin, Stone thought. He leaned forward and grasped the railing in front of him.

"Barron," Barker began, "I know you were as shocked as we all were at the disappearance and probable death of Sasha Nijinsky, who was to have been your co-anchor on the evening news."

"Yes, I certainly was," Harkness said, looking a little uncomfortable. He crossed his legs and tugged at the knot of his necktie. "A horrible and tragic event."

"You were . . . elsewhere at the time all this happened, I believe."

That's right, Stone thought, let him set his own trap.

"Yes, I was. I had been reporting from the Middle East. Not for the first time, I might add—more like the twentieth—and I was returning to New York on a flight from Rome."

"I see," Barker said, looking regretful. "I'm extremely sorry to hear you say that, Barron; I had hoped for a little more candor on this subject."

Harkness looked alarmed. "I don't know what you mean," he said, as if he couldn't think of anything else to say.

Dino laughed aloud. "Sure, sure, Harkness; go ahead and paint yourself into the corner."

Barker shook his head. "Barron, in light of information that has come into my possession, I should warn you now to abandon this pretense."

"What pretense?" Harkness asked weakly. "What on earth are you talking about?"

"Barron, I have it on the authority of an unimpeachable source that you were not on the flight from Rome that day, that your ticket was used by another person. Tell us, now, Barron, where were you when Sasha Nijinsky was thrown from her balcony?"

Harkness said nothing for a moment, clearly stunned; then his eyes narrowed and he sat up straight.

Stone was reminded of a contentious interview with Richard Nixon many years before, when Harkness had gotten angry with good effect. What was he up to?

"Let me tell you something, Hi," Harkness said, with tightly controlled ire. "I don't know who has misinformed you, but I have made that particular flight from Rome six times in the past twelve months, and I've gotten to know some of the crew. When that airplane landed at Kennedy, I was sitting in the cockpit jump seat, watching the captain execute an instrument approach. His name is Bob Martinez, he's a senior captain with the airline, and he will vouch for my presence in his cockpit during that flight." Harkness took a breath. "What's more, I was traveling on that occasion in the company of Herman Bateman, the president of Continental Network News, and *he* will vouch for my presence on that flight. Now, do you have any other questions?"

Dino leaned forward and looked at Stone. "What the fuck is going on?"

"Shhh," Stone said. He took a folded sheet of paper from his pocket and handed it to the director. "Please get this to Hi at once."

Jimmy nodded and handed it to the young woman. "Just walk out on camera, and hand it to him."

The woman left as Hi Barker continued his questioning.

"Yes, I do have another question, Barron," Barker said, not intimidated. "A police source has informed me that when detectives went through Sasha Nijinsky's financial records, it was discovered that a sum of two million dollars was missing from her funds. Another source has now told me that Sasha had transferred those funds to you for investment, and that they have not been seen since, that you have been unable to return these funds. Would you care to comment on that?"

"I certainly would," Harkness said, not missing a beat. "It is true that Sasha asked me to invest such a sum for her; she had considerable faith in my financial judgment. In January of last year, she gave me a cashier's check for two million dollars made payable to an offshore bank with which I sometimes invest. In the autumn of last year, she asked me to withdraw her cash in the investment, so that she could purchase a cooperative apartment. I did, in fact, receive into my account on the day Sasha disappeared the full amount of her investment, plus a considerable profit. The following day, not knowing of Sasha's whereabouts or condition, I personally delivered a cashier's check in the amount of two million, four hundred and thirty-nine thousand dollars to Mr. Frank Woodman, Sasha's personal attorney."

Before Harkness had finished speaking, Stone was dialing Frank Woodman's home number.

"Hello?"

"Frank, it's Stone; I must be brief—are you watching *The Hi Barker Show*, by any chance?"

"As a matter of fact, I am."

"Is what Harkness just said true? Did he deliver those funds to you?"

"Yes, he did. They were disbursed as a part of Sasha's estate."

"Thanks." He hung up and watched as the young

woman walked onto the set and handed Barker the unfolded sheet of paper. Last chance.

Barker read the paper, and his eyebrows shot up. "Barron," he said, "I have just received a news bulletin, and I wonder if you would like to modify any of your statements in the light of this." He read from the paper. " 'The New York City Police Department has just announced that Sasha Nijinsky has been found in a downtown Manhattan loft, alive and well.' That's all it says. What is your response?"

Barron Harkness smiled. "Why, that's wonderful news! Is there anything about where she's been?"

"No, but clearly Sasha will now be able to identify the person who threw her from that balcony to the street."

Stone missed Harkness's response to this, because his attention had been caught by a movement near the set. Cary Hilliard had stood up. Her eyes as wide as those of a frightened deer, she stood still for a moment, then walked quickly across the set, directly in front of the cameras. Barker and Harkness, distracted by the movement, both turned and watched her. The director pushed a button, and the show's theme music came up again.

The announcer spoke up. "This has been the first *Hi Barker Show*. Tune in next Sunday night when Hi's guest will be . . ."

Stone burst out of the control room and ran for the elevators. Cary was banging on the button as he approached, and, when she saw him, she bolted.

"Cary!" he shouted down the length of the hallway. "Stop! Wait!"

She ducked down another corridor, out of his sight. He followed and was met with an expanse of closed doors. He began trying them.

A dozen doors down the hall, one was unlocked. He opened it and heard the clang of footsteps on fire stairs. He stopped for a moment and leaned against the wall. The memory of another set of steel stairs in another building flooded back to him. Now he knew whose footsteps those had been.

He started down, only to realize that the sound of footsteps was coming from above. He reversed his direction and followed the sound.

One floor up, the exit door stood open, and he found himself on a gravel roof. A gust of wind nearly knocked him off his feet. He grabbed at a ventilator pipe and held on. The view was all the more spectacular because there was nothing between him and the lights of the city but blustery air. Twenty feet away, only the modern building's low railing separated him from the lights. He looked around and saw a flash of mink coat disappear behind an air-conditioning unit. He followed.

He came around the unit, and she stood perhaps thirty feet from him, her feet spread in something like a fighting stance, leaning against the wind. She was no more than six feet from the low railing. Stone began walking toward her.

"Stop, Stone," she said. "Stop right there, or I'll jump."

He stopped, but he had already covered twenty feet; only ten separated them.

"You made me believe you were protecting him, but all along you were protecting yourself, weren't you? Right from the very beginning," he shouted over the wind.

"No," she said.

"You wanted to be with me so you would know what I knew about Sasha's case, that's all."

"No, Stone," she said. "I loved you from the start. I love you now, believe me. Get me out of this, and I'm yours. Barron can go to hell. Just get me out of this, and I'll make your life wonderful. Really, I will."

"You were sleeping with Sasha, weren't you?"

"Yes, but it meant nothing. It was just another erotic experience, don't you see?"

It was coming together for him now. "You were fucking Sasha, and so was Harkness. Harkness wanted her, not you, didn't he?"

"We were all fucking each other, sometimes all at once," she said. "She wanted him—not because she loved him, but because she could destroy him if she was married to him. She only wanted to cut off his balls, and then the evening news would have been all hers."

"And you, what did you want?" He edged a little closer.

She backed up a couple of steps. The edge was nearer now. The wind was gusting, and she leaned into it for a moment. "Well, you were useless, weren't you?" She spat. "You wouldn't free your-self of that dead-end job, so that you could get ahead. Barron was simply the best alternative. I didn't love him, though; I loved you. Why do you think I kept seeing you?"

"You didn't love me any more than you loved Barron or Sasha, Cary." He stepped closer; he could grab her now. He put a foot forward but kept his weight on the rear one. He reached out and snaked a hand around her waist.

There was a howl from behind him, and the wind struck his back. Involuntarily, his weight shifted onto the forward foot, and then to the toe. He let go of Cary. Slowly waving his arms for balance, he fell toward her, still pushed by the wind. Cary stepped instinctively back from him, and her calf struck the railing. In desperation, she reached out and grabbed at his coat lapel. Then they both toppled over the railing, out into the night. Sixty-five stories of thin air welcomed them.

Stone stopped short; something had his ankle. He ignored it, watched Cary slip from him and fall, facing him, revealed by flashes from lighted windows, all the way down until she struck the top of what looked like a Yellow cab.

Chunks of gravel were spilling from the top of the building now, falling past Stone to the street. Whoever had him was slipping over the side with him. He'll let go, Stone thought, and I'll join her. Then he stopped moving.

There was a chorus of grunts and muffled shouts from above, and, inch by inch, he was hauled back to the top of the building, scraping his shin quite badly. When he was back on top, lying with his cheek pressed gratefully to the gravel, he could see Dino hanging on to his ankle, and Barron Harkness and Hi Barker hanging on to Dino. They let go of each other reluctantly.

Stone crawled over to a ventilator and sat down with his back to it. "Thanks, Dino," he was finally able to say. "You did it again."

"And it's the first time you ever thanked me for it," Dino puffed.

"I don't believe any of this," Hi Barker said to nobody in particular. "But it's going to make one hell of a story."

Only Barron Harkness seemed to give a thought to Cary. "She's gone," he said absently. "My wife is gone."

Dino was the first to answer him. "Get used to it, pal." He snorted. "She's New York Dead."

52

Stone sat with his client and watched the jury file back into the courtroom. He had a sinking feeling about this. He didn't like his client much, and he wasn't sure the man was innocent. He was afraid the jury didn't share his indecision.

"Has the jury reached a verdict?" Judge O'Neal asked.

Stone thought she was looking particularly attractive today, as much as she could in judicial robes.

The foreman stood. "We have, Your Honor," he replied.

"The foreman will hand the verdict to the clerk."

The clerk received the verdict, read it to himself, then handed it to Judge O'Neal. She read it and handed it back to him.

"The defendant will rise and look upon the jury; the jury will look upon the defendant."

Stone stood with his client.

"The clerk will read the verdict."

The clerk looked at the piece of paper. "We, the jury, unanimously find the defendant guilty as charged."

Stone's client sighed audibly.

Well you might sigh, Stone thought. I tried to get you to plead to the lesser charge, you dumb schmuck. But you thought you could beat it.

"The jury is released with the thanks of the court for a job well done," Judge O'Neal said. "Sentencing is set for the twenty-fifth of this month; bail is continued pending." She struck the bench with her gavel and rose. The courtroom rose with her.

Stone turned to his client. "I'm sorry we couldn't get a better verdict."

"You warned me," the man said. "Can I go home now?"

"Yes. We have to decide whether to appeal; I really think you should consider the expense."

The man sighed again. "Why bother? I'll do the time."

"You're free until sentencing, but you'd better be prepared not to go home after that. Bring a toothbrush."

They shook hands, and the man walked sadly away. Stone began gathering his notes.

"Mr. Barrington?"

Stone looked up. Judge O'Neal was standing to one side of the bench, behind the railing.

"In my office, please," she said primly.

Stone groaned. He had pressed his luck often in cross-examining the prosecution's witnesses, and she had repeatedly called him down for it.

Now, the lecture. Hell, he thought, I'm lucky not to have been held in contempt. He trudged into her chambers, ready to take his medicine.

She had perched on an arm of the big leather sofa. She undid her robes, and they fell aside to reveal a bright red dress that went particularly well with her blonde hair. She crossed her legs.

They look awfully good, he thought. Something stirred in him for the first time in a long while.

"I read about the Nijinsky case, of course," she said. "I believe you discovered Ms. Nijinsky in a thoroughly dead condition."

"That's right, Judge. She was what a friend of mine calls 'New York Dead.'"

"In that case, I will remind you of our wager of some time past," O'Neal said, uncrossing her legs and recrossing them in the other direction.

He had forgotten.

"You, sir, owe me a dinner," she said.

Stone smiled. "Yes, Your Honor," he replied.

Acknowledgments

The Public Affairs Department of the New York City Police Department was not helpful in the research for this book. Individual officers were, however, and I would particularly like to thank Detective Jerry Giorgio of the 34th Squad Homicide Team for some enlightening conversations.

I thank Elaine Kaufman for keeping the home fires burning on Second Avenue and for running a place where a writer can get a decent table.

I am grateful to my editor, Ed Breslin, my London publisher, Eddie Bell, and all their colleagues at HarperCollins for their appreciation of this book and their hard work on its behalf.

Once again, I want to extend my gratitude to my agent, Morton Janklow, his associate, Anne Sibbald, and all the people at Janklow & Nesbit for their continuing care and concern for my career.

Author's Note

I am happy to hear from readers, but you should know that if you write to me in care of my publisher, three to six months will pass before I receive your letter, and when it finally arrives it will be one among many, and I will not be able to reply.

However, if you have access to the Internet, you may visit my website at *www.stuartwoods.com*, where there is a button for sending me e-mail. So far, I have been able to reply to all of my e-mail, and I will continue to try to do so.

If you send me an e-mail and do not receive a reply, it is because you are among an alarming number of people who have entered their e-mail address incorrectly in their mail software. I have many of my replies returned as undeliverable.

Remember: e-mail, reply; snail mail, no reply.

When you e-mail, please do not send attachments, as I *never* open these. They can take twenty minutes to download, and they often contain viruses.

Please do not place me on your mailing lists for funny stories, prayers, political causes, charitable fund-raising, petitions, or sentimental claptrap. I get enough of that from people I already know. Generally speaking, when I get e-mail addressed to a large number of people, I immediately delete it without reading it.

Please do not send me your ideas for a book, as I have a policy of writing only what I myself invent. If you send me story ideas, I will immediately delete them without reading them. If you have a good idea for a book, write it yourself, but I will not be able to advise you on how to get it published. Buy a copy of *Writer's Market* at any bookstore; that will tell you how.

Anyone with a request concerning events or appearances may e-mail it to me or send it to: Publicity Department, Penguin Group (USA) Inc., 375 Hudson Street, New York, NY 10014.

Those ambitious folk who wish to buy film, dramatic, or television rights to my books should contact Matthew Snyder, Creative Artists Agency, 2000 Avenue of the Stars, Los Angeles, CA 90067.

Those who wish to make offers for rights of a literary nature should contact Anne Sibbald, Janklow & Nesbit, 445 Park Avenue, New York, NY 10022. (Note: This is not an invitation for you to send her your manuscript or to solicit her to be your agent.)

If you want to know if I will be signing books in your city, please visit my website, *www.stuart woods.com*, where the tour schedule will be published a month or so in advance. If you wish me to do a book signing in your locality, ask your favorite bookseller to contact his Penguin representative or the Penguin publicity department with the request.

If you find typographical or editorial errors in my book and feel an irresistible urge to tell someone, please write to David Highfill at HarperCollins Publishers, 10 East 53rd Street, New York, NY 10022. Do not e-mail your discoveries to me, as I will already have learned about them from others.

A list of my published works appears in the front of this book and on my website. All the novels are still in print in paperback and can be found at or ordered from any bookstore. If you wish to obtain hardcover copies of earlier novels or of the two nonfiction books, a good used-book store or one of the online bookstores can help you find them. Otherwise, you will have to go to a great many garage sales.